APPOINTMENT WITH YESTERDAY

APPOINTMENT WITH
YESTERDAY

CELIA FREMLIN

faber

First published in 1972 by Gollancz
This edition first published in 2024
by Faber & Faber Ltd
The Bindery, 51 Hatton Garden
London EC1N 8HN

Typeset by Typo•glyphix, Burton-on-Trent DE14 3HE
Printed and bound in the UK by CPI Group (UK) Ltd, Croydon CR0 4YY

A CIP record for this book
is available from the British Library

ISBN 978–0–571–39127–1

2 4 6 8 10 9 7 5 3 1

CHAPTER I

Milly, she felt, would be a good name. Quiet, undistin-
guished, and as different from her real name as it was
possible to be.

Real? Who needed to be real, travelling on the Inner
Circle at four o'clock on a Monday afternoon? Staring past
the blank, middle-aged faces opposite, she caught sight of
her own blank, middle-aged face reflected in the scurrying
blackness of the window beyond. She almost laughed at the
likeness between the whole lot of them, and at the feeling
of safety it gave her. It's because of London Passenger
Transport, she mused, dreamy and almost light-headed by
now from lack of food and sleep: we're just the Passenger
part of London Passenger Transport. How marvellous to be
just a swaying statistic, gently nodding, staring into space!
Statistical space. Nobody, she reflected, ever brings their
real selves with them on to a tube train. None of us have.
We have all left our identities behind in some vast spiritual
Left Luggage office: and no one could guess—no one, possibly, could ever guess, just by looking—that there is one
among all these glazed faces that has left its identity behind
not just for the duration of the tube journey, but for ever.

The train was slowing down now, the cold, underground
light of Euston Square platform was wiping her reflection
off the window opposite: and the fear—familiar now, and

as regular as labour pains, coming at three minute intervals throughout the day—nagged at her once again as the train sighed to a halt, and the doors slipped open. Suppose someone should get on who knew her! Suppose one or other of the station men were beginning to recognise her, as she travelled round and round the same circuit of stations, ever since seven o'clock this morning!

Oh, she varied herself for them, as best she could! Sometimes she took her hat off, and sat with wispy hair dangling; sometimes she put it on again; and sometimes she clutched it in her lap, and tied round her head a red silk square. Lucky, really, that this red silk square had happened to be in the bag that she snatched up as she fled out of the house before dawn this morning. Lucky, too, that there had been some money in the bag: a couple of pounds, anyway, and some odd silver: for she had thought of nothing—not of money nor anything else—as she tore up the basement stairs, her breath grating in her lungs with terror at what she had done. How she had wrenched and wrestled at the warped, obstinate front door, with its peeling paint and ancient, rusty bolts! Beyond that door was freedom—she seemed still to be tasting that first rush of icy air into her throat as the door lurched open. After that, all she could remember was the running. Running, running, running, the winter air searing into her lungs like gulps of fire, and her startled heart clamouring for mercy as it fought to keep pace with her terror, her instinctive, primitive certainty of being hunted down.

But she wasn't being hunted down, of course. Who goes hunting along the South London streets at six o'clock on a

January morning? And especially along a street like this, with not a light glimmering anywhere, in all those serried rows of windows. For this was not a street of bright, brisk, busy people, the sort who might get up at six to light the fire, to start the kids' breakfast, to get to the factory in time for the early shift. No, this was a street where people lie in bed till noon, till two, or three, or four in the afternoon: where milk bottles stand unwashed and uncollected on steps and landings, and where the names printed under the tiers of bells are yellow with age, and evoke no glimmer of recognition in the red-rimmed eyes of whichever current incumbent might drag himself to the door when you ring. Un-names. Just like hers. How appropriate, then, that she, an inhabitant of that street, should be finishing her life on the Inner Circle, going round, and round, and round, the one place in all the world where you will never need a name again.

She roused herself with a start. Now, Milly, she admonished herself—for it was imperative that *she* should get used to the name, herself, before she had to try it out on other people—now, Milly, pull yourself together! You mustn't keep dozing off like this, or people really *will* start noticing you! Some kind gentleman will come along and say, "Now, Lady, where d'you want to get off . . . ?" and then you'll have to say the name of some station, and actually get *off* there! You can't say to him, can you, that you're not going to get off *anywhere*, that you've come here to live, you've moved in, and you're going round and round the Inner Circle, on a ten pence ticket, for *ever*?

3

So come, now, Milly, what *are* you going to do? You have spent ten pence of the two pounds thirty-five that you had in your bag. You have the clothes you stand up in, including, luckily, your outdoor coat. You are forty-two years old. You have no skills, qualifications, references. Until these last terrible months, you led a life so protected, so narrow, so luxurious, that you are soft as pulp, through and through. You probably can't work at *anything*. You have no friends to turn to, no relatives, because you are Milly now, and nobody, nobody in all the wide world—must ever have the faintest inkling that you have any connection with that woman who ran all but screaming into a London street in the early hours of Monday, January the tenth.

It couldn't be in the papers yet. Not possibly. All the same, Milly felt her heart thumping horribly every time a new passenger got on the train, sat down opposite her, and unfolded before her eyes yet another copy of the back page of the evening paper.

Not that it would be on the back page. It would be on the front page, certainly, once it got into the papers at all; and so each time Milly waited, in growing trepidation, while the owner of the paper turned it this way and that, folding and refolding it as he read, until at last, with any luck, the front headline would swoop into view, often upside down.

Yes, it was still all right. PETROL PRICE SHOCK still occupied the place of honour. No one, yet, would be

4

surreptitiously studying her features round the edge of their paper. So far, so good.

But what would be the headlines tomorrow morning . . . ? and now, at last, into her slow mind, still numbed with shock, there seeped the idea that there was need for haste. What had she been thinking of, wasting the precious day-light hours crouched in a corner of the tube train like an abandoned kitten? She should have been hastening to find herself a job, lodgings, an employment card . . . a whole new identity. She should have done all this instantly, today, before her blurred picture began staring up at every strap-hanging commuter in London: before every employer, every landlady was on the alert, peering under the brim of her hat, wondering who it was she reminded them of . . . ?

In stumbling haste, she sprang from her seat as the train slowed down, and hobbled on stiff legs towards the sliding doors. Which station it was, she neither knew nor cared: she only knew that she must get out—get moving—*do* something! The long day's paralysis of will was succeeded now by an obsession for hurry. Hurry to anywhere, to do anything—it didn't matter, for the obsession was just as irrational as the paralysis had been, just another symptom of shock, not a real decision at all.

The Outside struck her full in the face, like a breaking wave. The cold, the speed, the people, and above all the bedlam of sounds, pounding against ears that had registered nothing all the live-long day except the endless soothing rumble of the Underground. She, Milly, new-born and newly christened, had been thrust forth from the safe womb of the Inner Circle, and must start living her new life.

Here. Now. In the Edgware Road. In the middle of the rush-hour, with darkness falling, and with two pounds twenty-five remaining in her bag.

Gradually, as she stood there, she realised that there wasn't anything she dared do. Not anything at all. Even if she had had the money for a hotel, she knew that she would never dare to push open any swing-door or walk up to any receptionist's desk. Imagine standing there, mouth open, while a polished, glittering girl insolently took it all in, from wispy, uncombed hair to lack of suitcase in grimy, un-gloved hand!

And a job—even worse! Imagine an interview right now . . . "Yes, Miss—er?" (Goodness, she hadn't even decided what her surname was to be yet, and whether she was to be Mrs or Miss!) "Yes, Miss K, and what was your last employment? What are your typing speeds? . . . Are you familiar with the use of a Something-ator? . . . Have you had experience on the sales side . . . ?"

As she ambled, almost in a trance, amid the pushing, scurrying crowds, Milly suddenly caught sight in a shop window of someone walking just as slowly as she was herself: an old woman with hair sticking out like straws from under her battered hat. For almost a second she didn't recognise her: and when she did, she stopped, her heart pounding. So *that* is what you looked like, after a single day on the run . . . ! She must buy a comb . . . a lipstick . . . ! Wildly she looked round for a Woolworths—a chemist—a supermarket.

But everywhere the shops were closing. London's day was over: night, and lights, and swarming people swept over the city as over a battlefield when the carnage is finished: and, more desolate than all, Milly knew that by now she not only didn't dare go into a hotel or apply for a job: she didn't even dare to go into a shop and ask for a comb.

A bus labelled VICTORIA was drawing up beside her, and instinctively, without any thought at all, Milly scrambled on to it. As a deer runs for cover to the undergrowth, or a mouse to dark holes in the wainscotting, so did the newborn Milly dart automatically into places packed tight with tired people. Anonymous, bored, preoccupied people, laden with parcels, fumbling for money, pushing and shoving, blank as zombies. Such places were her home from now on: and when the bus reached Victoria, she recognised another of them. The evening crowds, the queues, hundreds of feet long, for tickets, for taxis, for trains . . . Milly didn't mind which queue she stood in, provided it was very, very long: and when at last she neared the head of one, she just wandered off and joined in at the tail again.

What must her hair look like by now! And her haggard, sleepless face, devoid of make-up! She pulled her hat tight down over her forehead, and hung her head, so that presently all she could see was legs. Vistas of legs, like columns in a cathedral. No, like trees, like neat pollarded trees, rooted into the stone . . . and yet creeping . . . yes, the trees were creeping . . . flowing, growing, going, across the barren surface, wherefore . . .

Wherefore what? Was it some quotation from the Bible drifting into her mind? . . . "wherefore they shall creep upon the face of the earth" . . . something like that . . . ?

"*Where for?*" yelled the man in the ticket office, for the third time. "Where d'you want to go, lady?"

"Well—I—" In her horror at finding that she had inadvertently allowed herself to reach the head of the queue, Milly's mind had become a blank. "Well—I—Well, where do the trains go to?" she asked idiotically.

"Seacliffe and South Coast, this office," the man snapped tiredly. "Suburban line, opposite Platform Six. Now, come on, lady. Take your time! There's only a coupla thousand people waiting behind you!"

His weary sarcasm stung Milly to panic.

"Oh! Oh dear! Yes!—Seacliffe, please!" she gabbled, seizing like a drowning man on the name that the booking clerk had tossed her. "I want to go to Seacliffe!"

"Single or return?"

"Oh! Oh, single! Yes, single, please!"

Single. What a lovely word. It meant *no return*! No return at all, ever! Fancy being able to buy that, just for money, at a Southern Railway ticket office! With a strange, singing joy, Milly saw her last two pound notes in the world disappearing, to be replaced by a small handful of change, and a small oblong of cardboard. But *what* cardboard! Passport, visa, birth certificate all in one! "Single fare, £1.40" is what it said, but Milly worked out the translation fast enough. It meant that the new-minted Milly was now a citizen of Seacliffe, now and for ever. There, in that unknown town, she was to work, and live, and die, and no one she had known in all her former life would ever find her.

CHAPTER II

It was not quite ten when Milly stepped out of the train on to the dark, gusty platform of Seacliffe Station. Already it seemed late at night, as it could never have done in London, and the straggling remnant of passengers who had got off the train with her were scurrying head-down towards the ticket-barrier, as if they feared that the last buses, the last taxis, were already leaving.

Milly followed more slowly. Of what concern to her were last buses and last taxis—she who had no destination, nothing to be late for or in time for? If you are going nowhere, it cannot possibly be too far to walk; and so Milly strolled through the ticket-barrier like a queen, insulated from all the haste and anxiety by a despair so complete as to be indistinguishable from peace.

But once outside, she was compelled to rouse herself. The night wind howled in from the sea with a force which set her gasping for breath and clutching at her hat, her hair, her wildly billowing coat. Around her loomed a width of unknown road, dark and completely deserted, with here and there a street lamp glimmering greenly in the fury of the wind.

Milly set off, exactly as if she was going somewhere. Not with any idea of averting suspicion—whose suspicion was there to avert in this storm-swept emptiness? Rather, it was because there was nothing else that she knew how to do. All one's life, one has been doing things with some sort of small purpose; the mechanisms are built-in, and they cannot cease just because all purpose has suddenly disappeared.

So she plodded on, and though her legs ached with a dull weariness, it did not occur to her to stop; and presently she knew, from the dampness whipping against her face, that she was getting very near the sea.

Ah, here it was! In what a glory of desolation it shouldered its black vastness against the ramparts of the parade—again . . . again . . . again, with all its ancient strength! The spray stung against her face, the wet wind screamed round her icy, aching ears, and tugged and wrestled with the wild, damp strands of her hair. Heavens, what must she be looking like by now! Anyone passing by would think she was a mad-woman, dawdling along like this in the wind and storm, with her hair flying out like seaweed!

Well, and why *not* be mad? The newspapers could put *that* in the headlines, too! Let them! Why not? Why not dance, and laugh, and scream with the screaming wind? Why not hurl herself like spray into the darkness, until her laughter and her screams became one and the same, one with the thunder of the black waves against the stonework, and the long, grating suck of the shingle as the water drew back, pausing for slow, incredible seconds while it gathered up fresh fury from its secret, inexhaustible store?

Oh, but the cold was wicked! Milly pulled up the collar of her coat round her aching ears, and set off walking again.

But already the collar itself was soaked with spray, and the wind whistled through her earache as if laughing at this fatuous attempt at protection. She could no longer see any glory in the black waves rolling in; they looked icy and horrible, and she crossed the road to the side where she couldn't see them; where the blank fronts of hotels and shut-up amusement arcades gave at least an illusion of shelter.

As she walked, Milly presently became aware of a strange sense of nostalgia. Some memory, as of a dream, long, long ago, was all about her: and as she came abreast of a little lighted fish-and-chip shop, still open and busy, she realised what the memory was. It was the memory of food. How long was it since she had eaten? Yesterday? The day before? She couldn't remember: and even now she wasn't feeling hungry. She felt no temptation to spend any of her few remaining coins in that bright little bar. But all the same, the momentary smell of food as she passed had been comforting, like a stranger's smile: a reminder that for some people, somewhere, life was still going on.

It must have been after midnight when she finally came to rest, aimless as a blown leaf, in a shelter on the sea-front, a little way outside the town. It was a glass and iron-work affair, three-sided, and by creeping into the furthermost corner, Milly found a little protection from the spray, and from the black, terrible wind screaming in off the sea.

Oh, but the cold! It seemed almost worse in here than outside. Gusts of icy air whirled round her knees, and pierced the soaked fabric of her coat as if it was paper: and presently it began to dawn on her that if she went on sitting here throughout the bitter January night, she was quite likely to die.

Die. She tried to make the word mean something, and became aware, for the first time, of how much she had deteriorated since this morning. Then, she had been shocked, terrified, but biologically intact. She had been reacting to fear as a healthy mammal should—by flight, and by an overwhelming determination to survive. It seemed incredible now, that determination to survive, and all the trouble she had been prepared to take for it! She remembered, wonderingly, how it had made her run, gasping, panting, for the nearest Underground, like a mouse running for its hole. Like the mouse, too, she had been upheld and guided by sturdy and marvellous instincts, handed to her intact and perfect across millions of years of evolution. These instincts, basic to every living thing, had still been strong and vital in her even while she had sat paralysed— defence by immobility—going round and round the Inner Circle: as she had scanned, tirelessly, the relays of insurgent passengers, with every muscle tensed ready for further flight if she should catch sight of an acquaintance, however remote. How anxiously, and with what zestful sanity, she had counted and re-counted the money in her bag, trying to make it come to more than two pounds twenty-five just as if it actually mattered! And as she trundled round and round on the tube, hour after hour, how she had schemed, and daydreamed, and worried about how to establish a new identity, how to get a job, how to find a room . . . It seemed

13

like a dream, now, that fantastic will to live, and all the effort she had been prepared to make for it! Now, it seemed too much trouble even to pull the draggled edges of her coat together over her frozen knees: and as for the idea of getting up and walking again, of stirring the circulation in her numbed limbs—such purposeful effort seemed incredible now; it was beyond anything she could imagine . . .

She became aware, presently, of an ominous lethargy, creeping up from her frozen limbs, and beginning to probe, tentatively, into the very centre of her being. These were the fingers of death. She knew it. Strange how she had seemed to recognise them immediately, as though she had known, all her life, exactly what death would be like when it came.

She had stopped shivering, too, in the last few minutes, and that was the most sinister sign of all. One by one, the marvellous mechanisms for preserving body-heat were breaking down. Soon, her temperature itself would begin to drop, and the blood-supply to her brain would fall to a point where anoxia set in. How easily and naturally the old, familiar medical phrases still slid into her mind, even after all this time! A legacy from her first marriage, this: and from the time even longer ago when she had been trying to train as a nurse. Dropping things, mishandling sterilised instruments, so clumsy and nervous over injections that the patients would plead, with real fear in their eyes, for "the little nurse to do it!" Or "the tall nurse", or "the blonde nurse"—any nurse at all, so long as it wasn't Milly!

Only she hadn't been Milly then, of course, she had been Nurse Harris: soon—if only she had guessed it—to become Mrs Waggett, wife of Julian Waggett, the promising young house surgeon.

No one in the hospital could understand why he had picked on *her*. With his dark, arrogant good looks, his charm, his air of absolute assurance, he could have had any girl in the hospital—or outside it, for that matter. All the young student nurses were more or less in love with him; some, like Milly, with a day-dreaming adolescent passion that declared itself solely by tongue-tied paralysis whenever he appeared on the ward; others, bolder and more experienced, were seriously out to get him. These were the girls who knew how to flash provocation from their cool downcast eyes as they stood by a bedside receiving instructions about a saline drip; who knew how to wear their sober uniform as if it was part of a strip-tease. Some of these sorceresses even managed to date the great man, now and again, and subsequently dined out (or perhaps cocoa'd out would be more accurate) for weeks afterwards on tales of wine and orchids and whispered words of passion.

Not that Julian Waggett had been rich—not in those days. He was only a house-surgeon, two years qualified, and earning such a salary as protest marches are based on. But it made no difference. Although he was only twenty-six, and among the lowest-ranking doctors at the hospital, the indefinable bloom of success was already upon him. Already one felt that the deep-pile carpets of Harley Street were unrolling under his feet as he trod the wards; and when he glanced off-handedly at the bed-end chart, or threw out a casual syllable that would light up a pain-racked face, you knew, you knew without any doubt at all, that those unhurried steps were taking him into his future swifter than the speed of sound.

And the woman who was to step into the future with him? Not for her would be the harried existence of an overworked GP's wife—tied to the telephone, meals drying in the oven, never a night's unbroken sleep. No, whoever finally succeeded in capturing Julian was in for a life of pampered luxury and ease. Service-flats. A town house and a country house. Luxury holidays in the Bahamas. Did he know, Milly (Nurse Harris, that is to say) sometimes wondered, how many thousands of rollers were rolled into how many acres of hair at the Nurses' Home each night, just for him? How many little pots of eye-liner, eye-shiner, skin freshener, pore-cream and all the rest were lined up in sacrificial array on his hundreds of unknown altars in little cell-like bedrooms? And could he ever have believed that those fluffy little heads, which seemed to find it so impossible to understand the blood-plasma tables, were nevertheless capable of compiling timetables far more complicated than anything dealt with at head office, when it came to engineering "chance" meetings with him on corridors or in doorways? And did he know—did it perhaps even amuse him to know—that several young lives had been drastically reshaped—for good or ill—simply by the fact that it was rumoured that he didn't like virgins?

And after all the sound and fury, what happened? He married *Milly*—Nurse Harris, that is to say! Nurse Harris of the gingery hair, and the freckles. Nurse Harris of the thick waist, and the stubby fingers, who couldn't wear eye-make-up because it brought her out in styes. And a virgin to boot. It was no wonder that when the engagement was announced, the whole, vast humming hospital seemed to stop in its tracks for a moment, from the top consultant to the lowest-paid washer-up, all of them asking the same question. Why? *Why?*

All their guesses were wrong. Nurse Harris wasn't pregnant. She hadn't inherited half a million pounds from a deceased uncle. Nor was Julian trying to call the bluff of some disdainful glamour-puss by making her jealous. He really *did* want to marry Nurse Harris. He *did* marry her. There were flowers, champagne, congratulations, and after that, of course, all that the mystified well-wishers could do was to sit back and wait for the marriage to crack up. Six months, most of them gave it.

But it didn't break up. Not in six months, nor even in a year. Two years passed—three—even five; and during this time Julian went from strength to strength. House-Surgeon, Registrar, Senior Registrar . . . Before he was thirty-five he was a consultant, and with a private practice on the side that was rapidly becoming fashionable. His name, now and then, began to appear in the papers, in connection with some tricky operation on a minor celebrity. By now the prophets of doom were having to eat their words: they had to admit that a man isn't likely to achieve success like this if he is all the time wresting with an unhappy marriage. In some inexplicable way, drab little Nurse Harris must have been right for him. But why?

Milly, of course, knew why. She had known all along, but had had no intention of allowing the knowledge to mar her joy and excitement over her extraordinary good fortune. She had known right from the start that what Julian wanted— nay, *needed*—was a wife who would serve as a foil for his own brilliance. A woman so retiring, so inconspicuous, that in contrast to her dullness his own wit, his own charm, would shine out with redoubled radiance. A woman who never, ever, in any circumstances, would draw attention away from him and on to herself.

And for a while—indeed for a number of years—the lop-sided bargain seemed to work very well. Milly was not an ambitious woman, she had no desire for the limelight for herself. Besides, she loved Julian, and rejoiced genuinely to see him where she knew he so loved to be—in the centre of an admiring crowd. She was proud of his success, proud to know that this dazzling, sought-after figure was *her* husband: and she felt, too, a deep and not unjustified pride in the thought that it was she, herself, who in all sorts of dull little inconspicuous ways had provided the background against which his wit and charm could sparkle their bright- est, and his talents be displayed to best advantage.

Right from the beginning, Julian had loved to give important little dinner-parties. Even in the early years, when they could ill afford it, he had always insisted that there should be wine, and flowers, and at least four courses of excellent food for their guests. Luckily, Milly was a good cook, though slow, so by dint of anxious planning and long hours at the stove, she always managed to produce a meal that was inexpensive and yet came up to Julian's exacting standards: and if, by the time they sat down to table, the hostess was too flustered and exhausted to join much in the conversation, what matter? It was Julian who was the star of the evening, Julian who led the conversation, filled up the glasses, radiated hospitality and charm. Sometimes he would chide her, afterwards, for being "such a little mouse!" but she knew that he liked it really, and she exerted such womanly guile as she possessed to see that her inadequacies remained a joke between them, and never became a serious issue.

But they did become a serious issue, of course, in the end. As the years went by, and success followed success for Julian, the dinner parties became larger, and grander. Little lions from the social and artistic worlds were invited to them, and then bigger lions. Until, at last, secure in his own unassailable reputation, Julian began to feel the need of a wife who would be a credit to him. Not one who would outshine him, of course—as if such a thing were possible!—Oh no! But he needed someone elegant, sophisticated; a fitting hostess for a man in his position. And one night, he looked at his existing wife, nervously sipping her sweet sherry, boring the Finnish Ambassador, and allowing her anxieties about the chestnut soufflé to show on her round shiny face. He contemplated her faded ginger perm, her freckles, and her thickening figure bulging under her black velvet dinner dress; and that had been the beginning of the end.

Milly had seen it coming, of course. She had known, long before he did, that she wasn't going to be able to "keep up with him". It often happened, of course, in their sort of circle. She had seen it with her own eyes, over and over again, among their acquaintances: the brilliant, ambitious husband rocketing his way to the top and discarding his dowdy, middle-aged wife en route, like a snake shedding its outworn skin in springtime. She'd met the wives, too, after the amputation was over: drab, dejected creatures, moaning on and on about the meagreness of their alimony, and about "his" ingratitude after all they had done and all they had sacrificed for him during the early years of struggle.

Had they no pride? It was all true, of course—but even so, surely a woman could keep her lips closed and her head held high? And as for alimony, Milly had thought—and sometimes, to selected cronies, had actually said—that if *her* husband ever deserted her, she would starve in the gutter before she would take a single penny from him!

But she took it, of course, when the time came, just like all the others. When it came to the point, there didn't seem to be anything else she could do. There she was, in the Kensington flat, and with bills pouring in for services and commitments that she hadn't even known existed; and even while she drifted about looking for somewhere cheaper to live, with landladies laughing in her face when she mentioned the sort of rental she had in mind—even in that short time, the second round of bills had begun to

arrive. Demands, Final Demands, threats of legal action—
what could she do but accept the hundred and fifty pounds
a month offered by her former husband, so generously
and with such calculated spite? It was, in fact, a larger sum
than had been awarded by the Courts, and he explained
this gratuitous munificence in a letter written to Milly
just after his much-publicised marriage to Cora Grey, the
up-and-coming young movie star who had divorced her
nonentity of a husband specially for Julian. The two of
them had made the front page of the evening papers at the
time, and since then their bronzed faces, full of improb-
ably glittering teeth, had leered up against a background
of sea and sky in at least two of the colour supplements.
No doubt it had all gone to Julian's head a bit: and this
explained—or Milly supposed it did—the schoolboy
spite, the easy, throwaway cruelty, of the letter he chose
to write to her, from his honeymoon paradise, at the very
height of his triumph:

"I'm sorry, my dear," he wrote, "that things had to end this
way; but there it is. I suppose it's just one of those things,
and for my part I'm happier than I've ever been in my life
before. Cora is a marvellous girl, we are made for each
other. To show you what a marvellous girl she is, let me
tell you that it was *her* idea that I should allow you fifty
pounds a month more than I am legally obliged to do.
Wasn't that terrific of her?—she is the most generous-
minded person I have ever known, and just doesn't know
how to bear grudges.

"Needless to say, I agreed with her that you should have the money. As she says, a woman in her forties has little chance of starting a new life, and so she really *needs* money: whereas a man in his forties is still in his prime, with a whole marvellous life ahead of him, I'm sorry, my dear: it seems unfair of Nature to have arranged things like that, but that's the way it is: and as you see from this cheque, Cora and I are trying to do what we can to make up to you for the fact that hope and happiness are all on our side.

"Well, that's all for now. We're dining with Lord and Lady Erle tonight, on their new yacht, so must hurry and get into our glad rags. Cora joins me in sending greetings, and she asks me to tell you that she hopes that your remaining years will bring you some sort of contentment. She tells me that she once had a great-aunt who, when her life's work was over, derived a lot of pleasure from growing mustard and cress in the shapes of letters of the alphabet. It was very interesting, she says, waiting for it to come up.

Yours, with all good wishes

Julian."

"*I'll show* him!" Milly had thought, as she tore the letter into tiny shreds.

And show him she did. Which was how, all these months later, she came to be crouching here, in this freezing seaside shelter, battered by wind and spray, with no food, no home, and, very likely, only a few more hours to live.

What would Julian say, she wondered, when he read the whole story in the papers tomorrow, or perhaps the next day? Would he just say, with that familiar curl of the lip, "God, how sordid!" Or would he, perhaps, murmur, with a tiny glint of unwilling admiration in those self-satisfied eyes: "Good Lord! I'd never have thought she had it in her!"

CHAPTER III

Milly stirred infinitesimally on the hard bench, and found that by now even her hips were numb. What was the time? Two o'clock? Or even three? Could it be that she had evaded in sleep some appreciable fraction of her nightlong sentence? There was no knowing. No way of measuring the dreaming and the not-dreaming that wove in and out of her head from the darkness and the storm. When she dreamed of cold, of a cold sharper than human flesh could bear, it was only to wake and find that it was not a dream at all. Her limbs were still there, jutting out of her in four places, and enduring in reality what could not be endured in dreams. It was *their* suffering now, rather than her own, that troubled her; for she, herself, had become very, very tiny, and was moving inexorably, and at an accelerating rate, out of range of their sufferings. She was deserting them, leaving them to fight their losing battle as best they might . . . and then, from she knew not where, there would come upon her a fit of shivering so violent that her soul would be jerked back into its proper place again, in charge again, suffering again, sharing to its excruciating limit the agonies of every far-flung cell.

Strange lethargies intervened, and strange awakenings where there had been no sleep; until at last the darkness seemed to break like a dropped cup, and she felt in her dream that some mighty change, some unimaginable glory, was coming over the earth: and when she woke she found that it was so. For when she opened her numbed eyelids there was a faint yellow light spreading over the tumbled waters; the wind had dropped; and it was day.

The light grew, and Milly was aware of something akin to worship as she contemplated her own body. This was the body that had brought her alive through the incredible winter night by the application of first one marvellous mechanism and then another. She remembered how it had first withdrawn blood from the extremities, the hands and feet, in order to feed the vital machinery in the centre: and then, without her even noticing it, it had curled itself up into this bundle in which she now found herself, mathematically arranged so as to expose the absolute minimum of surface area to the searing cold. And after that, when her limbs were numb and all her willpower gone, it had kept her blood circulating and her heart minimally beating by means of bouts of shivering alternating with bouts of drowsing apathy. By these magical, unbelievable mechanisms it had kept death at bay all through the livelong night, and without any sort of help or co-operation from *her*—as far as *she* was concerned, she had been leaving herself to die. And with all this, it had launched at her no reproaches for having landed it in this desperate situation: it did not ask her *why* it had to be kept out like this all through the coldest night of the year, in wet clothes, and with no food inside it. Like a true and loving friend, it had accepted her decision without reproach, and then had put all its energies, all its varied and wonderful skills, into sustaining her through the consequences. I've never had a friend like it!—thought Milly, staring down at her bedraggled person in the growing light; and with this thought there came to her a blazing determination to survive. *She* die of exposure? Not on your life! Why, she hadn't even got a sore throat! Slowly, painfully, she set herself to restore the power of movement to this numbed, miraculous body of hers. As soon as she could move, she would buy it some hot coffee, a roll and butter . . . she felt almost dizzy at the thought of such wonders, and at the realisation that they were still within her reach. She still had *some* money, after all; eighty or ninety pence at least.

At the thought of this sum, the strangest thought imaginable came to her. There was something to spend it on even more important than food. She must have her hair set!

Wasn't this the least she could do? How could she allow her body, her faithful, miraculous body, which had protected and steered her through the deathly perils of the night, to go about looking like a scarecrow?

And it was only much later, as she sat staring at her transformed appearance in the hairdresser's mirror, that she realised that this way of spending her last shillings had also been downright sensible. Now she would be able to look for a job, bargain with landladies, invent stories about lost insurance cards. She was equipped now, to face the brand-new world.

26

CHAPTER IV

"Yes, well, can you start tomorrow?"

Choking back the rest of her imaginary life-story, Milly stared at her prospective employer incredulously. The woman wasn't even listening! When Milly had first seen the advertisement for a Daily Help, on a board outside a newsagent's, it had seemed obvious to her that the first thing to do was to think out some plausible sort of past for herself: and so for more than an hour she had loitered in an arcade of deserted slot-machines, concocting this wonderful tale which so cleverly explained just how it was that she happened to have no address, no references, and no employment card. And now here was this woman interrupting her in mid-sentence to offer her the job, just like that! For a moment, Milly felt affronted rather than relieved. All those carefully-plotted details about the invalid father, the requisitioning of the family home, the loss of all her personal papers in the move: and then the death-duties, and the mysterious Family Debts—all, all were wasted! Mrs Graham (for such it seemed was the name of this anxious, thirty-five-ish person who kept glancing at the clock and fidgeting with paperclips)—Mrs Graham didn't want to know one thing about any of it! She didn't want to know Milly's age, her capabilities, or why she had suddenly dropped into Seacliffe like a visitor from Mars. All she wanted, it seemed, was to clinch the deal before (to judge by her agitated glances) Milly should disappear into thin air with a rattle of ghostly chains, or re-embark in her flying saucer, or whatever. Were Daily Helps really as rare as that? Milly could only suppose that they must be, and her spirits rose a little. It was a long time since she had felt rare.

"Can you start tomorrow?" Mrs Graham repeated, torturing the inoffensive paper-clip with nervous fingers. "You see, my other woman let me down rather badly . . . not a question of money, it wasn't that at all. I'm willing to pay thirty-five pence an hour, and lunch as well, she always had a good lunch. And it's light work, Mrs—er—; nothing heavy, you'll find it's a thoroughly labour-saving kitchen, all the equipment and everything, brand new. And a Hoover! With fitments! And there's the Dustette, you can use it for the shelves and everything, you won't need to get your hands dirty . . ."

By this time, Milly had realised who it was who was interviewing whom, and she adjusted her posture accordingly, leaning back a little in the chair on whose extreme edge she had so far been timorously perching. Now, in her newly relaxed position, she set herself to listening graciously while her victim reeled off, with anxious haste, the variegated delights in store for Milly if she accepted the job. Up-to-date waste-disposal. Non-rub polishes. No scrubbing . . . There seemed no point in interrupting, though in fact Milly had already quite decided to take the job. Or, rather, it never occurred to her not to. From the first moment when she began scanning the newsagents' advertising boards this morning, she had taken it for granted that

28

she would take the very first job that she was offered—if, indeed, she was offered anything at all. Never, in her wildest dreams, had she supposed it would be as easy as this! She, an unknown woman, past forty, with no skills, no qualifications, no references, and wearing a coat still damp from sitting out in it all night! Why, for all this Mrs Graham knew, she might be a murderess . . . !

"You *will* turn up tomorrow, won't you?" Mrs Graham was saying anxiously. "So many of the women I've seen, they've said they'll come, and then they just don't turn up! You won't let me down, will you, Mrs—er—Oh dear, what *is* your name? I ought to have asked you before."

Milly was just opening her mouth to answer, when she realised that "Milly", alone, wasn't going to be enough. A surname! Quick, quick! She racked her brains to think of something . . . anything . . . Oh dear, Mrs Graham must already have noticed her hesitation in answering . . . !

And indeed, Mrs Graham had: but, as is so common with people in a state of anxiety, she had immediately integrated this new phenomenon into her own special network of worries, and imagined that Milly's hesitation meant that she was wavering over her decision to take the job.

"You *will* come tomorrow, won't you?" she urged, for the second time. "I'm counting on you! I get so tired of people who promise to come and then just disappear! Promise me you won't do that!"

Gleefully, Milly promised. Disappear!—when by this time tomorrow she could expect to have one pound forty

29

in her pocket and a free lunch inside her? Not likely! Besides, Milly had already done enough disappearing, in the last thirty-six hours, to last her a lifetime.

She spent the afternoon in the station cafeteria, where it was warm. She had gone there to steal food, but had found, rather to her surprise, that she couldn't bring herself to do it. Absurd, really, that a woman capable of the deed she had set her hand to yesterday, should today find herself unable to reach out that same hand just to purloin a two pence bread roll!

If she hadn't been so hungry, she would have laughed.

Oh, well. So she wouldn't be able to eat. But there were other bodily pleasures to be enjoyed—pleasures which were now for the first time being fully revealed to her in all their glory: and one of them was sitting down. The sight of a vacant seat in a corner by the radiator filled her with such a passion of longing that she almost fainted with the fear that someone else might get there first! Through trays and trolleys, and all the detritus of Consumer-Man, she battled her way towards the haven of her desires.

At last! Here she was, her head resting against the dark-green decor, and her legs, throbbing with sheer comfort, stretched out in front of her under the table. She felt her eyes closing, but it didn't matter, no one was going to notice. This was a *station*, wasn't it, an outpost of the wonderful, anonymous world she had inhabited yesterday? The world of commuters, where hurrying takes the place of existing—"I hurry, therefore I am!" If you aren't hurrying, then you aren't existing, and that makes it quite all right to sit with your eyes closed, your damp coat steaming—you can even snore—for a whole afternoon, and never a glazed eye will swivel in your direction, nor a single, screwed-up consciousness detach itself from its inner speedometer for long enough to wonder who you are and why you are so tired.

People came, they sat down opposite her, they ate their buns, looked at their watches, and went: and still Milly slept on, secure in the knowledge that she didn't exist. A black cat in the dark: white square on white: what an aeroplane looks like out of sight: you can't get much safer than that.

For two hours Milly slept like the dead, or like the not-yet born; and when she woke, there was an object in front of her so marvellous that for a second she thought she must have died and gone to Heaven. The object was white, and delicately carved; the edges formed a frieze of fantastic beauty and complexity—no, not a frieze exactly; more like petals, petals of a flower, opening out before her, offering itself, in total, smiling friendship.

Milly blinked. Her vision cleared (for one moment she would have said rather that it dulled), and she found herself gazing hungrily at a broken roll, partially buttered, that someone had left to go to waste on a crumb-strewn plate, only a foot away from her.

Milly was amazed. How could things be so easy? No one could call *this* stealing! She twitched the plate furtively towards her, and as she bit deep into the broken crust, and felt the soft, feather-whiteness of the bread against her teeth, she murmured a soundless prayer, she knew not to what or whom. Already the sense of revelation was fading: induced by starvation, and lowered blood-sugar, the vision was being systematically blotted out, gleam by evanescent gleam, with every delicious mouthful.

A shame, really, after all this, that she couldn't manage to finish the roll! After only a few bites, all her ravenous hunger was gone, and she felt quite bloated. She was just about to slip the remainder of the roll into her handbag, to eat later on—for tomorrow's breakfast, perhaps— when a tray lurched into her field of vision. It swayed for a few seconds in front of her eyes, and then came to rest on the table. The owner of the tray, a middle-aged man with greying hair, settled himself comfortably in the seat opposite Milly, reached first for salt and then for vinegar, and then, having besprinkled his sausage and chips liberally with both, he proceeded to unfold an evening paper, prop it against the vinegar bottle, and thereafter seemed to bury himself in it, ladling forkfuls of chips into his mouth like an automaton.

At first, all that the little scene meant to Milly was that she could now, perhaps, slip the rest of the roll into her handbag unobserved. Surreptitiously, she pulled the handbag into her lap, and opened it in readiness behind the screen of the table: then, just before snatching at the roll, she gave a quick final glance across the table to make sure that her companion was still thoroughly engrossed in his paper.

He was. Why, then, did Milly not seize her chance, grab the piece of roll, and snap her handbag shut on it? Instead, she just sat, staring.

... FOUND IN FLAT was all she could see of the headline, but it was enough: enough to freeze her hovering hand; to drive all thought of food from her shocked consciousness. Vainly she screwed herself this way and that, trying to see the hidden portion of the page: vainly she tried to assure herself that it was too early . . . too soon . . . they couldn't have discovered anything yet.

They could, though. It wasn't too early at all. This was a London paper. Of course the news could be in it—this was just exactly the length of time you would expect the thing to take, allowing for the snail-like reactions of the inhabitants of that haunted street. Or was it? How long would Mrs Roach, on the floor above, have sat listening inertly to the strange sounds in the basement? How long would it be before her dulled senses became aware that something was amiss? And even after she was aware, how long would it have been before she dragged her bulk out of the ancient fusty chair in which she spent her days, and took herself, slip-slop in her downtrodden slippers, curlers twisted this way and that in her sparse hair, out of the front door and down the gusty street to the telephone box at the corner? For there was no telephone in the house—a deficiency which Gilbert had actually boasted of to Milly, in his gentle old voice, as if it was some rare and expensive luxury. "It's the only way to get any peace, these days," he'd said, that day when he took her to his home for the first time: and it was only afterwards, and gradually, that Milly had become aware of what it was that Gilbert meant by "peace".

33

How long had it taken her to understand? How long was it before she began to guess what it was that she had let herself in for by marrying Gilbert?

Marrying him had seemed, at the time, the answer to all her problems: and so, in a way, it was, for at that time all her problems had been simply the variegated facets of the same problem: the problem of how to "*show*" Julian! Show him that "a woman in her forties" is *not* finished and done for: show him that she, the discarded wife, could still attract, still find herself another man. Show him that what he had thrown away like an outworn glove was a treasure for which other men came begging. Show him, in fact, that she didn't care *that* for him and Cora, and for the divorce, and for all the humiliating publicity! Show him that she could still bounce up again, unquenched and unquenchable, ready to start life all over again. And to show him, above all, just what he could do with his alimony!

"I am returning your cheque," she had written—and the composing of this letter had given her, perhaps, the most exquisite ten minutes of her whole life. It seemed, looking back, that it was just for this ten minutes that she had undertaken the whole thing: had bartered, knowingly, the whole of her future life, with no doubt at all that a lifetime of frustration and boredom was a small price to pay for ten minutes of triumph so perfect and so complete. "I am returning your cheque," she wrote, "as I no longer have any need of—or indeed any right to—further support from you. You will be pleased to hear that I am getting married next week, and am happier than I have ever been in my life. Gilbert is a widower, just sixty, tall and most distinguished-looking, and has a pleasant home of his own in South London . . ."

She hadn't known, of course, at the time of writing, how much of all this was lies: though she had known that some of it was, and she hadn't cared. She knew, for example, that Gilbert wasn't sixty, but a good many years older: his stiff gait, his feathering of snow-white hair, and above all his hands, tortoise-slow and spotted with old age—all this had made it quite clear, from the very beginning, that he was deceiving her about his age. But so what? All she had felt at the time was a mild gratitude towards him for taking upon himself the burden of telling the lies, instead of leaving it to her. For, if he had not done it for her, she would, of course, have subtracted the decade herself in boasting about her suitor to Julian.

What she *hadn't* known, at that time, was what the "pleasant house in South London" was actually like. But even if she *had* known—even if she could have seen with her own eyes the boarded-up windows, the peeling, ancient paint, and could have heard the slip-slop of Mrs Roach's slippers on the stairs—even then, it probably wouldn't have made any difference. Because at that time she simply didn't *mind* what the rest of her life was going to be like, any more than she minded what Gilbert was like. All that mattered was that Julian should *think* she had made a catch and was living happily ever after. Real life seemed a trivial thing compared with impressing Julian.

And anyway, what the hell? How could life with this harmless old man possibly be worse than hanging on in the awful, well-appointed Kensington flat, pitied by the neighbours, avoided by her and Julian's former friends? Gilbert at least seemed to value her, in his mumbling, fumbling way. He was courteous and deferential to the point of incomprehensibility, and sometimes paid her stiff, complicated compliments, which she couldn't but find pleasing, starved as she had been of any words of approval during recent years.

Besides, she supposed, vaguely, that she would grow fond of him as time went on. He seemed to have led a miserable life—nagged by his first wife into a nervous breakdown, swindled out of his proper pension by the now defunct Indian Civil Service: and Milly rather fancied herself in the role of little ray of sunshine to brighten his declining years. And if, in the process of brightening someone's declining years, you can also administer a well-deserved kick in the backside to your ex-husband's inflated ego—well, what normal woman would hesitate?

Milly wouldn't, anyway. She promptly married Gilbert at a Brixton registry office, with two deaf old men captured from a nearby bowls club as witnesses: and she straightaway sent Julian a beautifully touched-up photograph of the wedding, with herself smiling a radiant smile that was quite unfeigned (and how should Julian guess that the joy irradiating her features was inspired not by love's young dream, but by the thought of his and Cora's faces as they received the news?)

Gilbert hadn't come out quite so well: he had a vulpine look which she hadn't noticed in real life, and his smile was glassy, and riddled with false teeth. Still, it wasn't too bad: at least the lines on his face were blurred and softened, so that he looked, in the picture, as if he really could be only sixty. And he was standing well, too, tall and spare, almost military. You couldn't say he looked handsome, exactly— and it was a pity that the fluffy whiteness of his hair was so in evidence—but at least he looked distinguished, in a bony, ghosty sort of a way.

The man opposite Milly suddenly lowered his newspaper, and it seemed, for one awful moment, that his glance rested on her face for just a little too long. Was her picture already in the paper, then?—that very same wedding photograph, perhaps, with the fixed, bridal smiles, now so eerily inappropriate. Just the sort of ghoulish touch that newspapermen love . . .

The man's glance had left Milly's face now; he looked merely irritable as he twitched over one page after another, folding and re-folding the paper as he searched for some small haven of print on which his flickering interest might rest awhile.

. . . FOUND IN FLAT . . . FOUND IN FLAT—twice more the tantalising letters flashed in front of Milly's eyes, until at last her luck was in, and the front page lay spread out before her in its totality:

STOLEN JEWELS FOUND IN FLAT, she read; and her whole body sagged in an ecstasy of relief.

Nothing to do with her at all! She was reprieved!

Because, whatever they were going to find in that basement flat in South London, it most certainly wasn't going to be jewels.

CHAPTER V

"Well, actually, I was wondering if I could pay by cheque?"

A cheque, signed with her new false name, naturally wouldn't be worth the paper it was written on, but Milly was calculating that, before it bounced back, she would have been able to pay the whole week's rent in full, in cash. She had never dealt in dud cheques before, and she wasn't sure how easy they were to laugh off—not to mention getting the landlady to laugh with you. But of one thing she was quite certain: a trendy little anecdote about the idiocies of the bank's newly installed computer would sound a lot funnier to a landlady's ears if Milly was already holding out three real, actual pound notes when she laughingly embarked on it.

"Is that all right, then?—who shall I make it out to?" Milly drew the futile, obsolete cheque-book from her bag with quite a flourish, and flicked it open with all the solid assurance of one who really *will* have one pound forty tomorrow, and another one pound forty the next day, and therefore isn't telling lies at all, not really. She was aware, though, as she stood, biro poised, and with an ingratiating smile on her lips, that the little woman who had advertised the vacant room upstairs was now watching her, sharp as a sparrow, from under her grey fringe: assessing her, totting her up, and wasting no time in coming up with the answer.

"I'm sorry. No, I don't take cheques. I'm sorry."

So she didn't take cheques. Just like some people don't take whisky. The tiny interlude of hope was over. Milly found herself being edged expertly back along the narrow entrance hall, past the bicycle, and the gum-boots, and the umbrella-stand, to where the front door still stood open, as if it had known, ever since Milly arrived, that she was one of the ones who would not be staying.

But on the threshold, Milly paused. When she had arrived here (attracted not only by the Rooms to Let sign, but also by the dirty curtains, which suggested that it might be cheap), it had still been afternoon, with faint gleams of sunlight on the tips of the slated roofs. Now, the air was full of dusk. The landlady shivered as she held the door open for Milly's departure: you could see she was impatient, longing to get the door closed again. As for Milly, her mind was empty of further plans. It all seemed too difficult.

"Well, goodbye, then," she said, vaguely, backing out of the little lighted hall. As she moved out of the shelter of the doorway, the icy chill of the coming night flicked at her: the first blades of the cold that was to come touched at her knees and at her throat: and straightaway her body remembered. Before any thought of hers could direct it, it was back through the already-closing door, back into the warm hallway, and fighting for its life.

She *quite* understood, she gabbled, that a person letting rooms has to be careful: she'd be just the same herself . . . the words rattled from Milly's lips like ticker-tape, racing to get it all said before righteous fury took the place of stupefaction in the startled face in front of her. So how would it be, Milly babbled on—and here she smiled into the still-dazed blue eyes with a frank, phoney charm worthy of Julian himself—how would it be if she gave references? She had a job locally . . . her employer . . . a Mrs Graham . . . ?

What on earth would happen if this suggestion was actually taken up, she had no time to consider. But at least Mrs Graham would have heard of her, and would have to say so: wasn't it quite something to have been heard of by someone, in this big empty world?

As it happened, the matter was never put to test. At the word "references", the indignant little body in front of her nearly exploded.

"References!" she spat. "What's the good of references? Anyone can fake a reference! D'you think I was born yesterday?" She didn't, of course, expect an answer to this question, least of all the answer "No, but I was!" which was what almost sprang to Milly's lips, and had to be hastily suppressed.

"Some of the worst tenants I've ever had have come to me with a whole bag-load of posh references," the woman continued. "I wouldn't give tuppence for a reference from the Queen of England herself! And anyway," she finished truculently, "Where's your luggage? I never take anyone who arrives with no luggage!"

At this additional indictment, Milly's hopes suddenly revived. As soon as someone gives *two* reasons for not doing what you want, instead of one, he has as good as lost the game already: unwittingly, he has put himself within range of argument on two fronts.

"My luggage? It's at the station," Milly said, with a dignity borne of having almost forgotten that everything she was saying was lies. "Naturally, I didn't want to drag it around with me before I was settled, and so . . ."

A small burst of derisory clapping from up above made both women whirl round and peer up into the half-darkness of the stairs. There, just at the bend of the banisters, two grinning faces had appeared, gleaming indistinctly out of a shadowy framework of beards and hair.

"Attagirl! You're winning!" called one cheery young voice, and the other: "Oh, come on, Mrs Mums, give her a chance! Remember the lies *we* had to tell before you'd let us in!"

The little woman thus addressed rushed like a small charging bull to the foot of the stairs.

"Off with you!" she yelled up into the darkness. "Both of you, off to your room! And I'll thank you to call me *Mrs Mumford*, if you please! Whatever's the lady going to think, hearing you go on like that? She'll think we keep a madhouse here! So off! *Off!*"

A shuffle of laughter, a thumping of heavy feet, and then the banging of a door. Mrs Mumford now turned to Milly almost apologetically, just exactly as if Milly had a right to be standing there in the hallway and passing judgement on the establishment.

"My students," she explained deprecatingly. "They'll be the death of me, I swear they will! Never a minute's peace . . ."

But Milly did not fail to notice the touch of pride in the

42

sharp voice. "My students . . ." whatever she might say, you could tell already that Mrs Mumford loved having them there.

"I've been taking in students for twelve years come September," Mrs Mumford informed Milly, temporarily suspending hostilities for the sake (presumably) of a few minutes' chat. "It's the University, you see, it's not more than twelve miles down the coast, they can get there in twenty minutes on the train. The money's not much, though, not when you consider the Sunday dinners as well. I've always done the Sunday dinners for my students, but when you consider the price of meat these days . . . And the way they eat, you wouldn't believe it, Mrs . . . Mrs . . . Excuse me, what *did* you say your name was?"

"Barnes," said Milly, who hadn't said anything of the kind, and had indeed only just this moment decided on it. "Milly Barnes."

"Ah. Yes, well, Mrs Barnes, like I was telling you, it's a big problem, running a house like this, especially for a woman on her own. Like when I started, you see, my Leslie—that's my son, you know—my Leslie was at home then, he wasn't married . . . Have *you* a son, Mrs Barnes?"

What a nice idea! Milly toyed with the thought of having a son—or even two sons. After all, they'd be past the troublesome stage by now, and out earning their own living. And what about a married daughter . . . ?

Milly sighed.

"No," she said. It was a pity, but the complications would be too great. These three young people would be expected

43

to come and see her now and again . . . unless of course they all had jobs abroad, in which case this little woman would be on the watch for airmail letters which never came. It was going to be difficult enough to explain why no letters came anyway, without that.

"No—" she enlarged on it cautiously. "I never had any children. Your son must be a great satisfaction to you," she went on, giving the sort of deft about-turn to the conversation which was going to have to become second-nature to her from now on.

"Well." Mrs Mumford paused heavily, pursing up her small mouth in thought. "Well. He's married into a funny family, you see. That's the trouble. It's not that I didn't warn him. I mean, it's not that I want to interfere, or anything like that, I'm not the interfering kind . . ."

At what point in the conversation had it become no longer possible to throw Milly into the street? These things are impossible to gauge in retrospect; but certain it is that the realisation that the critical moment was already past came to them both, suddenly. Mrs Mumford's voice abruptly trailed into silence, and she stared helplessly at Milly, almost as if appealing to her for advice. How, she seemed to be asking, are we to start quarrelling again *now*? By what route can we make our way back to the point when I was saying "No, I'm sorry," and holding the front door open for you to disappear into the night? It was a problem in etiquette to which Mrs Mumford's limited repertoire simply didn't extend.

"Well." She said at last, and then, when nothing came of

the remark, she tried again: "Well, I suppose."

"Yes," said Milly.

It still wasn't clear who had won: but all the same, they couldn't go on standing here in the hallway for ever, so after a bit, Mrs Mumford led the way upstairs, explaining, from long habit, that no one was allowed to run a bath after eleven p.m. because of the cistern. Only after she had completed this little admonition did she realise that every word of it had been insiduously strengthening Milly's hitherto tenuous claim on the tenancy.

"And of course, no late visitors!" she snapped, hitting out at random now, as she felt the initiative slipping from her grasp, and "No, of course not," said Milly heartily. "I say, what a gorgeous room!"

Nothing in her twelve years of landladyhood had prepared Mrs Mumford for this sort of reaction to her First Floor Back, Business Lady or Gentleman Only: and for a moment she stopped dead in the open doorway, staring first at Milly and then at the room, as if wondering who it was who was going mad. She couldn't, of course, guess that the dingy little carpetless room was irradiated with the primeval, almost-forgotten glory of having four walls, and a roof strong enough to keep out the rain and the savage winter wind; nor that the narrow lumpy bed with its old-fashioned white counterpane was holding out the promise of that most voluptuous of all human joys: lying down in safety, with blankets.

"Oh, I'm going to be so *happy* here!" cried Milly, feasting her eyes on the four solid walls holding up so marvellously against the sleet, and snow, and the bitter wind from the sea. The heartfelt sincerity in her voice seemed to bewilder her prospective landlady. After all these years in the business, Mrs Mumford knew well enough when she was being "got round". She could have taken her PhD any time, in identifying "soft soap" and "flannel", and all the other rent-postponing tricks that the wit of tenants could devise. But this sincere and unqualified admiration for one of her ugliest and most over-priced rooms was something that she could not place.

If you can't place it, it's dangerous. She watched Milly's incomprehensible enthusiasm through narrowed eyes. It was unnatural. And suspicious. And heart-warming.

"Yes, it's a nice little room, isn't it?" she found herself saying, proudly. "And if you look at those curtains, Mrs Barnes, you'll find they're lined. Properly lined. I had them done professionally, I don't believe in stinting, not where my tenants' comfort is concerned . . ."

Was it those lined curtains that decided the issue in the end? Neither Milly nor Mrs Mumford could have put their finger on it, but by the time Milly had obediently examined the said linings, stroked them with her forefinger, and agreed about the superior quality of the material, not like the rubbish they sell you *these* days—by this time, the whole argument was plainly over. Milly was here to stay. Both of them knew it. Milly had won.

Aggrieved, and not a little bewildered at this turn of events, Mrs Mumford looked uneasily around for some small way of punishing Milly for whatever it was she had done to thus worm her way into the establishment. She expected co-operation from her tenants, she told Milly sharply, and she hoped Milly hadn't brought a radio? They caused a lot of trouble radios did, and she, Mrs Mumford, had always been one for avoiding trouble. Did Milly quite understand?

Having thus re-established her ascendancy, Mrs Mumford took her leave, and Milly was left in undisputed possession of the small cold room, with its bare electric-light bulb and the pale damp winding its slow tides among the brown criss-cross pattern of the wall-paper.

Victory! At last! The sense of victory was like a fever, and Milly was aware neither of cold nor of hunger as she pulled off her blouse and skirt and slid between the icy sheets. And as she lay there, in the darkness, she felt as an athlete must feel as he stumbles, exhausted, past the tape, with the cheering from a million throats ringing in his ears. Only for Milly there was no cheering, only the distant, changeless roaring of the winter sea, and the rattle of her ill-fitting windows as the wind battered against them out of the night.

Oh, but the triumph of it! The glory of lying here, safe, and dry, and victorious, her whole soul glowing, expanding with the consciousness of having faced almost impossible odds, and of having overcome them! What wonders she had performed in the past thirty-six hours! Had she not succeeded in disappearing, without trace, from the heart of a great civilisation which checks and counter-checks, which lists and dockets and supervises its citizens as no civilisation has ever done before? And had she not survived, and survived in perfect health, thirty-six hours of exposure and starvation such as might have brought a trained soldier to his knees? She, a flabby middle-aged woman, with no training, no money, and in a state of total shock, had succeeded not only in surviving, but in finding herself a job, a home, and a new way of life, and all without rousing a moment's suspicion in any of the people involved!

If only Julian could know! "Not fit to be out alone!" he used to say, with such withering scorn, when she happened to have left her gloves somewhere, or to have forgotten the special Polish olives, or whatever, for one of his important parties. "Out alone," indeed! Just let him look at her now!

The dim, unfamiliar shapes of the strange furniture in the strange room began to melt and swim before Milly's eyes as the deep drowsiness of prolonged fasting stole over her. How clever I am! she congratulated herself sleepily, and as she lay there, basking in the contemplation of her own cleverness, it never dawned on her that, for a person planning to vanish without trace, she had already made two glaring and awful mistakes: one of them so foolish that, really, even a child might have thought of it, and taken more care.

CHAPTER VI

Milly woke from a long, dreamless sleep with a vague sense that something was going on. For a while she lay, inert and tranquil, too sleepy to care. Then, slowly, recollection of yesterday's events came flooding back, and with it a realisation of where she was and how she had got here. Slowly, and with a degree of awakening curiosity, she opened her eyes.

At first, the sickening terror almost made her faint, right there as she lay. And the most ghastly thing of all was that the terror was so familiar: familiar like a madman's nightmare, that has to be lived through over and over again, for ever, and from which there is no escape. The shuffling, slippered footsteps; the striped pyjamas sagging from bony shoulders as the tall, stooping figure fumbled its way across the curtained room . . . The long hands groping, softly reaching into drawers and cupboards . . . searching, fumbling . . . The terror was so great that at first Milly could neither move nor cry out.

Had her escape all been a dream, then? Had these last two days never happened at all? All that cleverness, all those stratagems and strokes of luck by which she had launched herself so miraculously into a new life—had it really all been too good to be true, as it had at moments seemed?

A dream? A mere fevered, wishful fantasy, bred of the sick, stagnant air of that South London basement—an air thick with obsession, with strange miasmas of the mind, soaked up over the years into the very walls . . . ?

So it was all to do again? Her decision—her escape? Had she still to face it all in reality, having gone through it once in dreams . . . ? Milly forced herself to look again into the almost-darkness: and now, with the first shock beginning to subside in her limbs and in her knotted stomach, she was able to observe that the figure was not quite as she remembered. Where was the crest of white hair, gleaming moth-like through the darkness no matter how black the night or how closely-fastened the ancient, creaking shutters? And where was the low, barely audible mumbling, on and on without end or outcome, that always used to accompany these nightly prowlings . . . ?

Nightly? Why, it wasn't even night! At that very moment the pyjama'd figure had reached the windows . . . was drawing back the curtains, knocking over something as he did so, letting in the first white glitter of a winter day. In the cold, sharp light, the figure was revealed to be young, and lanky: tousled, fairish hair flopped this way and that around his ears, and in his right hand he swung a large, battered aluminium kettle. With unspeakable relief, Milly recognised him as one of the young men who had been peering over the banisters last night while she and Mrs Mumford fought out their life-and-death battle of wits.

"Oh!" said the young man, apparently noticing Milly's head on the pillow for the first time, and then "I say!"

He paused, as if for an answer, and then resumed his own train of thought: "I mean. That is. I say, I'm sorry! I didn't think there was anybody here."

Milly still couldn't think of anything to say. She was limp and speechless from relaxation, the aftermath of fear, so she just lay there, contentedly enough, waiting for some sense to emerge from the encounter. He looked quite a nice young man; bearded, and with amiable greenish eyes under shaggy beige eyebrows. Just now his mouth was open.

"It's the hotplate, you see," he volunteered at last, hitching up his pyjama trousers as he spoke. "I suppose you don't know what's happened to the hotplate?"

"I'm afraid—well, you see, I only came last night," essayed Milly, still dazed: and then she watched, quite unsurprised, while the intruder, with a muttered exclamation, flung open the door of a huge yellow-varnished wardrobe, and began rummaging in its depths. Clanking sounds . . . muffled thuds . . . and then he emerged, wild-eyed, and pushing the tumble of hair back from his face. For a second he glanced despairingly round the room, then he turned, and strode without a word to the door.

"Kev!" he yelled. "I say, Kev! The silly old cow's gone off with the hotplate! *Now* what are we going to do?"

Which hotplate? What silly old cow? Before any guesses could begin to form themselves in Milly's mind, there were suddenly *two* young men filling her doorway. The second one (Kev, presumably) was darker, and distinctly better groomed than his companion. His beard was trimmed, and his pyjamas firmly corded.

"I say, I'm sorry about this," said the newcomer to Milly. "Jacko had no idea there was anyone here, you see."

He paused, and looked thoughtfully round the room. "I say, do you mind if *I* come and have a look?—It must be somewhere." He paused politely for just long enough for Milly to have said "Yes, that's quite all right", if she had so wished: and then he set himself to flinging open drawers and cupboards, delving among hair-curlers, outworn gloves, and long-ago relics of somebody's gracious living—lace-edged table-mats, embroidered nightdress-cases—the sort of things that are too good to throw away and too bothersome to use, and so just right for lodgers.

"You *see*?" said the first boy, Jacko, with a sort of melancholy triumph, when it became clear that his friend's search was destined to be as fruitless as his own, and, "I *told* you you should have helped her pack!" retorted Kevin, "Then she'd never have . . ."

At this point, both seemed to recall simultaneously the existence of Milly, who was by now sitting up in bed with her winter coat clutched round her. They looked at her consideringly.

"Miss Childe," observed the one called Kevin, with just the faintest touch of reproach in his voice, "always used to let us make our tea in here. On the hotplate."

"Yes. On the hotplate."

Milly was beginning to hate the hotplate, whatever it was. She met the two pairs of mildly reproachful eyes boldly.

"I don't know anything about it," she declared. "I don't know what you're talking about. *What* hotplate?"

"For our morning tea," explained Kevin patiently. "We always made our morning tea on it. In here," he added explanatorily, and still with that more-in-sorrow-than-in-anger note to his voice. "*Now*, I don't know how we're to make our tea at all! That's the point."

"Yes. That's the point," agreed Jacko.

Both were now looking at her with a sort of guarded appeal, like puppies who know that they aren't *really* allowed to be fed at table. Jacko was clutching the big, useless kettle to his breast, just where his middle pyjama button was missing.

But what could Milly do?

"What about the gas-ring?" she suggested, her eyes lighting upon this appliance as she spoke. "I don't mind you using my gas-ring, if you like."

"You mean there's some *money* in it? In the meter?"

They both spoke together, and with such eager hope that Milly hated to have to disappoint them.

"No," she said regretfully, "I'm afraid not—That's to say, *I* didn't put any in, and I'm afraid, just at the moment, I haven't . . ."

"No. Oh, well . . ." Jacko shrugged, sadly, but no longer with any reproach in his manner. During the last minute or two she had imperceptibly become one of them, all in the same boat.

The three of them regarded each other sadly.

"Ah, but it was a great little gadget, that hotplate!" sighed Kev, nostalgically, like an old man reminiscing about the vanished joys of his youth. "You could plug it into the lights, you see, and it would hot up a treat, and never cost anybody a penny! I can't imagine what the old cow was thinking of, going off with it like that! I mean, whatever would make her do such a thing?"

"Perhaps it was hers?" suggested Milly mildly: and both boys stared at her as if she had taken leave of her senses. Clearly, the concept of private property simply wasn't applicable to something they wanted as much as this.

"But we've got nothing to make our tea on!" Jacko cried indignantly; while Kevin, with the inventiveness born of necessity, suddenly cried out: "The bed! Like she might have shoved it under the bed, with all the junk . . ."

By now, both of Milly's visitors were full-length on the floor, grovelling under her bed, throwing up debris like terriers in a rabbit-hole. Shoes. Laddered tights. More shoes. A copy of Nova. Half a candle . . .

"Hey!" came Kevin's voice, muffled by dust and blankets, "Hey! Look! Ricicles! Anybody like Ricicles?" He squirmed out and up into a sitting position, holding up his find in triumph.

How old they were, there was of course no way of guessing, but the packet was nearly full, and Milly, who till this moment had felt no sensations of hunger at all, was suddenly faint with longing.

"Yes! " she answered. "Oh yes . . . !" and when one of the boys recalled the existence somewhere among his belongings of half a tin of condensed milk, left from the time Janette was here, she felt that happiness could go no further.

Five minutes later she was sitting on Jacko's unmade bed in the cluttered barrack of a room that the two boys shared, and listening to the story of their lives while she shovelled spoonful after spoonful of ageing Ricicles into her starving frame.

The two life stories, it seemed to Milly, were both unusual and surprisingly similar. Both lads, it seemed, came of prosperous families: both had always wanted to be artists, but had unfortunately ended up like this, studying economics at a provincial university. So far, the story seemed a familiar one to Milly. In her young days, too, budding geniuses had been forced by soulless and insensitive parents into training for something dull and practical. But apparently, with these two, it wasn't quite like that. Far from being soulless and insensitive, both sets of parents had eagerly begged to be allowed to finance their budding young geniuses through art school for as many years as they wanted. Paris . . . Rome . . . Anywhere they liked . . . money should be no object.

"But of course," explained Kevin, "that would have been just art-school stuff. Not my scene at all."

"No," agreed Jacko. "That was the thing. It's a matter of integrity, you see. Personal integrity."

Integrity, it seemed, had stopped them doing a lot of things, such as getting a vacation job, or studying hard for their exams. As far as Milly could make out from the narrative, it was integrity, plus their abhorrence of material possessions, that had stood in the way of success at every turn.

"You see, Mrs Barnes, we just don't *want* success," Jacko explained, waving his spoon about to emphasise the point.

"Success is a form of death. You know——material possessions, and all that jazz. It's just not our scene."

But wasn't a hotplate a material possession? Milly asked, rather ill-advisedly——and there was a moment of pained silence, as if she had enquired after some unmentionable relative. Then Jacko pointed out, rather stiffly, that it was *their* Ricicles she was eating: they, Kev and himself, believed in sharing, and non-violence, and in respecting the beingness of every human person.

Milly, defeated by all this logic, humbly apologised.

They were very nice about it: and soon she felt that the three of them had been friends for years. She told them the fictional story of her life (the very same concoction that had been so insultingly brushed aside by Mrs Graham yesterday), and their rapt credulity went far to soothe the frustrated creative artist in her: so much so that the selling-up of the family heirlooms almost brought tears to her own eyes, and the thought of the non-existent haunts of her childhood being trampled now by the equally non-existent feet of strangers was wonderfully bitter.

Her good-natured hearers seemed to believe every word of it, and to have all the time in the world to listen: and when she came to the only truthful bit, about how hungry she was, their concern was quite touching. They rummaged around among their hi-fi equipment and their unironed shirts, and found her two starch-reduced rolls and some peanut butter. These, on top of the Ricicles, made her feel wonderful.

After this, they told her about sex, and how they were *through* with that sort of thing: kids' stuff. Yes, homosexuality too, and the perversions, and all that drag—they'd tried the lot: nothing to it. Integrity, that was the thing. Kevin, it seemed, was through with drugs as well: and when Milly asked if that was kids' stuff too, he said no, it wasn't quite that, but he'd been turned right off by going home one vacation and finding his grandmother smoking pot and saying she thought the younger generation was marvellous. It had turned him right off, it really had: and anyway, he informed Milly kindly, integrity, and the discovery of the true self, were possible *without* the aid of drugs. He knew, because he'd tried.

By this time there was not a crumb nor a scraping of anything eatable left, and Milly realised with sharp dismay that she had no idea what the time was! Why, she might already be hours late for her wonderful new job! Ten o'clock, Mrs Graham had said.

"What's the time?" she cried, rudely interrupting an account of Jacko's true self versus the Admissions Board, and for a moment her two companions seemed rather taken aback. They found her anxiety about being in time for work puzzling, and a little shocking: and though they were too kind actually to say it, it was plain enough to Milly that integrity was not really compatible with punctuality. However, they were broad-minded lads, and when they realised that Milly really *was* worried, they took counsel, and Jacko clattered amiably down the stairs to consult the household clocks. He came back with the reassuring news that since the kitchen clock said twenty to eleven, and the chiming clock in the dining room had just struck seven, it couldn't possibly be later than half past nine. Earlier, very likely. Milly would soon get the hang of it, he assured her, after she'd lived here a while.

"Off to work, Mrs Barnes?"

Whether by chance or cunning, Mrs Mumford had materialised in the hallway just as Milly was letting herself out of the front door, and Milly seized eagerly on the opportunity (such opportunities having become increasingly rare of late) of speaking the truth.

"Yes," she said happily, meeting the landlady's watchful eyes with a smile. "I have to be there by ten . . ." and so saying she stepped triumphantly forth into the frosty, silver-yellow morning.

"Off to work!" How safe, and solid, and successful the phrase sounded! Milly fairly danced along the icy, unfamiliar street, the sea-wind whipping at her scarlet head-scarf, and her ungloved hands pushed deep into the pockets of her winter coat. Off to work! Off to work! What price mustard-and-cress *now*, eh, Julian?

CHAPTER VII

"Ah, good morning, Mrs—er—! Do you think you could start in the kitchen? There's not much to do really, just one or two things that don't go in the dishwasher; and then if you could just go over the floor with the Squeejee? That's all it needs, it's specially surfaced, you see. I don't believe in hard scrubbing, do you, Mrs Er—all that down-on-hands-and-knees business? I believe in labour-saving, my kitchen is modern throughout, all the latest equipment. I don't believe in *making* work . . ."

By the time Mrs Graham had reached this point in her credo, the two of them had reached the kitchen doorway, and Milly came into full view of the one or two things that wouldn't go in the dishwasher. Grease-caked saucepans, burnt baking-tins and frying pans . . . and on every surface in sight lay mountainous, half-dismantled mechanisms, each trailing a greasy length of electric flex, and most of them plastered with ancient remnants of food, each in accordance with its function.

"Yes . . . yes, of course," agreed Milly faintly, trying to conceal her dismay as she contemplated all these rejects from the labour-saving paradise about which Mrs Graham was still prattling so blithely:

". . . can take up to four loads in a morning!" she was saying proudly, patting the dishwasher as if it was a favourite pony, and Milly now turned her awed gaze towards the subject of this eulogy. It dominated the scene like a queen termite, its huge white bulk throned on what had once been a roomy draining-board, but whose effective area had now been reduced to a strip two or three inches wide, on which (Milly could see already) it would be impossible to balance anything much bigger than a teacup.

"The washing-up is *nothing* now! " Mrs Graham was explaining happily. "Just a few cooking things which can be left till it's convenient" (like now, I suppose, thought Milly) "and all the rest goes straight into the dishwasher! All the cups, saucers, spoons, plates—unless they're *very* greasy, of course . . ."

It seemed to Milly that the thing liked washing up exactly the same things as everyone else likes washing up, and it avoided anything at all difficult or unpleasant: the only difference being that *it* got away with it. Mrs Graham was right now beaming on it with loving pride, as if it had just passed its O-levels . . .

"It cost me £200!" she informed Milly in hushed tones, "and it's been worth every penny! It's *time*, you see, Mrs Er, that I'm short of: for a person like me, time *is* money!"

It was for Milly, too, of course: in her case, an hour equalled seven shillings, as Mrs Graham of all people, should have known. But Mrs Graham seemed to feel that the predicament was so specially *hers* that Milly hadn't the heart to point out its universality. Instead, she listened with respectful attention while her employer continued:

"You see, I happen to have a degree in Sociology, and if a woman has had any sort of higher education I feel she has an obligation to *use* it, even after she's married, don't you agree, Mrs Er? It's difficult, though, working at home: people seem to think that just because you're at home, they can interrupt you just as much as ever they like. They think they can come in and out bothering you about every tiny thing! My other woman was like that."

Her voice trailed off into a deprecatory little laugh, and she shot an anxious glance at Milly. Clearly, she wanted to make sure that the point had got across, but was fearful lest it might have offended her new Mrs Er in the process. Milly suppressed a tiny smile and was agreeably aware of the first stirrings of a sense of power. Mrs Er's were few and far between.

But after Mrs Graham had gone, and she found herself alone in the messy, alien kitchen, the brief feeling of confidence left her, and she felt something approaching panic. Where should she start? Where was everything supposed to go? Where was the Vim . . . the washing-up liquid . . . ? In the weeks to come, she was to learn that this attack of panic when confronted by a strange kitchen was one of the occupational hazards of being a Daily, and she was to learn, too, how quickly it passed: how, if one set oneself quietly to doing just one thing, however trivial, the other tasks would mysteriously sort themselves out and become manageable while one wasn't looking. But this morning, in her very first job, she didn't know any of this: she thought it was herself, her own inadequacy, that was to blame.

I can't! she thought, I can't! Her hands were trembling, and her mouth was dry, exactly like someone about to make a public speech for the first time: yet even while she panicked, she began, whether by good luck or instinct, to do the right thing. That is, to do *something*. She began blindly pulling the pans out of the sink and stacking them on the floor beside her.

And suddenly, wonderfully, she found that a miracle had happened! She had done one thing! She had cleared the sink! Now all things were possible.

Humming a little tune in sheer relief, she turned on the hot tap to its fullest extent, and as it surged clean and steaming against the stainless steel, she began with real enthusiasm to select an assortment of objects to begin on: she was now positively enjoying the enormity of the mess confronting her. She had joined battle with it, and she was going to win!

But here came the next setback. No dishcloth. Not just that she couldn't *find* a dishcloth: there simply wasn't one. Not anywhere. Nor a floorcloth either, nor any rag of any kind. How on earth was she to wash up all this stuff without one—not to mention the wiping of all these streamlined labour-saving surfaces, now revealed as a mass of grease, old tea-leaves, and smears of gravy? Milly's fingers itched to get at it all with a lovely, hot, well-wrung-out cloth, and for a moment she stood motionless, surveying the smears and spills, weighing them up against Mrs Graham's degree in Sociology.

Then, her decision made, she marched boldly out of the kitchen and knocked firmly on the sitting-room door.

"No dishcloth?" Mrs Graham was blinking, vaguely, as she looked up from her typewriter, like a kitten just roused from sleep. "No *dishcloth*? But of course there isn't a dish cloth. We have a dishwasher—I showed you, Mrs Er—and so we don't *need* a dishcloth. It's an *automatic* machine, don't you see? The washing up is done *automatically*."

She spoke wearily, as if it was the twentieth time she had had to repeat this same elementary fact. You could see her visibly resigning herself to the idea that Mrs Er was going to prove just as stupid as My Other Woman.

"It's an *automatic* dishwasher," she repeated, stealing an impatient glance down at her typewriter, but Milly stood her ground.

"It's all those saucepans," she pointed out. "The things that won't go in the dishwasher. The baking-tins. And the mincer. And the burnt chip-pan. And all that white, sticky stuff in the Mouli-Mixer—"

"Oh dear. Well." You could see that Mrs Graham was interrupting the recital because she knew it by heart. She must have gone through it many a time with My Other Woman and her predecessors, and she had learned, the hard way, that stupidity has to be humoured.

"You want a rag, I suppose?" she diagnosed wearily. "I'll see what I can find." And with a huge sigh she got up from her typewriter and began rummaging in the bottom drawer of a big mahogany desk. Embroidery silks—hem-stitched tray-cloths—postcards—cotton wool—they boiled up like soapsuds round her elbows as she stirred and prodded, and at last, in weary triumph, she produced

63

a torn nylon slip and the half-unravelled sleeve of a knitted sweater.

"*Here* you are," she said, and such was her air of having secured these objects against unimaginable odds that Milly hadn't the heart to point out that they were almost useless for the job in hand, and that what she needed was something absorbent, like an old towel or piece of sheeting.

So she simply thanked her employer meekly, and went back to the kitchen. It took much longer than it would have done, if only she'd had a proper rag, and the final result was not all that she could have wished: but it was certainly greatly improved, and Milly fairly glowed with pride when her employer came in, an hour later, and surveyed the clean and shining surfaces with real approval.

"They're marvellous, aren't they, these dishwashers?" she observed, looking blandly round at the results of Milly's labours. "See how clean and tidy they keep the kitchen! You've no idea the mess we used to be in, before we had one! I'm going to make a cup of coffee now, Mrs Er, could you put the kettle on? I drink a lot of coffee when I'm working. I expect you'd rather have tea, Mrs Er, wouldn't you?"

Milly thought quickly. Did this mean simply that My Other Woman had preferred tea? Or was it a veiled command—coffee in short supply, or more expensive, or something?

Well, and suppose it *was* a veiled command? Who was it, anyway, who had to be careful not to annoy whom? At this invigorating thought, Milly's courage returned.

"No—actually I prefer coffee," she declared boldly, and registering only the faintest flicker of surprise, Mrs Graham took the Nescafé from the shelf, and proceeded to make coffee for the two of them.

"I'm on a special diet, I don't take sugar," she observed, stirring two heaped teaspoonfuls into Milly's cup as she spoke; and Milly accepted the sickly-sweet concoction without protest. In the first place, she could quite see how the specialness of Mrs Graham's diet would be spoiled by other people not taking sugar either, and in the second, she could feel in her body an unwonted craving for sweetness. Even after all those Ricicles, she still felt half-starved, and she watched, almost dizzy with greed, as Mrs Graham reached for a tin of biscuits, opened it, and peered inside.

"All sweet ones!" she said disgustedly. "Arnold— Professor Graham, that is to say—he *will* buy the sweet ones! I've told him a million times . . . ! For two pins I'd do the shopping myself, but it's so convenient for him, the supermarket's right on his way back from the University . . ."

Milly watched, sick with disappointment, as Mrs Graham began replacing the lid—but just at that moment, something seemed to arrest Mrs Graham's attention. She cocked her head on one side, and set the biscuit tin absently on the table: and Milly, pretending to think it had been passed to her, snatched greedily into the tin.

Had this behaviour looked very odd? Mrs Graham was staring at Milly unbelievingly, and Milly, covered with shame and confusion, was just about to apologise, when Mrs Graham herself began to speak.

"I can't understand it!" she was saying, "I can't understand it at all! Alison *always* sleeps till lunch time! *Now* what am I going to do?"

By now Milly could hear the sounds too—the unmistakeable protests of a baby who considers that her morning sleep is over. Mrs Graham pressed her hand against her white forehead despairingly.

"And Arnold will be back at one, wanting his lunch, and I've still got my correlations to finish! Look, Mrs Er, would you mind seeing to her for me? Do you know anything about babies? If you could just get her up, and change her nappy? And then keep her with you while you do the dining-room? She's no trouble: you just have to see that she doesn't pull down the ornaments, or open the sideboard, or put anything in her mouth, or interfere with the papers on the couch, or get at the china in the cabinet, or play with the lamp flex, or pull the books out of the bottom shelf, or pinch her fingers in the door—Oh, and watch out for the vases, won't you, Mrs Er? She's mad about flowers. And the clock too: now that she can climb up to the clock I just don't know *what* we are going to do. And whatever you do, don't let her cry, because I *must* get on with my correlations, I just *can't* be interrupted any more this morning."

With which instructions, she whisked up her cup of coffee and fairly fled into the sitting-room, shutting the door behind her with a finality that was almost a slam. Milly was left to locate the baby as best she could.

Not that it was difficult. The screams were reaching a crescendo now, and Milly opened the door behind which they resounded with a good deal of trepidation. She was no automatic baby-lover: she only liked them if they were nice, and there was so far no evidence at all that this one was going to fall into any such category.

At the sight of the furious, red-faced little creature, standing up clutching the bars of its cot and jigging up and down in its rage, all Milly's most non-maternal feelings surged into her breast.

"There, there! Now, come along, then!" she forced herself to squeak ingratiatingly across the uproar: and at the sound of her voice Alison at once stopped screaming, presumably from sheer shock. For a moment the two glowered at each other in mutual dismay. Traumatic, that's what it must be, thought Milly glumly, to have a complete stranger walk in like this and yank you out of your cot and start changing your nappy. Surely, even a mother *without* a degree in Sociology might have thought twice about it?

Still, everything has its bright side: it seemed, mercifully, that the effect of traumatic experiences on Alison was to stop her screaming for minutes on end: long enough for Milly to change her nappy, get her leggings on, carry her into the dining-room, and set her down on a rug, where she sat, sucking the plug of the Hoover with ferocious intensity, and following Milly's every movement with unblinking concentration. She remained in this felicitous state of shock for long enough to allow Milly to dust all the furniture, and even to wipe the window-sills and mantelpiece with a damp cloth. After that, inevitably, recovery set in, and Alison began to feel well enough to screw up her face ready for a new bout of crying. At this unwelcome sign of returning vitality, Milly hastily gave the child a pair of nutcrackers out of the sideboard drawer, together with a small brass tray to bash them against, and while Alison was thus employed, she herself got on with the hoovering. By now, she was feeling really pleased with herself. She was managing the job splendidly. Mrs Graham had been really pleased with the kitchen, and surely she would be pleased with this room, too: it was beginning to look very nice, with all the furniture polished and shining, and the last of the crumbs disappearing off the floor like a dream . . . and it was just then, just as she switched the Hoover off, that the telephone began to ring.

It was ridiculous, of course: why on earth *shouldn't* Mrs Graham's phone ring now and again? Why in all the world should it be anything to do with Milly? And yet, as she stood there, behind the closed door of the dining-room, Milly felt her pulse quicken. Her palms began sweating . . . soon her heart was leaping in her throat with great, panicky thuds, and her legs trembled so that she could hardly go on standing. She heard Mrs Graham cross the room, lift the receiver . . .

"Seacliffe 49901," Milly heard her say briskly, and held her breath as she listened. In a moment now it would be all right. She would hear Mrs Graham saying something like: "Oh hul*lo*, Christine . . . !" or "Thank you *so* much, Tuesday will do splendidly . . . !" something of that sort, something to show conclusively that it was nothing whatsoever to do with Milly. Well, of course it wasn't. How could it be? No

68

one in all the world knew she was here . . . how ridiculous to panic like this about nothing!

"Ye-es," she heard Mrs Graham saying, in a guarded sort of voice, and then, more decisively: "Yes, she's been here since ten o'clock . . ." And after that came a pause, which to Milly's ringing ears seemed to last a lifetime. Then Mrs Graham's voice again: "Well, I can't help that, can I? But who told you about her? How did you know?"

By this time, if only her legs would have carried her so far, Milly would have been out of the dining-room window and sliding down whatever drainpipe there might or might not be to the ground three storeys below: but so paralysed was she with the sheer, incredible horror of it, that she could only stand there. Who had traced her . . . ? How . . . ? Or had it all been a plot, a police trap carefully laid for her? What a fool she had been . . . ! Why hadn't her suspicions been aroused by the incredible ease with which she had walked into this job . . . ? Why hadn't she realised that it was a trap, that Mrs Graham must be in league with the police . . . ? Even as these speculations rang and rattled through her whirling brain, she realised that the telephone conversation had broken off: Mrs Graham was crossing the hall . . . opening the dining-room door . . . and now she was standing there, in the doorway, fixing Milly with a hard, suspicious stare: and behind the suspicion, there was the faint, unmistakeable flicker of fear . . .

"A phone call, Mrs Er," she said accusingly, "from a neighbour of mine. She's heard I've got a new woman, someone seems to have seen you coming in this morning, and she wants to know if you've got any time left to work for *her*? She wants to talk to you about it. Now, you will remember, won't you, Mrs Er, that you undertook to do mornings for *me*. You won't let me down, will you? From what Mrs Day tells me, I think she may be going to offer you forty-pence an hour, but you *will* remember, won't you, Mrs Er, that you get your *lunches* here. A really good lunch, every day . . ."

Luckily, Mrs Graham was so thoroughly wrapped up in these anxieties that she did not notice the way Milly almost danced across the hall to the telephone; nor did she hear the breathless relief in Milly's voice as she settled for three afternoons a week with this Mrs Day. It was her *own* sense of relief, not Milly's, that was engaging Mrs Graham's whole attention: the colour was visibly returning to her cheeks as it slowly became clear from Milly's side of the conversation that there was to be no real betrayal. It was only *afternoons* Mrs Er was engaging herself for with the perfidious Mrs Day!

But the suspense, while it lasted, had made Mrs Graham irritable.

"It's incredible, isn't it?" she grumbled, as Milly put the phone down. "The way you can't keep anything to yourself in a place like this! *I* never told anyone I'd got a woman . . . I don't know how these things get about! I mean, you've hardly been in the place two hours, and she has to phone up . . . ! Oh, well . . ."—Mrs Graham made a visible effort to recover her poise. "It's not that I *mind* Mrs Day having you in the afternoons, Mrs Er, not a bit, I'm only too glad, if that's what suits you both. It's only that I do wish people wouldn't go round *telling* everybody . . . You *won't* let me down, Mrs Er, will you?"

And Milly, graciously, as became the great lady she had so recently become, promised that she would not.

CHAPTER VIII

Milly had rarely in her life felt happier than she did that afternoon, as she walked home along the seafront with one pound forty in her pocket, and with a lunch of lamb chops, mashed potatoes and sprouts still warming her through and through, like remembered joy. The wind had dropped, and through the gathering mist of the winter afternoon Milly could hear the invisible small waves slapping and sighing along the shingle, and she felt herself alive, and tingling with hope, in a way that she had not known since her teens. Oh, she had experienced hope all right, in adult life: wild, desperate, frenzied hopes, sometimes to be fulfilled for a while, more often to be disappointed, to be shattered and destroyed under her very eyes. But this was something different. Adult hopes are hopes *of* something . . . that this or that will happen or not happen. What Milly was experiencing now was the sort of hope that belongs normally only to the very young: not hope *of* anything in particular, but just Hope, its very essence, huge, unfocused, as undefined and as ungraspable as Eternity itself.

It was because she *was* young, of course: younger than she could ever remember, only three days old. Propelled by disaster grown too big to grasp, she had finally been hurled like a thunderbolt out of all her worries, all her fears, out of all the burden of her mistakes and crimes, and had crashed down into peace: into the still, golden winter mist, by the side of the quiet sea. It was like dying and going to heaven . . . it was like dying as a peculiarly intense form of life . . . it was new, new! And in all this new heaven or new earth, whichever it might be, Milly was the newest thing of all!

What a success she had made of her new life, so far! Last night's euphoria was still with her, quite undiminished by that brief panic over the telephone call this morning. Rather, that moment of overwhelming terror and guilt seemed to have done something to her which had wiped out guilt and terror for ever. Because her fears at that particular moment had proved unfounded, she now felt immunised against fear.

It was like being vaccinated—something like that. She was innoculated, now, against trouble, in some way that the doctors don't know of. The sea-mist gleaming all around her was like the lifting of the anaesthetic after an operation . . . there was that same dazed, exalted feeling that the pain is all over . . . when in fact it may sometimes be only just beginning.

But not all the gains were illusory: Milly was sure of that. She *had* done well as a Daily Help: astonishingly, unprecedentedly well, considering how few things she had succeeded in doing well in her former life. She had cleaned Mrs Graham's kitchen and dining-room really thoroughly, she had kept Alison quiet, she had helped cook lunch; and (she was sure of it) provided real moral support to her employer when, at twelve-fifty or thereabouts, disaster struck, in the form of Professor Graham coming home to lunch a full ten minutes earlier than expected.

"Oh, God!" his wife had greeted him, glancing up from her typewriter with a hunted look. "What's happened, Arnold? You said one o'clock! You said you wouldn't be back for lunch till one!"

Milly, peering through the kitchen door, saw a tall, scholarly looking man with greying hair settling his umbrella carefully in the umbrella stand. Then he straightened up and walked towards the sitting-room door. At the door he paused, took off his horn-rimmed glasses, all steamed-up from the sudden change from outdoors to the central-heated flat, and set himself to polishing them assiduously with his handkerchief. His mild brown eyes blinked owlishly without them, creating a barrier of gentle non-seeing-ness between himself and his aggrieved wife. Only after he had settled the glasses on his face again and returned the handkerchief to his pocket, did he seem constrained to answer her.

"I got a lift," he explained. "Carstairs has to go to the Library Committee lunch, and so he offered to drop me on the way. But don't worry, dear, finish what you're doing, I'm in no hurry."

"Finish what I'm doing!" His wife, with a huge sigh, pushed her papers aside and ostentatiously fitted the lid back on to the typewriter. "I sometimes think I'll *never* finish *anything* I'm doing! First Alison woke up early from her morning sleep—and now *you're* home! You don't know how lucky you are, Arnold, being allowed to *work* when you're working! How I envy you that room of yours at the University . . . all your things to hand . . . No one bothering you . . . !"

"They *do* bother me, you know, dear, sometimes," he pointed out mildly. "The telephone goes a lot in my room, you'd be surprised. Committees. Visiting lecturers. Trouble in the typing pool. All sorts of things. I can't always get on with my work as I'd like to."

"But you don't have Alison screaming her head off!" countered Mrs Graham. "And lunch to see to . . . and then I've got this new woman this morning, I've had to settle *her* in. It's amazing how many questions they seem to have to ask . . . *Mrs Er!*"—here she raised her voice to a ringing shout to reach Milly in the kitchen—though in fact Milly could already hear every word of her clear, carrying, complaining voice—"Mrs Er! Could you hurry the potatoes a bit? Professor Graham is back earlier than he planned . . ."

How one hurried potatoes, Milly wasn't quite sure. They boiled at the speed they did boil, no matter who went down on their knees to them. But she judged (rightly) that the shouted instruction was meant more as a reproof to Professor Graham than as a command to Milly: and so she simply went on with her preparations for the meal as quickly as she could, and radiated respectful sympathy— on, off, on, off—as Mrs Graham flapped in and out of the kitchen bemoaning her unfinished correlations.

Thanks to Milly, lunch was on the table, and Alison strapped in her high-chair, on the dot of one, and so Professor Graham had nothing to complain of, as his wife assured him, three or four times in succession. He'd *said* one o'clock, hadn't he?

And indeed he wasn't complaining. He sat consuming his lamb chops, mashed potatoes and sprouts with obvious enjoyment, a copy of *Scientific American* propped against the bottle of ketchup in front of him, and on his face the look of a man at peace with the world: a look off which his wife's barbed attempts at conversation bounced harmlessly.

So after a bit she turned her attention to Milly, and began explaining to her about Alison's diet, and how important it was that she should have plenty of salad now that she was eleven months old and on mixed feeding. She pointed out to Milly, with modest maternal pride, that a tomato and a shredded lettuce leaf had been added to Alison's share of the meal, and Milly murmured suitable words of approval, meanwhile watching with fascinated admiration, Alison's skill in extracting from the mush in front of her every scrap of tomato and lettuce leaf and throwing it on the floor. Like most babies in this diet-conscious age, she had a passion for all non-protein, non-vitamin foods, and it seemed to Milly that she and her mother had evolved a very good working arrangement: Mrs Graham talked fluently and enthusiastically to all comers about how much salad she gave Alison and how many vitamins it contained, and what a good effect they had on the child's teeth and complexion (which were indeed perfectly all right), while Alison stuffed herself contentedly on mashed potato flavoured with ketchup. This way, they were both happy. The only loser was Milly, whose task it proved to be to sweep, wipe and scrub Alison's vitamins from the floor after the meal was over.

Still, one pound forty! Not to mention Mrs Graham's heartfelt "Well, thank you, Mrs Er! You *will* be back tomorrow, won't you? Ten o'clock, as usual?"

Rich, and successful, and sought-after, Milly had sailed down in the lift to the ground floor, and swept like royalty out of the central-heated building and into the sudden, exhilarating cold of a January afternoon, with the white, glittering fog rolling in from the sea.

By the time she had re-lived this triumphant morning in every detail, as she strolled along, Milly had reached the point where she must leave the sea front and turn inland. Actually, this was by no means the quickest way from Mrs Graham's to Milly's lodgings, but somehow she had wanted, in her happiness, to walk along by the side of the sea; to let the sea share it with her, its soft waves rippling in through the mist, just as it had shared with her, thirty-six hours ago, the long night of storm, and darkness, and despair.

CHAPTER IX

When Milly arrived home—for this was how she already felt about No. 32 Leinster Terrace—she was greeted by a wonderful smell of freshly-baked cakes. Very tentatively—because she didn't yet know what, apart from not having baths after eleven, lodgers were allowed to do or where they were allowed to go—she peered in through the half-open kitchen door. Mrs Mumford, in a torn but colourful print overall, was at that moment up-ending a large round cake-tin over a rack on the scrubbed wooden table. Delicious steam, like incense, rose all around the tin and on either side, intent as acolytes at some holy rite, sat Jacko and Kevin, sniffing the sacred fumes and watching the mystic procedures with reverent adoration.

"I tell you, I'm not touching it till Sunday!" Mrs Mumford was scolding. "It's for Sunday, this cake, d'you think I'm going to be shamed in front of them all by serving a cake for Sunday tea that's been cut into? What d'you think I am? And it's not a scrap of good the two of you looking at me like that, you can keep sitting there till they come and take you away in your coffins, I'm not giving you a single crumb . . . !"

All the while this tirade had been pouring from her lips, Mrs Mumford had been scrabbling about in the table drawer. Now she brought out a long, sharp knife, and, still scolding, she proceeded to cut two generous slices from the big golden brown cake. Steam surged up from the incisions, and as Mrs Mumford planked the slices in front of her two devotees, Milly could see the lightness of the texture and the thick scattering of raisins.

"Ah, that's the stuff!"

"Good old Mums!"

Both boys spoke with their grateful mouths already crammed; and Mrs Mumford pursed up her lips in an attempt to hide the smile of pleasure and culinary pride that was threatening to undermine her authority.

"Not a scrap more, not one scrap!" she was beginning threateningly when Jacko at that moment caught sight of Milly hovering outside the door.

"Barney!" he managed to choke out hospitably through his mouthful of cake. "Hi! Barney!" Then, turning back to Mrs Mumford, he cleared a space in his mouth to enunciate more intelligibly: "Hi, Mums, Mrs Barnes is back! Let's have her in to the tea party! Come on in, Barney!"

At this, Milly could hardly do less than put her face round the door and apologise (for what, she was not quite sure, as she had done nothing at all, but it was obvious that an apology was called for). Mrs Mumford meantime contemplated this new arrival with an air of both irritation and relief. "There goes another slice of my cake!" she seemed to be thinking sourly, and also "Thank goodness, another woman, *she'll* understand how put-upon I am!" Accordingly, she set a large slice of cake before Milly, put on the kettle for tea, meanwhile enlarging on the trials and tribulations of being landlady to a pair of idle layabouts who thought that cakes grew on trees, and that three pounds fifty a week entitled them to pester the life out of her all day long, and to eat her out of house and home into the bargain. "See what I mean?" she finished, planting two further slices of cake on to the boys' plates. "Now I'm going to have to make another cake for my son and that minx on Sunday! I can say goodbye to this one, that's for sure!" She gazed with ill-concealed satisfaction at the remnant of her much-appreciated creation, poured Milly a cup of strong, hot tea, and then settled down to telling her visitor about the price of raisins, and how her daughter-in-law had never even written to thank her for the Christmas pudding she'd taken over last year. "Full of best brandy, too!" she grumbled. "It's the last time I'm making the Christmas pudding for *that* lot, and that's a promise . . . !"

Milly, beginning to suspect that this was a promise that had been made, and broken, ever since the son's marriage, answered non-committally, but with all due sympathy. She was beginning to like this snappy little woman and her warm, untidy kitchen, and as for Jacko and Kevin, she felt that she had known them all her life. This was her home. This was where she belonged.

So it was all the more of a shock, when she went up to her room half an hour later, to find a strange suitcase standing just inside her door. It was large, and shabby, tightly strapped, and covered with foreign labels . . . Geneva . . . Beirut . . . Delhi . . . Milly stared at the exotic names in a sort of trance of dismay, while her mind slowly came to grips with the idea that someone else must be moving into

her room! Some horrible person with real money instead
of a dud cheque-book . . . with real luggage instead of an
implausible story about the left-luggage office! The sense of
betrayal rose in Milly's throat like sickness. Why had Mrs
Mumford said nothing?—Why had she welcomed Milly
into the kitchen to cake and tea, like an old friend, and
never a word about this plot to throw her out into the
street? Out into the street, right back to the beginning, all
her efforts, all her achievements, fallen about her like a
house of cards! Had Mrs Mumford heard some rumour
about her new lodger—had she guessed something? There
had been nothing in the papers this morning, of that Milly
had made sure: but what about the evening papers? The
evening papers from London? Had there been a photograph? Had Mrs Mumford, seeing the likeness, decided that
Better Safe than Sorry, that When in Doubt, Don't—any
one of those countless depressing maxims which make life
so difficult for anyone trying to get away with anything, and
so boring for everyone else? But in that case, why the cake
and tea, and the friendly conversation? . . . Least Said,
Soonest Mended, no doubt . . . Milly felt fury boil up inside
her, only to curdle slowly into despair. To roam once again
homeless through the winter night . . . To fight death off yet
again, for what, for what . . . ? And at this moment a clatter
of feet on the stairs announced the arrival of Kevin and
Jacko from the kitchen. Were *they* in the plot, too? After all
their friendliness this morning, after all that exchange of
inmost thoughts, of life-stories true and false, not to
mention the Ricicles . . . had they, too, connived at her

betrayal? She came out on to the landing to confront them: she tried to speak, but something as big as a billiard-ball in her throat seemed to choke her.

"What ho, Barney!" Jacko greeted her gaily, and Kevin, close behind, added: "Have you looked in your room, Mrs Barnes? There's a surprise for you!"

"A surprise . . . !" Milly almost gagged on the word . . . but now the two young men were upon her, almost dragging her into her room.

"See?" Jacko was swinging the alien suitcase above his head like a trophy, and Kevin added, more soberly: "It was my idea, Mrs Barnes. I got it from a chap I know in Medical School. Old Mums fell for it like a monkey falling off a log . . ."

"Yes," interrupted Jacko, "she'd been going on half the morning, you see, about how funny it was that this Mrs Barnes hadn't fetched her luggage yet, and when the Mums starts saying something's funny, then you know it's serious. So we thought it over, Kev and l, and we came up with this idea—"

"*I* came up with it," Kevin interposed. "*You* only—"

"Yes. Well. Anyway." Jacko looked momentarily aggrieved at this interruption to the flow of his narrative: then his native ebullience took over again. "Anyway, like I said, we got this idea of borrowing some luggage for you. Something real classy, to stop the Mums in her tracks! And it so happens that Kev has this classy friend in Medic., so—"

"He's not a friend, I just happen to know him," interrupted Kevin defensively, and Milly understood at once that to admit to upper-class friends would be damaging to his status in the student community. Lads like Kevin and Jacko, busy trying to live-down their glaringly non-working-class backgrounds, had to be careful about this sort of thing.

"He's not a bad guy, though, in some ways." Kevin resumed. "He said it was OK about the suitcase, so long as he could have it back for the summer, and so—"

"We lugged it in as if it weighed a ton."—Jacko took up the story again, swinging the empty suitcase this way and that to emphasise the cleverness of the trick. "We made sure that the Mums heard us coming in, and when she stuck her nose out to see what was going on, we told her we'd fetched your case from the station for you. It was too heavy for you to fetch yourself, we said! Oh, you should have seen us, Barney, humping it up the stairs, gasping and straining at nothing—Look, like this!"

Swinging the empty case to the floor, Jacko reproduced the pantomime for Milly's benefit, bending to the imaginary weight, and panting for breath. "Good, isn't it?"

"As a comic turn, yes," observed Kevin drily. "But as a serious attempt to kid Mrs Mums that it was a respectable item of luggage belonging to a respectable lady—well, I don't know why you didn't dress up as a down and sling custard-pies around as well, just to make sure! I was scared every minute she was going to ask us what was in it to make it so heavy—That's all we needed, to have the Mums searching it for bombs, when the whole idea was to lull her suspicions!"

"Oh, gee, it was the best bit of acting outside of the West End for years! It had the Mums eating out of our hands! And was she impressed! Look, Barney! See the labels we've given you!"

Looking closer, Milly saw now that on each of the flamboyant foreign labels, some unknown name had been carefully erased, and "Milly Barnes" had been substituted, in small, neat capitals.

Her two knights-errant seemed so pleased with themselves, and were so obviously waiting for little cries of admiration and gratitude from her, that she hadn't the heart to reveal her qualms about the whole business, or to point out to them that the fictitious story of her life—hard enough to make watertight anyway—was henceforth going to be further complicated by the necessity for fitting into it spells of globe-trotting on this daunting scale. How was a life of devotion to her invalid father in the depths of the country to be reconciled with a giddy round of visits to half the capitals in Europe? Lisbon—Copenhagen—Athens—Madrid . . . her eyes scanned the array warily, and she tried to remember how much of the invalid-father stuff she had given Mrs Mumford . . . Or was that the story for Mrs Graham . . . ? Had she told Mrs Mumford merely that she was a widow . . . ? From now on, she would keep notes—if necessary in columns, on squared paper—so that she could see at a glance whom she had told what to. System and orderliness were clearly as necessary to a career of deception as to any other calling.

Meanwhile, the two eager young faces were beaming on her expectantly, awaiting suitably fulsome expressions of gratitude and of admiration for their cleverness: and she proferred both, wholeheartedly. The genuine friendship and concern for her that had gone into the prank were heartwarming: as to its wisdom, she kept her doubts to herself. She could only hope that the shrewd-eyed Mrs Mumford was as easily deceived as these two lads seemed to imagine.

After they had gone, all puffed-up and glowing with their good deed for the day, Milly kicked off her shoes, and settled herself on her bed to think. It was cold, but not unbearably so. With the eiderdown over her knees, and her coat clutched about her shoulders, she was comfortable enough, except for her feet, which were aching and tired. She had not noticed her tiredness while she was bustling about at Mrs Graham's, with one eye on Alison and the other on the clock, but she realised now how unaccustomed her body was to hard work. The months that lay behind her had seemed, in the living, to be months of almost intolerable strain; but in point of fact they had been months of rotting; of slow, insidious decay, a slackening of all the fibres, of mind as well as body, under the encroaching shadow of fear.

Shadows . . . shadows . . . a blotting out of daylight, a barricade, thicker than death itself, between herself and the sun . . . this had been Milly's first impression of the basement flat in Lady Street, when she and Gilbert Soames had returned to it after the strained, registry-office wedding, and the nearly silent wedding lunch which had followed for the two of them in the dark, expensive restaurant, both of them sunk in thoughts unmentionable to the other, and scarcely able to eat. Gilbert had paid the huge, futile bill for the uneaten food without the faintest quiver of dismay on his aristocratic face, and had then summoned a taxi and handed Milly into it as though she was a queen. In silence, they had driven back through the tired August streets, heavy with the fag-end of summer, and with the faint, South London haze blurring, ever so slightly, the heat of the afternoon. Milly (already she was thinking of herself, in retrospect, as Milly: her old name had become as remote as a dream)—Milly remembered how she had sat in the corner of the taxi feeling very tidy and compact, and vaguely surprised to find that she was feeling nothing else of any kind. She wasn't even feeling too hot, in spite of her new cream-coloured crimplene suit with its high neck and elbow-length sleeves. So she sat, staring out at the shopping crowds of the Brixton High Road, and at the heavy, muted sunshine, and waited to feel something. For she had not, as yet, given a name to the small, nagging sensation that had awakened somewhere inside her at the moment when she was saying "I will!" She had not recognised it as dismay, still less as horror, and she had, indeed, found it easy to forget about it, after those first few moments. What with the necessity for looking her best and happiest in that photograph that was to go to Julian; and then the difficulty of persuading the photographer to have the prints ready before the weekend—all this gave little time for speculation on such trivial matters as whether her marriage would be a success, and whether the rest of her life, and Gilbert's, was going to be worth living. If only the prints could be ready on Friday, before noon, then there was every chance that Julian would get his copy on Monday. The air-mails were pretty good, usually: letters often crossed the Atlantic faster than they crossed London, that's what everyone said. With luck, the photograph, proof of the wedding, would reach Boston (where Julian—the brightest star in all the glittering brain-drain of that year—had recently landed some kind of high-powered research job)—it would reach Boston first thing on Monday morning. That would be good. Monday morning, going off to work with the shock of it still raw in him, and with no time to go over it all with Cora, the two of them consoling themselves by thinking up catty remarks, and looking for secret strains in the bright-ness of the pictured smiles.

Yes, Monday morning would be the time. Milly leaned forward in the taxi, bracing herself, using all her willpower, as if that would somehow speed the photographer in his task, and get that thin blue letter airborne, winging its way to Julian almost at the speed of sound.

The taxi drew up half way down the grey length of Lady Street, and Milly felt her husband's—(No! No! how her mind had choked on the word, even in her thoughts!) No, she felt *Gilbert's* bony arm under her elbow, helping her cere-moniously to the pavement. She stood watching while he paid the driver, selected the correct tip, and handed it to the man with that air of authority, of unquestioned rightness, which had first attracted—Well, no, attracted was too strong a word—let us say which had first made Milly feel that it probably wouldn't be too bad being married to him. She liked men to be good with taxis. As she stood there, a sudden memory of Julian being good with taxis hit her like a blow out of the sullen August heat. For a moment she could hardly stand, and so she was glad enough of the steely old arm gliding along under her elbow, helping her across the pavement: helping her past a high iron railing . . . and now it was propelling her down the steep, shadowy area steps. Down, down . . . She was aware of a chill striking upwards as she left the sultry August heat behind . . . and as she went, the damp, shadowy stone seemed to march gravely upwards, on every side, until at last, here she was, at the bottom of a dank, narrow canyon, out of sight of the sunlight and of the passers-by. The tap-tapping of their unseen feet above her seemed suddenly far off, part of a vanished world.

And now Gilbert, at her side, was fingering through a bunch of heavy great keys . . . Selecting first the one for the mortice lock . . . Then for the yale lock . . . then for the special burglar-proof catch . . . until at last the basement door creaked open, and a smell of trapped mildew surged out towards her like water when the lock gates are opened.

Gilbert Soames did not lift his bride across the threshold. He held the peeling old door open for her, courteously, and waited for her to creep through ahead of him into the darkness.

It wasn't quite dark, of course, once your eyes got used to it. Gilbert's flat (Milly's flat too, of course, now, but as yet she wasn't facing that sort of thing) was well below ground-level, but on a bright day such as this a muted grey light managed to seep down and to find its way through the heavy iron bars that protected every window in the flat from burglars. That was Gilbert's explanation, anyway, and at first Milly had thought it plausible enough. In an area like this, he'd said, people living in basements or on the ground floor had to protect themselves as best they could.

But now, looking at the bars from inside, Milly became aware of that strange tremor again, right in the pit of her stomach. Just for one second, she experienced the first, faint quiver of realisation of just what it was that she had done in marrying Gilbert Soames. The knowledge that this place was now actually her home flicked at her mind for a moment, and was gone. Quickly, she thought about Julian, and the way he would off-handedly slit that envelope open on Monday morning, never guessing what was inside.

She became aware that Gilbert had come back into the room. Since their arrival a few minutes ago, he had been padding softly around the flat, almost sniffing at everything, like a cat that wants to make sure that all its familiar corners have been undisturbed. Now he was back in this front room, with its massive ancient, mahogany furniture, and he was looking at her with a curious bright intensity: and it came to her, with a sudden, overwhelming sense of revulsion, that he expected to kiss her.

89

The intensity of her revulsion took her totally by surprise. Because Gilbert had often kissed her, naturally, in the course of their decorous courtship, and she hadn't minded at all. But that had been different. A kiss, then, had usually been a goodbye kiss, heralding the fact that one more leaden-footed outing was safely over, and that she could now skip upstairs to her solitary flat and think about Julian, and about his and Cora's faces when they heard that she had hooked herself another husband. *Those* kisses had had the same sort of satisfying finality as putting a stamp on a letter—*there*, that's done! and they hadn't bothered her at all. But now . . .

"I'll make some tea!" she proposed quickly, and without waiting for an answer she darted off into the damp, windowless cavern which Gilbert (she had already learned) insisted on calling "the scullery". It served as the kitchen, though, and must have done for years, since it was here that an ancient, grease-caked gas-cooker kept its quiet vigil, undisturbed by the faint, ceaseless footsteps above, tap-tapping their way, unnoticed, out of the nineteenth century and far into the twentieth.

Tea. Afternoon tea. As she searched about for matches, kettle, teapot, Milly turned the phrase around in her mind and found it good. She was here for afternoon tea. For afternoon tea, you arrive at four (just as she was doing), and at half past five you begin to look at your watch and say you think you ought to be going. That's how it would be: she'd been invited to tea by this strange old man, and in a couple of hours she'd be home again, in the peace and solitude of the Kensington flat: maybe ringing up one of her friends to tell her, just for laughs, how she'd been to tea with this weird old man in such a strange, depressing flat, like something out of Dickens, my dear, it really was!

Milly knew quite well, in one part of her mind, that she was playing a game with herself, one of the most dangerous games in the world. She knew, too, that sooner or later the make-believe would come to an end, and the reality of what she had done would come crashing in: and yet, for the moment, she couldn't in any way worry about it.

Detached, even tranquil, in a strange way, Milly part-filled the great iron kettle at the cold tap above the ancient stone sink, and set it on the wavering small flame of the gas-cooker: and as she sat, patiently waiting for it to boil, she suddenly had the oddest feeling, that all this was really, actually happening. To *her*!

For one moment, she was seized by such panic as she had never dreamed or imagined; but instantly she fought it down. She fixed her mind on Julian, and on what he would be thinking next Monday, and on what Cora would be thinking; and very soon reality had shrunk back to its proper size. The size, that is, that would conveniently fit into the small compartment of her mind which was all she had had to spare for it of late.

Now, she looked around at the peeling plaster walls of the windowless kitchen, and at the strange shadows cast by the dim, fifteen-watt bulb, and wondered, for a moment, what it would feel like to realise that she would never cook by daylight again.

To her relief, she found she couldn't realise it. Well, of course she couldn't! All this wasn't happening to *her*. Not *herself*. It couldn't be.

CHAPTER X

How long had she succeeded in thus keeping reality at bay? Stirring restlessly on her narrow bed in Mrs Mumford's First Floor Back, Milly tried to recall the precise moment she had realised exactly what she had let herself in for by marrying Gilbert Soames: the moment when she had first faced, fairly and squarely, the fact that she had tied herself irrevocably to a dreary, ill-tempered old man whom she did not even like, and for whom she felt nothing but a powerful and disconcerting physical revulsion.

There had been no such moment, of course: such cataclysmic moments of self-revelation are rare. What happened to Milly was what happens to most people when they are confronted by mistakes or disasters too big to be borne: they let in the reality of it inch by inch, as it were, a little bit at a time, avoiding at all costs the full, total shock of it. And meanwhile, unnoticed and unallowed for, something in the inmost core of such a person's being is all the time quietly getting used to it. It starts in the body, the very bones and muscles imperceptibly accustoming themselves to the new patterns of movement through the day, the new doorways, the new steps up and down, the new weights and obstacles. Thus, long before she had in any degree resigned herself to her new state, or properly comprehended it, Milly found her hand giving just the right twist to the scullery tap to make it stop dripping: found her feet pausing, without any direction from her, when they came to the broken seventh tread of the dark, evil-smelling stairway down from Mrs Roach's part of the house: found her eyes shutting, of their own accord, just in time to escape the sight of Gilbert sucking the skin from his hot milk, greedily, spinning-out the pleasure of it with smacking lips. By the time full realisation had broken upon her of what she had done to her own life, it all seemed to have been going on for quite a long time.

The evenings had been the worst, in those early days. Strange how those first evenings of her marriage to Gilbert seemed, in retrospect, to have bunched themselves together like frightened sheep, so that they seemed like just one evening, with no beginning and no ending.

Certain episodes stuck out, though, sharp as flints, the horror of them catching at her breath even now, just as it had done at the time, but she could not place them chronologically or set them in any ordered sequence of day succeeding day. Was it the first evening, for instance—or the second?—or maybe later still?—that she had first noticed the earliness of the hour at which Gilbert was accustomed to lock up for the night? She remembered listening to the pad-pad of his ancient gym shoes as he roamed from room to room, locking the doors, drawing the hinged wooden shutters across the windows, fastening the great bolts, and only after he had finished, and had settled down in his big leather chair, with the green-shaded reading-lamp casting a strange cat-glitter into the gloom of the great room——only then did it dawn on Milly, with a sickening stab of sheer horror, that outside the sun was still shining; that toddlers with bare legs and sunsuits clutched their mothers' hands as they wove their way homewards, with prams and shopping, through the heat of the late afternoon.

That was one memory. Was it that same evening, or a later one, when she had found herself in the scullery, rinsing the two teacups meticulously under the cold tap, and setting them upside down on the old wooden draining-board, spongy with the wetness of years? And then the two saucers . . . the two plates . . . And then just standing there, wondering how on earth to make the task take longer, so that she would not have to go back, just yet, to the room where Gilbert was waiting for her in the green-ish lamplight, leaning back in his great leather chair, stroking the tips of his long mottled fingers together gently while he waited.

Waited for what? It was many weeks before Milly began to guess at the answer——or, indeed, to realise that there was any particular need to pose the question. These first evenings, all she was clearly aware of was an intense need to procrastinate: to put off, by any means, the moment when she must join him: when she must push open the heavy door and make her way across the big, shadowy room, aware of his eyes on her continuously as she edged her way between the vast mahogany side-board and the dusty great mahogany table, piled high with bundles of yellowing newspapers, each carefully tied round with string.

"Finished in the scullery, my dear?" he would say politely, as she settled herself in the sagging cretonne-covered arm-chair that stood across the empty hearth from his leather one. "Yes," would reply Milly, or perhaps "Yes, it's all done", and this, somehow, signalled the end of the little tableau. Gilbert would at last take his eyes off her, and almost with an air of relief would pick up his newspaper and disappear behind it, sometimes for two hours or more.

He didn't like Milly to read, though. If he should look up from his paper and notice that she had a book or a magazine in her lap, he would frown, and mutter, and finally make a great show of folding up his own paper; and then he would sit there, silently, waiting for her to say something.

Had conversation always been as difficult as this? Sitting there tongue-tied in the sombre great room that Gilbert called the dining-room, Milly had racked her brains trying to remember what they used to talk about before they were married? Those Tuesdays and Fridays when they had gone off to a tea shop together after the Industrial Archaeology class—what on earth had they found to say to each other? She could remember that the afternoons had been dullish, and that she had usually been relieved rather than sorry when it was time to go home—but it hadn't been as bad as *this*. Surely not—it couldn't have been. Had they talked about the class, then, and their fellow-students, and the snippets of homework they were sometimes set? Now and again, she remembered, the conversation had become quite interesting, and Gilbert had revealed little bits about his past life: about the house he had been forced to sell at a loss when he went abroad; about the brother he hadn't spoken to for forty years because of some sort of quarrel about their father's estate. Nothing very exciting, but still, it had made conversation of a sort. But now, when Milly tried, in desperation, to revive these topics, throwing bright little questions into the oppressive silence of the great room, something killed them even as they left her lips. They fell, heavy as stones, into the gloom, and the silence surged back, sometimes with a strange hostility in it, as if she had interrupted something.

Around nine o'clock—or sometimes even earlier—Gilbert would lower his paper slowly and rub his eyes with his bony knuckles, prolonging the gesture until Milly's own eyes felt bruised and she had to look away. Then he would unfold his stiff length from the old chair and stand upright.

"I think I'll be turning in now," he would say, and they would exchange a dutiful goodnight kiss, and he would go padding off, around and around the flat, in and out of the rooms, until at last his bedroom door clicked shut with an air of finality, and Milly would let her breath go in a long, shuddering sigh.

As the days went by, her dread lest more than the goodnight kiss would sooner or later be required of her, begun gradually to lessen. He was an old man, after all. But, disconcertingly, her distaste for even the kiss seemed to grow greater, not less, as time went by. The curious feeling of his moustache against her cheek, like a damp nailbrush: the touch of his flabby skin . . . sometimes it was all she could do not to jerk her head away, or raise her hands in front of her face, as if warding off a blow.

And then, nearly a week after the wedding, there had come an evening which Milly would never forget or forgive—though who was the one to be forgiven, she would never know.

It was an evening just like the ones that had gone before, with Milly sitting in her now familiar chair at the side of the fireless grate, watching the faint twitchings of Gilbert's outspread newspaper, and listening to his heavy breathing behind it. She had not dared to pick up her own book, for fear of provoking him to lay down his newspaper and wait for her to embark on one of those awful attempts at conversation; and as she sat thus, totally without occupation, it slowly dawned on her that this was Monday. It was the evening of the day when Julian and Cora should have received the wedding photograph: and she had forgotten it!

Forgotten it! The moment of supreme triumph, for which she had casually bartered her life, her happiness, and her self-respect, was over. It had come, and it had gone, and it was finished; and she hadn't even noticed it! All that remained now of that flamboyant gesture of defiance was the price of it: the life-long price which she had contracted, so off-handedly, to pay.

CHAPTER XI

"Barney! I say, Barney—Oh, I'm sorry! Are you asleep, or something?"

Jacko had switched the light on: now, in deference to Milly's supposed state of slumber, he disconcertingly snapped it off again.

"There's a visitor for you!" he whispered considerately through the darkness. "Shall I say you're asleep?"

By now, Jacko's highly idiosyncratic technique for not waking people had brought Milly bolt upright on the bed, her heart pounding. Like anyone roused suddenly in unfamiliar surroundings, she was taking a few moments to collect her wits and remember where she was: but in her case, there was the additional problem of having to remember *who* she was, as well.

Milly Barnes! That's who! The relief that flooded through her was succeeded by puzzlement. What was the time? Had she been sleeping, or merely deep in reverie? The winter afternoon had still been bright through the window when she had settled on to the bed: now, it was quite dark.

"Put the light on, Jacko, do!" she urged; and then, as he obeyed, she focused her mind on what he had been saying. "A visitor? What sort of a visitor?"

"I say! You look as if the police were after you!" Jacko remarked sympathetically, as the sharp yellow light revealed

Milly sitting poised on the very edge of the bed, her outdoor coat clutched round her as if in readiness for flight. Her eyes were still blinking from the alternations of light and dark: under Jacko's scrutiny, she tried to shake the dazed look from her face, and pushed her hair into place as best she could.

"What sort of a visitor?" she repeated, uneasiness stirring in her as full consciousness returned. "A man or a woman?"

Why it mattered so much, she could not think. Either way, it could mean that she had been tracked down by someone out of her past. But the fact remains that as soon as she heard that the visitor was female, she felt the fear draining out of her limbs, leaving them firm and springy, ready for anything.

"I'll come down," she said; and full of curiosity, now, rather than alarm, she set off down the stairs.

The visitor, a rather untidy-looking woman of about forty, in raincoat and trousers, had been left standing in the hall while Jacko came in search of Milly. When she saw Milly coming down the stairs towards her, she looked quite frightened.

"Yes?" said Milly, and then, when the woman still didn't speak, she went on: "Did you want to see me? I'm Mrs Barnes. Milly Barnes."

At this, the stranger looked more frightened still, and for one awful moment Milly wondered if she had made some awful mistake . . . had said the wrong name? had revealed, in some inexplicable way, her true identity? For the first time it dawned on her (in her urgent concern for her own safety, this aspect of her situation had hitherto escaped her) that if people knew who she really was, they would be *frightened*.

"You wanted to see me?" she repeated, warily; and now at last the woman spoke, her face twitching with sheer nerves.

"Yes, that's right. Mrs Barnes. It *is* Mrs Barnes, isn't it? Yes. You see. That is. I hope you don't mind my coming round like this?"

Milly hoped so too, fervently. It depended so much on who the woman was, why she had come.

"No, not at all," she said guardedly, and then listened, with growing puzzlement, while her visitor circled round and round the reason for her presence, never quite daring to pounce.

"I'd like you to be quite, quite honest with me," she was saying. "I shall quite understand. I mean, I wouldn't like. That is, I do realise what a very great deal . . . And how it is nowadays, I mean for everyone, isn't it?" Here she looked wildly round the little hall as if for moral support. "I hate to ask you, really," she plunged on: "And of course I know you haven't . . . That is, your time must be . . . Well, we all are, aren't we? And of course. I mean, I do realise that it's very short notice. It's not giving you a lot of time, and I'd never have suggested it, only. But I shall quite understand, Mrs Barnes. I should never have asked you, really. But you see, my other woman . . ."

At the mention of this familiar character, all Milly's bewilderment cleared.

"When do you want me to come?" she asked; and straightaway all became plain. It seemed that Mrs Lane (for such was the trousered woman's name) belonged on the same grapevine as the Mrs Day who was a friend of whoever it was who had spied Milly going to work at Mrs Graham's this morning: she had, Mrs Lane said, heard from "everybody" that Milly was a wonderful worker, reliable, and very quick, and after a little more flattery it became clear that Mrs Lane was wondering—she was just *wondering*—if all that speed, reliability, and wonderfulness could be hers for forty pence an hour?

How many hours? Why, as many as Milly could condescend to spare . . .

So that was another two afternoons a week, starting tomorrow! Milly went upstairs her mind awhirl with multiples of forty pence and thoughts of what they would buy after the three pounds rent had been subtracted. Why, by the end of tomorrow afternoon, with Mrs Graham's one pound forty as well, she would be able to pay the week's rent *and* put a shilling in the gas-meter! *And* buy fish and chips . . . !

"Kevin!" she called, as she reached the top of the stairs. "Jacko! Guess what's happened!"

They were as delighted for her as she had known they would be; and after a brief and jubilant consultation, it was decided that if she would contribute a shilling for the gas fire, and find some matches somewhere, then they, Jacko and Kevin, would go out and buy pork pies and a tin of

Nescafé to celebrate. In Milly's room, because it was smaller than theirs, and so a shilling's-worth of heat would go further.

It was the nicest celebration Milly had attended for years; and ended with her helping Jacko and Kevin to write their long-overdue essays on Agrarian Reform in the second half of the Nineteenth Century. She didn't know anything about Agrarian Reform, but then Kevin and Jacko didn't either, and of the three of them, she proved to be the most adept at re-wording passages from the textbook so that they wouldn't show up as bare-faced copying. Also, she could spell.

She thought idly about taking an economics degree herself; but would it bring in thirty-five pence an hour as *reliably* as her present avocation? And would a single half-day's work at it make you famous overnight, as *her* morning's work seemed to have done? Would people come round begging you, almost with tears in their eyes, to accept lectureships, the way they came begging for *her*?

No. On second thoughts, Milly decided against it; and instead, she studied Kevin's street-map to find the quickest way from Mrs Graham's flat to Mrs Lane's home on Castle Hill. It seemed that if she left Mrs Graham's promptly at two, and took the short cut through the arcade, and then down under the railway arch into the Old Town . . . "Fifteen minutes," predicted Kevin, "No, I've done it in seven," boasted Jacko, "all the way from the bus depot to the top of the Old High Street . . ." While they bickered, and the last of the shilling's-worth of gas gulped and died in the hearth,

Milly worked out the mileage for herself. Twenty minutes, allowing for getting slightly lost on the way.

Actually, she got more than slightly lost, and as she had not managed to leave Mrs Graham's till ten past two, she was nearly fifteen minutes late, and very out of breath, by the time she lifted the blackened brass door-knocker of The Cedars, Castle Hill. The Old High Street had been steep and winding, and Castle Hill came off it nearly at the top— much further up than it had looked on the map. Milly was very conscious of her flushed face and untidy hair, as well as of her lateness; and she prepared to launch into abject apologies the moment the door should open.

"Call me Phyllis!" was Mrs Lane's immediate greeting; and before Milly could get out a word, she had added fervently *"Please* do!" She was wearing the same trousers as yesterday, topped now by a heavy knitted jersey with a much-stretched polo-neck, and almost worn through at the elbows. Brushing aside Milly's flow of apologies with deprecating little chirrups, she led the way through a cold, lofty hall into a back room which felt even colder, in spite of a small, guttering paraffin heater in the corner.

"Just till we get the coal fires going," Mrs Lane apologised vaguely, gesturing towards this appliance: and then, looking around her with an air of defeat, she continued: "I don't know where to ask you to start, Mrs Barnes. I really don't. It's got out of hand, it really has. Oh dear!"

Milly tried to think of some way of disagreeing, for politeness' sake, but the words dried on her lips. The room looked as if nothing had been cleared away or dusted for months. Books and papers loomed top-heavy on every visible surface, and, interlaced among them, stood mugs of congealed tea, lengths of balsa wood, a dismantled tape-recorder, and empty bottles of gin. Over all lay a sort of top-dressing of crumpled garments: shirts, torn vests, ancient corduroy trousers—all waiting to be washed? Ironed? Mended? By Milly?

"This is my husband's study," said Phyllis. "His den," she amended hopefully, as if that might make some sort of difference. "You know what men are!" she added, with a sidelong glance to see how Milly was taking it. "Do you think?" she proceeded; "I mean, the thing is. Well, it's Eric, you see. My husband. What I want is, Mrs Barnes, if you could try and clean it up a bit? You know—just get it all nice and tidy, but you'll be careful not to touch anything, won't you? Eric just goes mad if anything gets touched."

These instructions made Milly a little thoughtful. Still, forty pence an hour! Besides, this poor woman, with threads of wool dangling from her jersey, seemed so distraught, and was already gazing yearningly at Milly as if she was grateful to her for even *looking* at the room.

"You couldn't start straight away, could you?" Phyllis was saying. "Or would you rather have some coffee?"

The alternatives were a little disconcerting, thus presented, but after her long walk up the hill, as well as the four hours' work that had preceded it, Milly found the courage to settle for the coffee. Besides, she wanted time to think out the task ahead of her, and to learn more about her employer. Already she had sized-up Mrs Lane (or Phyllis, as she must remember to call her) as one of those employers who have at the back of their minds an imaginary dream-home: one which has no relation to the one they are actually living in, but which they believe—and continue to believe—will one day suddenly materialise if they only go on faithfully paying someone forty pence an hour, like sacrificing enough sheep at the temple of Athene. With an employer of this type, a Daily Help's first task is to get as clear a picture of this imaginary dream-home as she possibly can, so that she can then make all her efforts tend in this direction, or at least appear to do so.

So over coffee, Milly reconnoitred the situation. She discovered that Phyllis Lane saw herself as the presiding genius of a warm, welcoming home, where the atmosphere was easy-going and casual. A home where husband and teenage sons were positively encouraged in their messy hobbies, and were never nagged. In her mind's eye, Phyllis saw a blazing log fire in that icy hall; she saw an ever-open front door, and a larder bursting with food, so that friends could drop in and find a welcome at any hour of the day or night. All this, it seemed, had been on the verge of realisation for the last eighteen years: and if only Phyllis could manage not to run out of sugar, and to be in when the coal-man called; and if only it wasn't so difficult parking the car, so that she could shop in bulk . . . And if only Eric would understand how difficult it all was . . .

Her faith that all this would change now that Milly was here, was terrifying: and when, in something like panic,

Milly pressed for details of her duties, all she could extract from her new employer was that she, Phyllis, felt that a house should be a home, and so would Milly make sure, when she did the boys' rooms, not to shift the spare parts of the bicycle Martin had taken to pieces last summer? He had them carefully arranged on the carpet, and so would Milly hoover in between them, being careful of nuts as she went? And if she *wouldn't* mind putting clean sheets on Michael's bed?—they should have been done ages ago, really, but she, Phyllis, hadn't been able to do it herself, because Michael kept his collection of Bright-O packet-tops on his bed, they were all arranged in sequence, and when he had a hundred of them he was going to send off for an airgun: so would Milly be specially careful not to disarrange them? And the Origami cut-outs they'd had such a craze for over Christmas, they were on the bed too. Oh, and above all, when Milly vacuumed, would she be very careful about the electric train set that was laid out all over the floor? Michael hadn't played with it since he was eleven, but he was still very particular about people not interfering with it. Milly *did* understand, didn't she? Apparently My Other Woman hadn't grasped the point at all.

"It'll be nice having the boys' rooms looking really nice again!" Phyllis concluded wistfully. "It gets beyond me, sometimes, it really does. Boys are so . . . After they've stopped being children, I mean."

She smiled, and sighed, and closed her tired eyes for a moment. Behind those drooping lids lay visions of colour-ful teenage rooms in the Sunday colour-supplements, with

Scandinavian wood window-seats, and bright cushions, and one or two brand-new pop records lying carefully casual on the plain white wood table. My Other Woman had failed to effect the transformation, it was true; but surely this Mrs Barnes would bring it off? After all, she was getting five pence an hour more than My Other Woman.

With a good many qualms, Milly set to work. But first there was the usual problem about dusters, and cleaning rags. Like ninety-nine per cent of other employers, Phyllis Lane proffered, with pathetic eagerness to please, bits of torn nylon, and lumps of abandoned knitting. She listened sadly, like a dispirited child, to Milly's explanation of why they would not do.

"But I've got *drawers* full of them: can't you use them for *anything?*" she pleaded, when Milly turned down the third remnant of tattered quick-knit cardigan, with the buttons still on: and at last, in sorrow and bewilderment, she succumbed to Milly's by now ruthless demand for something like a piece of old towel. Under further pressure, she unearthed a plastic bucket without a handle, and a cannister of spray-on polish that wouldn't spray. Silently, Milly promised herself that she would use her very first bit of surplus earnings to buy herself dusters, rags, and proper tins of polish: she would go round equipped with the tools of her trade, like a piano-tuner, or any other specialist.

Mrs Lane had asked her to start in Mr Lane's study, the room she had first been shown: and for a minute Milly stood looking at it, and felt the panic growing in her. But she defied it. Out of her experience, she whispered to herself: "Do *something*. Do just one thing. Then your heart will stop beating like this, and you will see your way."

While she was still standing like this, waiting for the courage to put her own excellent advice into practice, Phyllis put her untidy head round the door.

"Oh, that's *much* better. Oh you *are* getting on!" she lied desperately, and seeing her employer's panic, Milly almost forgot about her own.

"I'm just getting down to it," replied Milly, soothingly, and even as she spoke, she felt welling up in her the strength to start. Already she had caught sight of the One Thing that could be done.

The dirty mugs and cups. Let them be her salvation. Dregs of tea. Dregs of coffee. Some fresh, some almost mildewed. Milly collected them all up and carried them out to the kitchen—and by the time she came back, she knew that her faith in the One Thing had once again been vindicated. She could see, now, exactly how to tackle the room.

First, the scattered garments. Nothing like clothes for making a room look sordid. She had not forgotten that the absent Mr Lane was due to go mad if she touched anything, but she was using her own discretion as to what a man— particularly a husband—would think of as a *thing*. Certainly not clothes in need of ironing. Nor a hunk of beige knitting in a paper bag. Nor half a wizened grapefruit in a pie-dish. Milly also surmised that the unknown Mr Lane might be prepared to overlook the disappearance of the glum little collection of objects awaiting his manly attention: the broken electric iron, the Teasmaid that didn't make tea any more, the dust-caked Do-It-Yourself china-mending outfit, complete with several cardboard boxes containing all the crockery that had been broken in the Lane household during the last eleven years. She set herself, bit by bit, to remove all the things which, in her experience, a man is happier without. Soon, some surfaces appeared, which could be wiped or dusted. She only wished that her employer wouldn't keep popping her head round the door and telling her how marvellous it looked. It didn't, yet, and by the time it did there would be nothing left to say.

By half past three, Milly was facing a new problem—one that, foolishly, she hadn't foreseen. She was tired. Not pleasantly, satisfyingly tired, as one might be after a long walk, but tired with an aching, urgent intensity that was like nothing she had ever experienced before. Of course, she should have realised that her middle-aged, out-of-condition body would at some point rebel: that aching in her legs last night, after just Mrs Graham's, should have been a warning. What a fool she had been! Gaily, and without a thought for anything but the extra money, she had taken on afternoon jobs for every day of the week, and had never for one moment pondered on whether she would be physically able to do them!

Typical!—she scolded herself. Typical! This is how I've been all my life: this has been at the root of every trouble I've ever had. Why don't I ever learn?

Learn what? That she must be careful in future to take account of her own limitations? Or that anyone can do anything if they once put themselves into a situation where they've *got* to? There is never only one lesson.

And so it came about that, since Milly had *got* to go on working for another two hours, she *did* go on working. She finished the study, and even started on the boys' rooms. She found that her legs would carry her here and there whether they thought they could or not; that her back would bend, and bend again, long after she thought it had reached the limit of its endurance.

And after about an hour, a strange thing began to happen. At half past four, or thereabouts, she became aware, with a dawning, incredulous wonder, that she was becoming unmistakably *less* tired, not more, as she went on working! Psychosomatic? Second wind? Some sort of physiological adaptation to stress? For the second time in her new-born existence, Milly whispered a prayer of gratitude to her own body, with its extraordinary, untapped powers. Once more it had been put to the test, and it had not failed: she and it, in partnership, had beaten tiredness at its own game, and they need never fear it again. For the next half hour Milly worked on, as painlessly as in a dream, her limbs moving in some rhythm which seemed to come from quite outside herself. Only a faint buzzing in her ears, and a certain slowness of thought, still reminded her how near she had been to collapse from exhaustion.

"Would you like some tea?" came Phyllis' voice from downstairs. "Or would you rather finish the boys' rooms first?"

Milly was finding these double-barrelled invitations a little disconcerting, but since the tea was already made, and the two cups and saucers set ready on the kitchen table, she could only suppose that she was meant to accept.

"Tea? Oh, yes, please, I'd love it," she said, and straight-away Phyllis went into paroxysms of apology.

No lump sugar, only granulated. Oh dear. Did Milly mind? And, Oh dear, there was no cake in the tin. No cake at all, things had been a bit . . . But there was plenty of Wonderloaf. And jam. And peanut butter. And marmalade. And smoked salmon . . . While Phyllis scrabbled thus hap-hazardly in her store-cupboard, throwing suggestions over her shoulder with the abandon of someone trying to lighten a sinking balloon, Milly listened greedily. She would like them all, actually. Except the peanut butter . . . And the jam turned out to have mould on top. Still, marmalade, and smoked salmon, and four slices of Wonderloaf, were not at all bad for a high tea. Milly felt her strength returning, and would readily have resumed her task in the boys' rooms, but Phyllis wouldn't let her.

"It's half past five—well, just on," Phyllis insisted, though in fact it was not yet twenty past. "I don't want you to over-stay your time, Mrs Barnes, you've worked very hard. Yes. You'll come again on Monday, won't you . . . ?"

All the while she was speaking, Phyllis was steering Milly out of the kitchen . . . urging her into her coat . . . pressing money into her hand. "Thank you" she kept saying, over and over again, "Thank you so much . . ." It was as if it was she, and not Milly, who was on the run from something . . .

Why, you'd think, from her frantic glances at the clock as she hurried Milly towards the front door, that the police were expected at any moment . . . And just then, as if on cue, there came a knock on the front door.

Phyllis had gone quite white. She looked wildly round, as if for a way of escape. Then, pulling herself together, she stepped forward and opened the door.

No policemen. Just a harmless-looking woman in a fur coat and stylish boots. A flurry of greetings, in the course of which Milly found herself being hastily introduced as "A friend of mine, Milly Barnes, I'm afraid she's just going . . ." And so, to avert deeper confusion and embarrassment all round, Milly snatched up her bag and went.

At the time, Milly found the episode puzzling, even slightly alarming—did Phyllis feel there was something suspicious about her new daily, which should be hidden from her friends? It was only when she came to know the Lanes better, and had learned just how rich they were, that she understood Phyllis' embarrassment. Like so many rich people these days, Phyllis Lane hated to admit that she could afford anything, least of all a daily help. She liked to think of herself as one of those joyous, infinitely capable mother-figures, who bake bread, whitewash ceilings, and collect driftwood for the fires, as well as running the home single-handed, with happy-go-lucky efficiency.

Not that any of this ever happened—she couldn't even get the coalman to call, and the supermarket only ever sold Wonderloaf. But one day—quite soon, if only this, that and the other wouldn't keep going wrong—one day, her vision was going to come true, and meantime, naturally, she didn't want to be caught red-handed paying the daily help. And caught, too, by one of the most penniless of all her New Poor acquaintances (witness the fur coat and the fashionable boots). If, in that moment of confusion and embarrassment, she had had any time for philosophising, she might have reflected, as she contemplated her fashionably dressed visitor, that Poverty, these days, is every bit as difficult to ape as Riches used to be.

CHAPTER XII

By the end of the second week, Milly's life had fallen into a pattern which she already felt had been going on for ever. The day started with Kevin's and Jacko's arrival in her room for their morning tea; and always, as part of the ritual, there was the fuss about the gas. The boys seemed to take a pride in never having a shilling for the gas—it made them feel like genuine poor students, and subtly removed the stigma of wealth from the Hi Fi set, and the piles of LP's, and the cine-camera that Jacko's father had given him for Christmas. And since the non-possession of a shilling seemed to mean so much to them, Milly went along with it, and listened obligingly each morning to the small fuss about it, followed by the small injustice of her always being the one to produce the shilling. Thirty-five pence a week—only an hour's work, when all was said and done. Rarely has so comfortable a friendship been bought so cheaply.

Then, at nine thirty, under the attentive gaze of Mrs Mumford (who always managed to be flicking a duster around the hall at just this hour) she set off for work.

"Well, goodbye, Mrs Mumford," she would say, as she unbolted the front door, and, "Ta ta," Mrs Mumford would reply if she was in a good mood, and, "*Goodbye*, Mrs Barnes," if she was not. Either way, she always added, "Back at the usual time, then?"

How lovely, already to have a usual time to be back at!

"*Yes!*"—Milly would cry jubilantly: and then, off into the icy winter morning.

She loved this morning walk to Mrs Graham's: she loved the cold, salty air on her face, and the sensation in her limbs of not being tired yet. This was now a positive, joyous sensation such as she had never before experienced: but then she had never experienced, either, the leaden, desperate tiredness that regularly assailed her in the middle of her working afternoons. Since taking up manual work, she seemed to be living in a new dimension of physical awareness: every muscle in her body seemed to have come alive, to be alert to the stresses and joys of movement; and she was conscious, as never before, of *herself* in charge. It was she, and she alone, who could give the order—"Move!" to an exhausted limb—and it would move.

But at this time, in the bright morning time, nothing of this sort was necessary. Her rested body would swing along through the low mist, or maybe the gleams of struggling sunshine, like the body of a dancer. That's how it felt, anyway; and if it looked more like the body of a middle-aged woman in a head-scarf plodding off to work, what cared Milly? The more unremarkable she looked, the better she was pleased. Then no one would bother to notice the way she always stopped for a few moments at the newsagent on the corner, glancing along the headlines, turning a page here, giving a quick look at the back of a copy there, as if trying to decide which of them all to buy . . . and then moving on, with a new bounce in her step, a new assurance in the set of her shoulders, without having bought any of them at all.

And as the days passed, and the headline Milly was dreading never appeared, the morning ritual became gradually more and more perfunctory until, by the fourth week, her assurance had become so great that she hardly bothered to look at the papers at all. Now, she pranced past the newsagent with only the most cursory glance. Yes, they were still on about the London bus strike—as if anyone cared—where *was* London, anyway? She felt remote from it all, and marvellous, and at last totally secure. Nearly a month now, and still nothing about her at all! She must have got away with it—though how, she could not imagine.

And it was then that the first signs began to appear that all was not quite as she hoped.

The day had started just like any other day. She set off for Mrs Graham's in as carefree a mood as ever, with no weightier problem on her mind than the question whether Mrs Graham would, or would not, be going to the library this morning. It was Mrs Graham's habit, once or twice a week, to spend a morning at the University library looking up the current sociological journals, leaving Alison in Milly's care. On these occasions, she evinced so much maternal anxiety, and gave Milly so many instructions, that anyone would have thought that Milly didn't always look after Alison anyway. Because by now it was part of the routine of Milly's mornings that at eleven-fifteen, just as Milly and Mrs Graham were settling down with their coffee, Alison would start crying, and Mrs Graham would frown, and set her cup down, and stare at Milly in a dazed sort of way.

"But she *never* wakes up till lunch time!" she would exclaim, incredulously. "She *always* sleeps through! Look, Mrs Er, would you mind, just this once . . . ?"—and Milly, just as on all the other mornings, would reluctantly gulp down the rest of her coffee, go and get Alison out of her cot, change her, and thereafter endure her unrelieved company for the rest of the morning, while trying to get the work done.

The only difference about the library mornings was that the drama began earlier. At half past ten, or thereabouts, Mrs Graham would start scuttling softly about the flat, glancing at the clock, stuffing papers secretively into her briefcase, speaking to Milly in whispers . . . for all the world as if she was plotting an escape from the Tower. What she was really plotting, of course (as Milly soon realised), was to make her getaway from the flat *before* Alison began crying. She liked to be safely out of the front door and calling over her shoulder . . . "And Alison will sleep till lunch-time . . ." *before* the first wails rent the air.

All the same, Milly preferred the library mornings, on the whole. For one thing, it meant that she could plan her coffee-break to suit herself—if necessary leaving Alison to scream for five minutes while she reclined in luxury, sipping coffee that she had made exactly as she wanted it, with exactly the right amount of sugar. For another—and this was the big thing—it meant that she didn't have to use any of the labour-saving equipment in the kitchen at all, and could get on with the work as fast as she liked. On the mornings that Mrs Graham was at home there was always the risk that she would grow bored with the correlations, and come wandering in to say: "But Mrs Er, why aren't you using the . . . ?"—dragging from its hiding-place yet another bulky, grease-caked contraption for making a simple task complicated. And by the time that had happened, there was never any going back. In general, and for most of the time, Mrs Graham was as vague and abstracted an employer as one could hope to find, drifting through her housewifely duties with her degree in Sociology clinging about her like a mist, blurring her awareness of any but the most glaring deficiencies on Milly's part. But once she had a labour-saving appliance in her hands she was like a gangster with a gun, nothing could turn her from her purpose. On such occasions she would quite forget how busy she was, and how nobody ever gave her any peace, and would ungrudgingly devote half a morning to following Milly about making sure that she used the Dust-Rite instead of a duster: and while the dust puffed leisurely this way and that around the rooms, and the correlations languished un-cared-for in the typewriter, Mrs Graham would deliver long lectures to Milly about the principle of suction, and how the furniture wasn't *really* clean unless you'd used the Dust-Rite. Nor really dirty unless you hadn't—this last provoked by Milly's incautious demonstration of how much less dusty the table looked after she had done it with an ordinary duster.

So the game, as Milly saw it, was to get the dusting finished before Mrs Graham got around to noticing what she was doing; to get the potatoes peeled with the nice little sharp knife before Mrs Graham came and unearthed the potato-peeler; to wrap the resultant peelings in newspaper and rush them out to the dustbin before Mrs Graham wandered in and caught her not using the waste-disposal unit. She had caught Milly thus on her second morning, and snatching the newspaper-full of peelings just as Milly was about to put it in the dustbin, she had tossed the whole lot triumphantly into the sink.

"There, Mrs Er!" she had exclaimed. "No need to bother with the dustbin! It all just goes down the sink! See?"—and at the flick of a switch an awful whirring noise filled the room. The potato peelings stirred faintly, as if in their sleep, and then settled down again.

"Sometimes it needs both taps on!" Mrs Graham screamed into Milly's ear, above the racket, and they both leaned over the sink and watched the water cascading down among the potato peelings. They were moving around nicely now, and Mrs Graham and Milly leaned over further still. The suspense was awful.

"Look, look!" Mrs Graham cried excitedly. "See? There's one going down! But you have to work them towards the outlet, Mrs Er, don't you see? . . . Isn't there a stick, or something?"

An old mop handle was pressed into service; and after that a wooden spoon; and gradually, with coaxing and prodding from both women, the mound of potato peelings began to diminish. Presently there were only a very few, very obstinate ones left, and Mrs Graham's exultation knew no bounds.

"See?" she screamed, at the top of her voice, in order to be heard above the uproar: "See that, Mrs Er?"—as she spoke, she switched off the machine, so that the final syllable gouged into the sudden silence like a pneumatic drill—"See? They're almost all gone! No need to bother with dustbins in *my* flat, Mrs Er! *Everything* goes down the waste-disposal!"

But not dead matches. Or milk-bottle tops. Or paper bags. Or chicken-bones. And so each day, when she arrived, Milly's first duty was to extract these and similar items from the horrible mush that Mrs Graham always had waiting for her in the sink. With the sort of unquestioning faith that an Early Christian might have envied, Mrs Graham hurled everything, including rancid fat, into the precincts of her waste-disposal unit, and then waited, in total trust, for the magic to begin.

Which it did, of course, punctually every morning when Milly arrived. Since there was no way of scooping it out at this stage in the process, Milly usually spent the first twenty minutes of her working day poking and prodding at it with assorted implements, with taps and machinery all on at full blast.

Mrs Graham loved it. Often she would leave her typewriter and come and watch, screeching advice and encouragement like a supporter of Manchester United; and the longer it all went on, the better she was pleased. She seemed to feel that having the thing on for twenty minutes was somehow twenty times as labour-saving as having it on for only one.

And so, what with one thing and another, Milly was distinctly relieved to find on this particular morning, that it was to be a library morning. Mrs Graham was on the telephone telling someone all about it when Milly arrived (she had her own key to the flat now, as she had to the homes of all her employers: lucky, really, that her crimes had been what they were, and did not include burglary). As she came into the flat, she heard Mrs Graham's voice, loud and clear, from the sitting-room:

"I shan't be back till one," she was saying. "But my woman will be here. She'll let you in, and then you can pick up the lot. And the yellow wool as well, if you like, I don't ever wear it. No, really: it's only cluttering up the wardrobe. As a matter of fact, I'd thought of giving the whole lot to my woman, but you know what they are these days. I daren't risk offending her!"

How do you make a noise like not being offended? Outside the door, Milly was wringing her hands. A yellow wool dress, and who knew what else besides, all going to waste to someone down a telephone! She thought forlornly about the endless drip-drying of her only garments in front of the coin-devouring monster of a gas-fire: she thought of Mrs Mumford's ever more speculative eyes watching her as she set off to work in the same outfit every morning: any day now, she would be prowling round Milly's room, drawing her own conclusions from the empty drawers, and from the locked, feather-light suit-case with its absurd labels.

But what could Milly do? Rush into the room crying "No offence! No offence!"? Or simply "*I* want them!", like a spoilt toddler? Or how about: "My *other* lady *always* used to give me her old dresses"? When you came to think of it, there was no reason why "My Other Lady" should not be built up into just as powerful a folk-image as "My Other Woman".

But while Milly was still debating her unusual social dilemma, the "ping" of the phone told her that her chance was over: and now here was Mrs Graham out in the hall, and telling Milly all about this Mrs Innes, and how she would arrive at midday, and must be persuaded, somehow, to take the lot.

"She's getting fat, that's the trouble," Mrs Graham con-fided. "It's compensatory eating, I keep telling her, but she won't do anything about it, and now she's going to start complaining, saying everything's too small . . ."

By this time, they had reached the bedroom, and Milly's shoulders under her thin blouse fairly shivered with longing when she saw the pile of woollen garments on the bed. Wool dresses . . . cardigans . . . all near enough the right size!

"Get her to take them *all*, won't you, Mrs Er?" her employer was urging. "Don't let her pick them about . . . she'll have this . . . she won't have that . . . all that sort of nonsense! Oh dear, it's so difficult getting rid of things these days, isn't it, Mrs Er?"

Since this was not really a problem for Milly, now or in the foreseeable future, she made no answer. Besides, her mind was already full of scheming . . . If only this Mrs Innes could have grown as fat as fat, and fussy with it!

"If you *really* can't get rid of them——" she opened the subject cautiously, improvising as she went along. "I mean, if you want just to *give* them away, then I wonder if the Bring-and-Buy sale at our Church——they have one every," (here she did a quick calculation) "——every third Saturday in the month, and I've been asked——"

But Mrs Graham had clinched the deal before Milly could round off the lie properly. "I wish I'd known!" she exclaimed, with just the faintest edge of reproach in her voice. "Then I'd never have bothered about this Innes woman at all. It only ends in having her stay to lunch, or something: you know what these people with troubles *are*. Look, Mrs Er, this Baptists' Pete of yours, do you think they'd be interested in a few books as well . . . ?" Her voice blurred abruptly as she swung open a cupboard door and dived into the dusty interior.

"There's several volumes of the 1910 Children's Encyclopaedia, that might interest them," she called hopefully over her shoulder: "And a complete set of——I can't read the name, the backs are a bit torn, but anyway, a complete set of Somebody's Meditation and Reflections, in twelve volumes. Oh, and my old sewing-machine, I've got one that works now, so perhaps this other one might come in useful to somebody . . ."

The semicircle of floor around Mrs Graham's crouching form was filling up fast; but she continued her explorations with undiminished zest.

"Do they ski at all?" she continued, plunging deeper into the recesses. "There's Arnold's old skis somewhere at the back, he does hoard things so. Ah, here they are! And his army uniform, too, I'd forgotten about that. And what about the portrait of his mother, in oils? I could never stand having it on the walls, so if they'd like it . . . ?"

She straightened up, pushing the hair back from her forehead, and surveying the chaos around her with a satisfied air.

"There you are, Mrs Er! you can take all those! Oh, and while you're about it, the old carpet-sweeper—"

At last, Milly interrupted.

"But—but I can't carry all that!" she protested, and at this Mrs Graham looked up, and stared at her in a sort of vague surprise, looking her up and down as if this was the first time she had really got around to counting how many arms Milly had.

"Oh," she said, and thought for a moment, painfully, picking away at the bit of her brain, long-disused, which concerned itself with other people's affairs.

"Yes, well," she said at last, reluctantly. "Well, perhaps you could bring something round to put them in, could you, Mrs Er? I've been trying to get this cupboard clear for ages. Oh, and Mrs Er, are these Mission people at all interested in fossils? Arnold has . . ."

Mercifully, at this point the first tentative protests began to sound from Alison's room. Straightaway Mrs Graham abandoned her discourse, and went into paroxysms of deafness: racing from room to room, head down, as if in a high wind, shovelling papers pell-mell into her briefcase . . . flinging on coat and scarf . . .

"And Alison will sleep till lunch-time," she shrieked, in the nick of time, and managed to get the front door closed before the first real yell of fury resounded through the flats.

Alison loved the old sewing-machine. She spent the whole of the two hours till lunch time contentedly wrecking it, screw by screw, and Milly was able to get on with her work in unprecedented peace and quiet.

By quarter to one, everything was clean, and the lunch was ready in the oven: and—to crown Milly's satisfaction—the unknown Mrs Innes with her unknown troubles hadn't turned up at all: and so Milly had gleefully parcelled up all those woollies for herself. They were already waiting, neat and inconspicuous, behind the kitchen door.

Now, with Mrs Graham's return imminent, she stuffed the sewing-machine back into the cupboard with the rest of the things, silencing Alison's screeches on the subject by a judicious mixture of savagery and blandishments. Then she washed the child's black and oily face and hands, put her into a clean frock, and forced her (by dint of monstrous subterfuge and sleight of hand) to sit and play with a nice clean toy till Mummy returned.

Disconcertingly, it was Daddy who returned first. He looked for a moment utterly panic-stricken when he realised that his wife wasn't back, and that he was therefore going to have to make conversation with the Daily Help. Then, summoning up all his resources as a gentleman and a scholar, he plunged recklessly into speech.

"Good morning!" he said, and fingered his folded newspaper longingly. Was that enough, he seemed to be wondering, or did one have to say something else before one could decently sit down and read?

"Nice day," he ventured, plunging yet further into the uncharted territory of conversation with Daily Helps. "A bit cold, that is. Looks like snow."

"It does," agreed Milly modestly, wondering whether she ought to call him "sir"? Or was it going to be possible always to frame her sentences in such a way that she never had to call him anything?

"Yes. Hm. Yes, indeed. Look, Mrs——" Professor Graham stopped unhappily, and Milly realised suddenly that her problem about what to call him was as nothing to *his* problem about what to call *her*. Unlike his wife, he seemed to be miserably aware that her name couldn't really be Mrs Er, not possibly.

"Look, Mrs——" he began again, and this time Milly came to his rescue.

"Barnes," she prompted cheerfully. "Milly Barnes."

"Barnes. Ah, of course . . . Mrs Barnes . . . So stupid, do forgive me. Look, Mrs Barnes, did my wife—did Mrs Graham say when she'd be back?"

One o'clock. You'll be off the hook at one o'clock, Milly almost told him; but changed it, hastily, to "Mrs Graham

127

told me she hoped to be back by one. Would you like to wait, or shall I . . . ?"

"Oh no! No thank you! Oh, no, no!"—Professor Graham's horror at the possibility of having to talk to Milly all through his lunch stuck out through his natural mildness like a snapped twig—"No, no! That's all right. Don't put yourself to any trouble. I'll just . . ."—and under cover of such politenesses he succeeded in getting himself into the chair by the window, safely hidden behind the protective expanse of *The Times Business News*.

Silly, really, to let it affect her. There was no real resemblance at all. Just a man's legs, topped by an outspread copy of *The Times*—framed, this time, by an expanse of winter sky, swept white by the sea-wind, and empty of clouds. How could such a sweep of pure, unsullied distance bring back to her, as if it was right here and now, a choking sense of claustrophobia . . . of encroaching darkness . . . ?

The back page of the paper quivered, just as Gilbert used to make it quiver, in the moment before he softly lowered it, and peered over the top to see, with those strange, silvery eyes of his, what his wife was doing. And now the paper lurched, as it used to lurch in the greenish lamplight . . . it swung to the left . . . to the right . . . it swooped downwards, and once again eyes, questioning eyes, were fastened upon her . . .

"Did you want something, Mrs Barnes?"

Professor Graham's pleasant, puzzled voice jerked Milly into an awareness of how oddly she was behaving . . . standing here staring, like a hypnotised rabbit, with no snake anywhere.

"No—no, it's quite all right," she stammered, and fled into the kitchen. Once there, she leaned against the sink for a minute, trying to steady her racing heart, to control her gasping breath. One of these days, she scolded herself, I shall be giving myself away! How many times, in these last weeks, have I let myself get into a panic over nothing? First that man in the café, and the headline in his paper about . . . FOUND IN FLAT. And then that first morning at Mrs Mumford's, with Jacko—as it turned out to be— bumbling around her room in the dark. And after that the telephone call at Mrs Graham's . . . Oh, the occasions were too many to count, and each time, it had been sheer luck that no one had happened to notice her state of shock and inexplicable terror. One day, if she didn't control these reactions, she would find she had given herself away, utterly and irrevocably. When would her body learn not to flood her system with adrenalin at every tiny surprise? When would her brain learn that these trivial little incidents, these chance reminders, were fortuitous, not aimed at her at all?

Aimed at her! How ironic that it should be *she*, now, who should find herself constantly interpreting the bright, pre-occupied world in terms of her own fears! Would there not be a strange, twisted justice about it if, in the end, it should be just such an attack of irrational, deluded panic that brought her to her own doom? How Gilbert would have laughed, that strange, silent laugh of his, like a small clockwork motor jerking away somewhere inside him.

It was just as if he was still there, waiting for her, in the black, bottomless past; waiting, in the quiet certainty that, in the end, she would lose her footing in the bright, precarious present, and come slithering back: back into the darkness, into Gilbert's own special darkness, which at first had seemed to be merely the darkness of a gloomy London basement, and had only later been revealed as the black, irreversible darkness of his own disintegrating mind.

For many weeks after her marriage, Milly had refused to recognise the special quality of the darkness: she had tried to fight it off with new fabrics, and higher-watt bulbs. By the time she had nerved herself to go to the doctor about her husband, it was too late.

Perhaps it had always been too late. After waiting all that dark November morning in the overcrowded surgery, among the humped, coughing people, Milly had in the end seen the exhausted young doctor, eyes red-rimmed from lack of sleep, for barely two minutes. He hadn't said much, he was too weary and dispirited, and what he did say wasn't really a lot of use. For by the time she had got around to consulting him, Milly already knew as much about delusional paranoia as any doctor. She knew more or less everything there was to know about it, except how to face it: and that no doctor could tell her.

CHAPTER XIII

He hadn't been as bad as that at the beginning. Well, of course he hadn't, or Milly would never have married him. And yet, even then, even in the days of the decorous, best-behaviour outings to tea-shops, there had been signs—tiny, warning flashes—which might have put a more astute woman on her guard. No, not a more astute one, necessarily; simply one who was more *interested* in Gilbert, as a person: one who was contemplating marrying him for himself, and not merely as a stick with which to prod her former husband into some sort of reaction.

Yes, the warnings had been there, all right; and Milly, in the throes of her plans for impressing Julian, had not given a thought to any of them. There was Gilbert's life-story, for a start: swindled out of his inheritance, estranged from his only brother, bullied by his wife, deprived of his rightful pension—what sort of a man is it who has *all* these things happen to him, unrelieved by any spark of generosity from *anyone*? And then there was the matter of his friends—his lack of them, that is to say. It was this, actually—this strange, dignified solitariness—that had attracted Milly's attention to him in the first place. Long before she knew who he was, or anything at all about him, she had noticed the way he always arrived at the Industrial Archaeology class alone: tall and silent, looking neither to left nor right, he would make his way to the furthermost desk of the back row; and throughout the session he would focus an almost disconcerting intensity of attention on the teacher: fixing his light grey eyes—so light as to be almost silvery, Milly had already noticed, before she knew so much as his name—fixing them on the teacher with unblinking concentration, broken only by the occasional need to copy a diagram off the blackboard, or the correct spelling of some little-known technical term. Since Milly herself was bored to death by the classes (her motive in enrolling had been the despairing one advocated in so many advice columns—"to meet people") she thus found herself with plenty of time, in between doodling and daydreaming, to watch this mysterious, white-haired man, and idly to wonder about him. He seemed so alert, and attentive, and purposeful, and yet he never spoke—neither at question-time in the class, nor afterwards, when the rest of the students were gathering in twos and threes, chatting, comparing unfinished homework, waiting for one another to come out for a cup of tea, or to catch the same bus home. Instead of joining in any of this, the inscrutable Mr Soames (this much Milly had learned by now, from the class register) would silently gather up his notes and edge his way out of the classroom, without a word to anyone.

Milly had been intrigued, and, since she had come to the class with the sole purpose of meeting unattached men, she determined (since nothing better offered) to cultivate the acquaintance of this one; and so, for three classes in succession, she made a point of greeting him boldly, with a smile, as he came into the room. He had seemed startled—almost affronted—the first time: the second, he acknowledged her greeting with a politely embarrassed murmur: and on the third, he had actually paused to say "Good afternoon", before retreating to the far corner of the room.

So far, so good. Slow-ish: but then, if the whole of the rest of your life is to spare, then where is the advantage of speed?

It was not until the next Class Outing that she really got a chance to speak to him. Twice a term, or there-abouts, on freezing winter Saturday afternoons, the whole group would go off in a coach to look at some blackish bit of brickwork at the edge of a canal, or something; and Milly would stand, bored to death and freezing cold, with her hands in her coat pockets, and sustained only by the thought that she was *out*. She was *doing* something: no sharp-eyed mutual friend would now have the chance of reporting back to Julian that his poor ex-wife spent all her weekends moping about the flat, alone. It was as she stood thus, one February afternoon, that the silent Mr Soames had approached her, and, after some minutes' hesitation, had asked her, in a voice stiff with unease but still smooth and cultivated, if she wouldn't like a cup of tea? And she, filled with a mixture of triumph at the success of her campaign, and boredom at the prospect of carrying it any further, had followed him into a waterside café. They had sat opposite one another at the slopped, plastic-topped table, and sipped the strong, tepid tea; and he had let out for her—hesitantly, as through a rusty gate—little bits of information about his troubles.

Troubles, even the dullest, are always mildly interesting at the first hearing; and Milly had been mildly interested. He wasn't too bad, he was better than nothing; and so, from then on, she had allowed the tepid relationship to take its course without any special effort on her part, either to foster it or to bring it to an end. Until, suddenly—it would have been about the middle of June—she realised that under cover of her inattention, the thing had been surreptitiously growing: she realised, with a little shock, that if she chose she could now give Gilbert that last little push that would get him asking her to be Mrs Soames!

Mrs Soames . . . ! Dear Julian, I am now Mrs Soames . . . From then on, it had all been as irreversible as falling down a precipice.

Including the bump at the bottom. The utter, stunning shock . . . followed by the slow awakening . . . the painful flexing of limbs to see what has been broken, what merely bruised and sprained; and finally the dazed survey of the strange, utterly new landscape . . . the rocks, the boulders, with here and there the possibility of a path, to somewhere or nowhere, as the case might be.

It must have been two or three weeks after her marriage to Gilbert that Milly began thus to pick herself up after the shock, and to take stock of her situation. She began by facing the enormity of her own folly in marrying him at all: and then, when that quickly proved futile, she began looking for ways to escape.

There were none. None, that is, which would not involve Julian and Cora learning, with gleeful pity, of the failure of her new marriage.

"Poor thing, isn't it pathetic?" Cora would say, tasting the words on her palate, like rare wine, and "The unwanted wife syndrome," Julian would comment, with a shrug. He loved to put things in categories.

No. Escape was out of the question. What was left, then, was endurance. What she had brought upon herself, she must live with. Live, and make something of it.

Make something of it? Milly remembered how she had looked around the underground dungeon that Gilbert called the dining-room: she looked at the mountainous mahogany furniture looming out of the grey light that she must henceforth think of as daylight; and for a moment she had covered her eyes. Make something of it? She must be mad!

Yet Milly was not without a certain dogged courage even then—even in those days, when she had not been Milly at all, and her body had not yet undergone the experience of being tested to the uttermost limit, and not found wanting. Yes, even in those days she had had inside her something almost as useful as courage—a defiant uncrushable pride. The sort of pride that can be used—as a mallet can be used if you haven't got a hammer—as a useful substitute for courage.

And so Milly had uncovered her eyes, and looked again into the lowering shadows which, down here, was all you had of noonday.

"*I'll show you!*" she said out loud, into the gloomy great room, her voice sounding reedy and thin in the oppressive silence. "I'll show you! You won't defeat *me*! Just you wait . . . !"

And straightaway there came into her head a scheme of such boldness, of such devil-may-care bravado, that she caught her breath.

Cushions! For this black cavern of a room she would make bright cushions, scarlet, flame, and emerald! She would scatter them here and there on the black horsehair sofa, and in the shabby great chairs! And flowers, too— dahlias, asters—all the reds and golds and purples of late summer, massed in the centre of that gloomy great table! She would defy the great deathly room, she would hurl colour into its shadows, fling glory into the very face of its darkness: with her own hands, dripping brilliance, she would bring it to its knees!

For a moment, her spirit wavered. Surely there must be some ordinary, practical reason why she couldn't do anything of the kind?

But there wasn't. Gilbert was out today, on one of his mysterious errands "to see a man" about something (the days were as yet far off when Gilbert would no longer go out anywhere, but would stay at home, behind closed shutters, watching her) and he had left her plenty of money for the household shopping. He wasn't mean—one must allow him that, at any rate—and as she stuffed the wad of pound notes into her bag and bustled about getting ready to go shopping for the cushion material and the flowers, Milly found herself indulging in the pious exercise which she had been practising ever more frequently of late—that of listing Gilbert's good qualities to herself in the faint hope that, if only she could make the list long enough, it might somehow add up to *liking* him.

Liberal with money. Undemanding. Unfailingly courteous, even when she had angered him. Affectionate—yes, she must allow him that—it was not *his* fault, after all, if her flesh shrank back at the merest brush of his hand in passing. Helpful about the house, too—sometimes taking over the entire cooking of an evening meal, closeting himself in the scullery for long, mysterious hours, at the end of which he would bring out strange, sour-smelling curries in covered dishes or bitter, spicy vegetable stews. And afterwards, all through the meal, he would watch her face, alert for some tiny grimace, some small, involuntary twist of her mouth, to belie her over-enthusiastic words of praise.

He was helpful, too, about the washing-up—if only she had appreciated that kind of help. It was her fault, not his, if irritation rose into her throat like heartburn as he padded softly about behind her, in and out of the scullery, putting things away, muttering to himself, sometimes, as he did so. Not much, as yet: the muttering seemed, in these early stages, like a mere mannerism, albeit an irritating one.

What else? As she made her way up the area steps, shopping basket in hand, into the unbelievable sunshine, Milly tried to add to the list.

Kind? Well, not *un*kind, anyway. He had awkward moods sometimes; occasional fits of explosive irritability about nothing; and strange, unpredictable spells of sulking—but in general he was quite nice to Milly, in his stiff, inhibited way. Considerate, too; opening doors for her, carrying trays, inquiring after her comfort. And as to sex, his demands were absolutely nil—whether by his own choice or because he had sensed her distaste, Milly did not know, and the last thing she wanted was to find out. Mercifully, he belonged to a generation which does not expect to talk about these things, and Milly could only feel grateful for the repression—neurosis—whatever it was—which made it possible for them to go to their separate rooms each night without ever having to engage in one single word of discussion about it.

As she hurried through the golden September sunshine towards the main road, Milly added up these qualities for the twentieth time, struggling to make the answer come out different for once. She made herself visualise Gilbert's pleasure and surprise when he saw the new cushions . . . and then—who knew?—the sight of his pleasure might make *her* feel pleased? For a few moments, they would be pleased in unison . . . and perhaps this would be the beginning of some vague sort of friendliness between them? Or something?

The new cushions gleamed out of the darkness like jewels in the deep earth; crimson, scarlet, gold and peacock blue: and the flowers on the great mahogany table seemed to be reflected in a deep pool of colour. She had polished the table as it hadn't been polished in years, stacking the old bundles of newspaper all up at one end as she worked: and now the old wood shone darkly beneath the blaze of reds and purples, picking up the colours, and throwing them back with a strange, coppery sheen, as though they were on fire.

Gilbert stood in the doorway, not speaking, staring in what seemed to be a sort of trance. He stood there so long, and with such a complete absence of reaction, that Milly began to feel quite scared. In the quietness, she began to hear her own heart beating. Was he struck dumb with surprise? Shocked, in some way, by the sudden loss of familiar ugliness? Or was he pleased—so pleased as to be at a loss for words? He seemed to be looking with particular intensity at the table, in its unaccustomed glory.

At last he spoke.

"Why have you been disturbing my papers!" he barked out, in a voice Milly had never heard him use before. "What were you looking for?"

For a moment, Milly was so taken aback that she couldn't speak. Then: "I wasn't looking for anything, Gilbert! Truly I wasn't!" (Why so defensive, though, like a schoolgirl accused of cheating?) "All I was doing . . . That is . . ." (Again this idiotic inflexion of guilt.) "All I was doing was clearing the table . . . To make it look nice, Gilbert, for the flowers! I've polished it, don't you see? Don't you think it looks nice, Gilbert? Now it's polished? With the flowers . . . ?"

Not even for one second did his glance flicker towards the flowers, to see if they looked nice. The light, shining, silvery eyes remained fixed on Milly. They were so bright, one might have imagined they were lit up by mercury lighting from within.

"You didn't find anything, then? You didn't untie any of the bundles?"—his voice was still high and strange—"Remember, my dear, it will be best if you tell me the truth!"

"But—but Gilbert, there isn't anything to tell! *Of course* I didn't untie the bundles—why should I?—They're only old newspapers . . . !"

Her voice stumbled into silence. Under the strange intensity of his gaze she found herself fidgeting, hanging her head. "I—I'm sorry, Gilbert!" she finished, absurdly humble.

Whether it was because of this humbleness, or whether he had somehow satisfied himself that she was speaking the truth, Gilbert began to relax.

"Very well, my dear," he said stiffly. "I shall have to accept your assurances. But please remember, for the future, that I don't like *anyone* to interfere with my papers. Not anyone at all. Do you understand?"

For the next hour or so, he occupied himself in sorting the bundles, and restoring them to their original places on the table.

He would not let Milly help him, and so she sat, idle and ill-at-ease, while he groaned and fumbled through his self-imposed task, peering closely at each dog-eared package, and muttering: sometimes testing the string, to see if it had become rotten over the years: arranging and rearranging, and sighing heavily to himself, until at last he seemed satisfied. He straightened up, and turned to look at Milly.

"There," he said. "Everything is back in its proper place now, and so that is the end of the matter. We will say no more about it."

He paused, and as Milly watched, a curious look of cunning came over his face, narrowing and sharpening his features until she was reminded of a weasel.

"I've arranged them in a very special way," he said, watching her closely, "so that I'll know immediately if you touch them again."

"But—But of course I wouldn't dream . . . !" Milly was beginning indignantly; but Gilbert raised his hand in a small gesture which somehow reduced her to instant silence.

"I said, we will say no more about it," he repeated, with a strange edge to his voice: and the argument was at an end.

It seemed a long time till bedtime. Gilbert made no further reference to the disturbing of his papers, and as to the flowers and the new cushions, he said absolutely nothing at all. The cushion that was in his arm chair—a brilliant scarlet one—he lifted out carefully, and without comment, and set it on the floor, as if it was a cat that had usurped the best seat; and then he settled down, as usual, behind the newspaper.

Milly, sitting opposite, seethed silently with anger and bewilderment; but since she dared not speak, much less argue, her feelings had nothing to feed on, and so gradually, as the evening ticked by, they withered to a small knot of resentment and incomprehension.

Oh, well. Gilbert was in one of his funny moods. He often got crabby and unreasonable in the evening. Evenings were his worst time.

Or that's what she thought at the time, anyway. She did not know yet, of course, what the nights were going to be like, a little later on.

CHAPTER XIV

With an effort, Milly roused herself. It was quarter past one now, and Mrs Graham still wasn't back. Milly was going to be late for her next job. By the time Mrs Graham had come in, and by the time she had finished reproaching Professor Graham for whatever it was he was doing wrong there behind the newspaper . . .

"*Arnold!*"

Mrs Graham's voice and the slam of the flat door came almost simultaneously:

"Arnold! Why on earth haven't you started lunch? Whatever are you waiting for?"

A swirl of briskness and frosty air flicked for a moment at Milly's domain in the kitchen, and then moved on. Mrs Graham might be reckless in some ways, but not so reckless that she would risk annoying the Daily Help when there was a perfectly good husband available.

"It's such a waste of *time!*" she rounded on him again. "There's no need to wait for me, I've told you a million times! You could practically have finished your lunch by now, and given yourself a bit of time to relax before you have to rush back!"

"I *am* relaxing," the professor pointed out, placidly. "At least, I was till you came in, my love. And I never have to rush back, as you know very well, dearest. I always leave myself plenty of time."

He had lowered his newspaper as he spoke, and was blinking at his wife over the top of it with a sort of innocent wonder. Or was he annoying her on purpose?

It was hard to tell, for by now Mrs Graham was launched on a saga of grievance so fluent that nothing he could say, annoying or otherwise, could deflect it even for a moment from its (obviously) well-worn channels:

"If we had a *car*——" she was saying—and from her tone of voice Milly knew that she must have been saying it for years—"If you'd only get a car, Arnold, we wouldn't *have* all this trouble! It would cut your travelling time by an hour a day, at least . . ."

"But I *like* my hour's travelling time," the professor explained, maddeningly. "It gives me time to collect my thoughts. It's peaceful."

"*Peaceful!*" The word seemed to have touched the very core of Mrs Graham's annoyance. She flung her coat and scarf on to a peg and came right into the room. "Peaceful! And how peaceful do you think *I* find it, slogging about in all weathers? Do you realise that I had to wait *forty minutes* for the bus this morning? Forty minutes, on that icy corner by the library gardens?"

"You must have just missed the twelve twenty-five, then," observed her husband, consulting his watch interestedly. "If you miss the twelve twenty-five there's nothing till after one. I find that myself, when I'm coming from the library."

Whoever it was who first suggested turning swords into ploughshares must have had a shrewd idea of how devastating, in skilled hands, the weapons of sweetness and light can be.

"Oh—you!" cried Mrs Graham, fast losing control of the situation. "I've never known anyone so . . . ! Ah, thank you, Mrs Er, we're just ready . . . !"

The complete change in her voice and manner, from fishwife to lady of the house, almost made Milly drop the joint, from sheer admiration. What acting! And what made it even more of a tour-de-force was that Mrs Graham surely knew—and knew that Milly knew that she knew—that Milly had heard every word of the dispute across the four feet of space dividing the kitchen from the dining-room.

Pure atavism, of course: a race-memory of the days when servants weren't quite real, and so it didn't matter what they heard. And more appropriate—had Mrs Graham but known it—than anyone could have guessed, because Milly, of course, *wasn't* quite real. Not her name, nor her way of life, not anything about her. She was a construct: a figment of her own imagination: a splinter off the final, shattering explosion of her former self, shot out into space, and now somehow taken root, like a dragon's tooth, in Mrs Graham's kitchen . . .

". . . And did you chop up Alison's lettuce and mix it in as I showed you, Mrs Er?"

Mrs Graham's rather school-mistressy tone, and the exaggerated concern with which she peered into her daughter's plate, annoyed Milly for a moment. Had she not been chopping Alison's lettuce for a long time now, and never a word of complaint from either the carpet or the plastic seat of the high chair? For a moment, intoxicated by that consciousness of power which is part and parcel of being a Daily Help, she toyed with the idea of Taking Offence: of watching them grovel and squirm, pumping out flattery and blandishments on an absurd scale, in a desperate effort to placate her.

But, *noblesse oblige*. Like other ruling classes before them, the Daily Helps of today must learn to wield their power decorously, and to resist its heady corruptions.

Besides, by now Milly realised that the fuss about the lettuce wasn't really about the lettuce at all, nor was it really addressed to her. Mrs Graham was simply trying to re-establish her own image of herself after the quarrel. Out-matched by her husband, she was going to show herself in control at least of a lettuce leaf.

Lunch was necessarily a rather subdued affair after all this. Mrs Graham took over the carving, as she always did when she wanted to show her husband how late it was, and how there was no time to have *him* fumbling about at the job; and while the knife flashed this message across the table in a morse-code of lightning strokes, and slices fell from the leg of lamb like grass before the blades of a mower, conversation would have seemed discourteous: a boorish interruption of this fine flow of communication. Even Alison messed her dinner about more quietly than usual, refraining from saying "Da!", with craftsman's satisfaction, as each handful landed on the floor. And as to Professor Graham, he showed no signs of being aware of anything at all. With the loose-leaf notebook of his afternoon's lecture propped in front of him, he accepted with apparent contentment whatever food was set before him, and ate it with good appetite. The only sign he made of being aware that anyone else existed was in the way he clutched absently at his plate and glass every time Milly passed behind his chair on her errands to and from the kitchen: a legacy, this, of years of eating in university canteens, where zealous clearing-up women, like seagulls on the Embankment, snatch food from under the very knife and fork of the unwary. Milly wondered if he would ever learn that she, at least, was not as zealous as all that? Or were the long-term effects of Higher Education irreversible?

It was nearly three o'clock by the time Milly got to Mrs Day's that afternoon, but it didn't really matter, because Mrs Day was never in. Milly had, in fact, never met her, and apart from that initial telephone call, and later on a message about where to find the key, she had never spoken to her. Thus she didn't know her at all—or rather, the only Mrs Day she knew was the one she had gradually constructed, clue by clue, from the trail of evidence left around the flat.

A typewriter, with always the same dusty page jutting from the roller:

> This may seem, on the face of it, a rather extreme position to adopt, or at least to savour of the disingenuous; but it must be borne in mind that congruence rather than equivalence should be our aim.

Yes, indeed! Good, safe stuff, congruence! Milly used to wonder about it sometimes, when, at her lowest ebb of after-noon tiredness, she reached this point in the dusting, and to wonder, too, if it wouldn't be rather fun to go on with it—say to half way down the page—and see if her employer noticed? Why, the poor woman might even be grateful; it was obviously something waiting to be finished.

What, though? A highbrow novel—with a publisher's deadline being missed while the crucial pages sat thus immobilised in the typewriter? Or an article for some spe-cialist journal on almost any subject whatsoever with the Editor ringing up, more and more irate, as press day drew near? Or could it even be a love-letter—there *were* couples, Milly knew, who in the heat of passion wrote this sort of thing to each other endlessly, in the interests of analysing their relationship to shreds. She imagined the poor man sitting alone in his attic/boarding-house/loveless mansion, rushing for the post each morning, his soul afire with longing for polysyllables that never came.

When she was at her very tiredest, Milly would toy idly with ways of continuing the passage that would fit all of these three possibilities. As she slumped over the dusting, taking the weight off her feet as best she could, appropriate sentences seemed to flow through her exhausted brain with extraordinary fluency:

But of course, as far as this is concerned, there are two ways of looking at the matter, neither of them entirely atypical, and neither (at least from the point of view of the onlooker) either more or less convincing than any other possible approach. For it must not be forgotten that the factors previously cited may well be only marginally relevant to the particular point at issue. In saying this, one is, of course, discounting the more obvious considerations: it is a matter, really, of the concepts applied, and the level of coherence aimed at . . .

Why, one could go on like this for ever! Milly was amazed that the clever Mrs Day should be finding any difficulty with it. She must be either a very busy sort of woman, or a very muddled one. Muddled, probably: a truly busy woman either finishes this sort of thing, or she refrains from starting.

Or perhaps the incomplete masterpiece wasn't hers at all? Perhaps she had a highbrow lover who had brought his typewriter to his assignations just once too often, and had thus found himself out on his ear, minus the end of his paragraph?

Yes, this seemed the most likely. It was more in keeping, too, with the Mrs Day revealed by the rest of the flat.

Her bedroom, for instance, strewn with fringed ponchos and psychedelic cat-suits. Four kinds of eye-shadow and a blonde hair-piece belied the learned pretensions of the typewriter: while flimsy shoes, kicked here and there as though the wearer had shed them triumphantly the moment she entered the flat, suggested that her feet were killing her more often than not—sure sign of an exciting social life. No one has ever been able to get far in the glamour stakes unless her feet are hurting.

What did *Mr* Day think of it all? So far, Milly had found no conclusive evidence of his existence, unless you counted the cigarette ash all over the place, and the permanent presence of a man's overcoat on a peg in the hall. Though this, of course, could just as easily have been left behind by the congruence man, when he leapt up from his typing and fled before the onslaught of Mrs Day's scarlet, inch-long nails.

If there *was* a Mr Day, then he must be a very tidy man, Milly decided, as day by day she tidied the all-feminine clutter from Mrs Day's bedroom floor. The bed, too, though a double one, had a decidedly feminine look, with its pink nylon sheets and matching frilled pillow cases; not to mention the pink panda night-dress case, with its simpering Walt Disney eyelashes and the zip coyly camouflaged along the length of its stomach. No doubt such a creature passed muster with the occasional lover—occasional lovers put up with almost anything, knowing that tomorrow they will be safe back in their own beds with their indigestion tablets to hand. No doubt such a one would easily bring himself to smile benignly on the awful panda, and to agree that it was cute. "You must *pander* to it, darling!" Mrs Day perhaps giggled, each time, as she shimmered out of her cat-suit . . . and each new lover in turn would be enchanted by such wit. But a *husband*? To have this sort of thing year in and year out . . . it would be an odd sort of man who would put up with it.

Well, and perhaps Mrs Day's husband *was* an odd sort of man? Perhaps it was he who had fixed up that great mirror opposite the foot of the bed, in which you could see yourself as you lay propped against the pillows (Milly had tried, and so she knew). The Days could sit and watch themselves drinking morning tea, if they liked. They could see not only their partner's ugly, contorted face during a quarrel, but their own as well. Lovely.

Sometimes, as she enlivened her solitary afternoons with this sort of thing, Milly felt it was rather sad that poor Mrs Day couldn't do that same sort of thing about *her*. But there were no clues that way round: no data on which to work. Just a clean flat in place of a dirty one, and, on Fridays, the removal of the envelope with two pounds forty in it. Even the most fanciful employer couldn't build much of a picture of her Daily Help out of that.

Just as well, actually. Every now and then Milly went quite hot and cold wondering what would happen if her unknown employer *did* walk in suddenly, and see what she was doing.

Not that she was doing any harm: nor, in the long run, was she skimping her work at all. She always did the two hours' work for which she was paid. It was the way she set about it—the way one *does* set about things when entirely alone and unobserved—that would have caused the raised eyebrows.

For the first thing Milly did, when she arrived tired, straight from Mrs Graham's, was to choose the most invit- ing of Mrs Day's new library books, and settle herself on the sofa with it. Mrs Day must belong to a very good library: the latest shiny best-sellers always seemed to be lying on her window-ledge almost as soon as they were published.

Sex, cancer, the end of life on earth—all the most popular topics were laid out for Milly's delectation week by week: and having made her choice, Milly would lie and read greedily, for twenty minutes or more, gobbling the pages with the uncritical gusto that comes from book-starvation. Access to books had been difficult for her of late.

And so there she lay, often till past three o'clock, in Byzantine luxury: central heating, absolute peace and quiet, and—if she cared to look out at it—a wonderful view through the picture window, right across the tiled roofs of the old town, to vistas of wintry sky and grey, tumbled sea. It was a lovely bit of the day, and Milly looked forward to it all morning. And later, as she bustled about the flat, she would often find herself stopping . . . to read a picture postcard that had arrived . . . to try on a pair of Mrs Day's gold sandals . . . to examine the framed photograph of a handsome young man who might be Mr Day and then again he might not . . . or to sit on the edge of the unmade bed reading an article in the *New Statesman* . . . This is what is called self-discipline, greatly lauded nowadays in contrast to discipline of the more old-fashioned kind. Its only disadvantage, for Milly, was that it made her two hours' work at Mrs Day's take at least four hours, which was very tiring, and got her home too late to put her feet up before going out for fish and chips with Jacko and Kevin.

The first thing Milly noticed, when she arrived on this particular Thursday, was that *Education for Death* was still there. She recognised it from right across the room, sleek and successful-looking, with its shiny red lettering and the crude silhouette, in vivid black, of a child with round white eyes, and round white buttons all down his front, and his hair sticking up all over his head—presumably with horror at the education he was receiving.

Milly noted its presence with relief (Mrs Day had a maddening habit of returning her books to the library just as Milly was getting properly into them), but before she settled down to it, she took a quick look round the flat to assess the nature of her afternoon's tasks. It was different every time. Sometimes the bedroom was a shambles, and the sitting-room virtually unused: sometimes the other way round. Sometimes the kitchen was so cluttered with dirty crockery that you could hardly move, at others the washing up had been done, but there were beer bottles all over the bathroom. You never knew. And what made it more complicated was that Mrs Day sometimes made hasty, last-minute efforts to make the place look a bit better—shoving dirty glasses behind the window-curtains, kicking crumpled paper handkerchiefs under the bed, or tossing a clean newspaper lightly over the place where the cat had been sick.

None of this helped at all, of course, but Milly presumed that her employer meant well. Anyway, it wasn't too bad this time. A saucepan had been burnt and not left to soak, and whichever character it was who threw his cigarette-ends into the electric fire as if it had been an open grate, had been visiting again, but otherwise everything was much as usual. There was one of Mrs Day's scribbled notes, though, propped up for Milly's attention against the flour-bin:

If Mr Plzpwrdge rings up, it read. *Please tell him to skrr the dgllrwn and not to rwrwll prrrn beivoose until I let him know.*

Thank you. A. L. Day

Milly sighed. Mrs Day was always leaving notes like this, and Milly often wondered what happened about them.

Please wash the strt grr thoroughly had been the first one, followed, the very next Tuesday, by *Please be careful not to rdvool the qumqmvruin gra pllooll without removing the plug.*

Milly had done her best. She had washed thoroughly everything that looked in the least like a *strt grr*; and as to the *qumqmvruin gra pllooll*, she had played for safety, and avoided anything that had a plug on it at all, for fear of *rdvooling* it.

So far, the method seemed to have worked all right. Anyway, she had not as yet found any fierce notes pointing out that the *strt grr* was still *filthy*. Thus it was with a fairly tranquil mind that she tossed this latest specimen into the waste-paper basket (if and when this Mr *Plzpwrdge did* phone, he would presumably know himself what he was talking about), and settled herself happily on the sofa to read.

CHAPTER XV

Bother Mr *Plzpwrdge*! The telephone was already shrilling through the flat before Milly had read so much as a page of her chosen volume. Why couldn't the wretched man have rung later on, when she'd only have been working? Dragging herself from her comfortable couch, she got herself reluctantly across the room, and picked up the receiver.

"I'm sorry, Mrs Day's not in," she said. "Can I give her a message?" She did not make her voice very encouraging. He had not even said he *was* Mr *Plzpwrdge* yet; with any luck she could avoid learning his name altogether, and then none of it could possibly be her fault. "She'll be back about half past six," she added, cautiously, and waited for the pleasant middle-aged voice to say very well, it would call again later.

But it didn't go like that at all.

"Who's that speaking?" the voice asked—and it seemed to Milly that a slight sharpness had come into it. "Who is it, please?"

"I—Oh, I'm just visiting here, I'm just—well—just a friend . . ." gabbled Milly, some instinct—or was it by now just habit?—preventing her telling the simple, innocuous truth about her role here.

"Oh. Oh, I see. Well, look, I'm sorry to bother you, but perhaps you can help us. Do you happen to know of a Mrs Barnes who works for Mrs Day? A Mrs Milly Barnes? We've been given to understand that she comes two or three afternoons a week and . . ."

"She doesn't! She isn't! There must be some mistake! Mrs Day doesn't know anyone called Barnes . . . !"

Only after she had got the receiver back on the hook did Milly realise what a complete fool she had made of herself. This man, whoever he was, might have been ringing up about something perfectly harmless—an offer of another job, perhaps, or to ask some market-research questions about detergent. *Now* what was he going to think? Frantically, she tried to recall the exact wording of her wild, muddled assertions, and to work out what an outsider would deduce therefrom. That she was lying, obviously, or else that she was half-witted. How could she—or anyone—know for certain that Mrs Day didn't know anyone called Barnes? You can know of your friends that they *do* know a Mrs Barnes, but how can you possibly know that they don't?

Oh, she had been a fool! A fool! And after her resolutions of only a couple of hours ago, too! Milly sat with her head in her hands, staring down at a crumb of ginger biscuit on the carpet, trying to understand what it was that had driven her to behaviour so insane.

Fear, of course. Some people might prefer to call it guilt. The ever-present knowledge that she was wanted for murder.

Murder. This was the first time that Milly had allowed the word to come into her mind uncensored. Murder. She waited for guilt, long repressed, to burst from her sub-conscious and wash over her in an intolerable tide.

Nothing happened. She said the word again, aloud, this time, into the empty flat. Murder. I have committed murder.

Still nothing. Nothing that could be identified as guilt, anyway. Fear, yes; and a lively determination not to be caught. These were familiar feelings by now, almost old friends, but they could not possibly be described as guilt.

This was ridiculous! Summoning up all the honesty she possessed, all the power of self-scrutiny, Milly probed deep into her inmost heart, searching for the black core of guilt that must lie there.

No good. The most profound and earnest piece of soul-searching that she had ever undertaken revealed absolutely nothing except a vague, generalised resentment about the whole business. "It's not *fair*," something inside her was childishly complaining, "why should *I* be a murderer when other people aren't? It's not *fair!*"

She tried again. "I have killed. I have committed the ultimate crime. I have taken a human life."

Still nothing. Human lives are being taken all the time, some by disease, some by cars, some by over-eating. To have contributed to one of these commonplace events seemed—well, not exactly trivial, but lacking in some essential element of evil. Somehow there was nothing there for guilt to feed on—it was like one of those imitation foods with no nourishment in them, that are designed to make you slim.

What was wrong? Why did she have no proper feelings? Was it that Gilbert's life had, in the end, been so divorced from reality that it was not a life at all? And did it follow from this that his death could not be a real death?

Was *this* the immortality that men have dreaded in their hearts since the beginning of time—the immortality conferred upon Tithonus as the ultimate vengeance of the gods?

Had Gilbert brought this ultimate vengeance upon himself as he sat in the thickening darkness behind the closed shutters in Lady Street? Towards the end, darkness was the only thing he trusted: he screamed at Milly, sometimes, if she so much as switched on the light in the scullery so that he could see it shining under the crack of the door. After such a denial of life, how could Death get him when the time came? On what could Death's skeleton hand get a sure grip in such a case? When bony hand encountered bony hand in the darkness, who would have been the one to flee in terror . . . ?

She should never have let her husband get into such a state: that's what the overworked young doctor had said, reprovingly, a month or two before Gilbert died. She should have brought him round to the surgery, and no, of course he couldn't prescribe anything without actually seeing the patient, how could he, it would be most unethical . . . And then, when the old man never turned up, and the wretched, jittery wife stopped pestering at the surgery, he must thankfully have written off the whole business. What could he have done, anyway? One more marriage foundering in the familiar welter of recriminations and mutual accusations of paranoia. What did people think doctors *were*?

And perhaps, if Milly had recognised the nature of her problem a little earlier, while Gilbert was still willing to walk in the light of the sun, she might perhaps have persuaded him, on some pretext, to go along to the surgery with her. Or even to allow the doctor to visit him at the flat, which had not yet become a fortress, barricaded against all comers. And perhaps, at that stage, medical treatment might have been able to achieve something. But while Gilbert was no worse than this, Milly was still viewing her disastrous marriage as just this—a disastrous marriage, which she must learn to live with and to alleviate as best she could. And unfortunately it so happened that the very ways she devised to improve her husband's spirits might just as well have been so many carefully graded provocations, each one a little more traumatic than the last—so little did she comprehend, at the beginning, the nature of the shadows she could feel gathering about her.

First, the matter of friends. According to her not very penetrating observation, it seemed obvious beyond all question that Gilbert was suffering from too dull and solitary an existence. Pottering about in this dreary flat all day . . . never seeing anyone but each other, no wonder it was driving them both up the wall!

Cheerful, varied company, then: that was the first necessity. A lively to-ing and fro-ing of visitors to brighten the poor chap up, take him out of himself.

Milly was not so blind, even in those days, as to suppose that she could let loose a chattering horde of her own former acquaintances on a man like Gilbert, with any hope of success, and so she tried, tactfully, to find out who *his* friends were, preparatory to bombarding them with invitations.

There were none. Absolutely none at all. When this fact was finally borne in upon Milly, she could not think what to do. Naturally, she hadn't supposed that Gilbert could boast any very scintillating circle of acquaintances, but she *had* imagined that there would be at least an old colonel or two, bumbling on about polo in the nineteen-twenties, and perhaps offering Gilbert an occasional game of chess, lasting for hours and hours under the green lamplight. She had expected to be bored by Gilbert's friends, but not as bored as she was by Gilbert on his own; and she was therefore quite ready to put a good face on it and make them warmly welcome.

But now it seemed that no sort of face, good or bad, was to be required of her: and when she pressed him, saying that there must be *someone* he'd like to have round, he gave her a strange, considering look, and did not answer. By evening he was in one of his sulks. He did not speak to her all through supper, and straight afterwards he retired to his armchair with the newspaper. He opened it and held it outspread before his face, as usual, but Milly knew that this time he wasn't reading it. Nor was he dozing, or letting his mind wander: rather he seemed to be more than usually alert and awake, as if he was waiting for something.

By the next morning he was his usual self again, and perhaps if Milly had taken the hint, and forthwith laid aside her plans for livening up his social life, things might have turned out differently. But unfortunately her enthusiasm for changing his way of life was only whetted by this setback, and she set her ingenuity to work to overcome it.

Her friends were out, obviously; *his* didn't exist, so what remained but to take matters into her own hands and invite, without consulting him, a pleasant, middle-aged couple who had been at the Industrial Archaeology class last term? Whether they were still there this term Milly didn't know, because she and Gilbert no longer went. Why they didn't she wasn't quite sure, and something warned her that if she asked him about it he would go into one of his moods. As yet, she was far from understanding what lay at the root of these "moods", but she was beginning to be just a little bit scared of them, and to have a vague sort of instinct about the things that would be likely to trigger them off.

Thus she said nothing to Gilbert of what was in her mind: instead she quietly wrote a letter to the Davidsons, c/o the Institute, and when Mrs Davidson's reply came, saying that she and her husband would be delighted to come to tea on Saturday, she made sure that she took it from the postman herself, without Gilbert seeing it. It would be better, she calculated, to spring it on him at the last minute, then he would not have time to work up a lot of silly objections.

Rarely can wifely miscalculation have had such disastrous consequences. That Saturday afternoon tea-party proved to be one of the most shocking experiences of Milly's whole life. Even now, months later, the thought of it still made her face grow hot. The scene was still as vivid in her memory as if it had only just happened . . . the scalding tea streaming in a brown tide across the clean white tablecloth and on to the floor . . . the two visitors, stiff as waxworks with shock . . . and herself, first stunned, and then rousing herself to a flurry of apologies . . . and then the mopping-up, as if it had been an ordinary accident, with the unfortunate Davidsons doing their appalled best to pretend that nothing much had happened . . .

It had been unfortunate, perhaps, that Gilbert had happened to be out when the visitors arrived. If he had been there when they came through the door, all smiles and hand-shaking, he might have reacted differently. As it was, even the brief forewarning that Milly had planned was denied him, and he walked into his wife's tea-party utterly unprepared.

For a moment, he just stood there, staring; just as he had stared when Milly had brightened his flat with flowers and cushions a week or two before. There was nothing actually very remarkable about his demeanour, and only Milly noticed the curious brightness that was coming into his eyes, a luminous look, as if a light had been switched on from within. The Davidsons, already giving little chirrups of appropriate greeting, noticed nothing: and so, as he padded swiftly towards the table, it was only Milly who was so paralysed with fear that she could not move. The Davidsons, naturally enough, assumed that their host was approaching to shake hands, and Mr Davidson had in fact already half-risen to his feet, and was saying something like "Ah, Soames, good to see you again——"——when Gilbert picked up the large earthenware teapot and smashed it down into the middle of the table: and then, without a word, turned on his heel and walked with the same soft, swift steps out of the room.

Of the flurry, and panic, and embarrassment which ensued, Milly could not remember much detail: the next thing that was clear in her mind was Gilbert's coming back into the room—was it ten minutes?—half an hour?—later, and mumbling some sort of apology, explaining, confusedly, that he "had had a lot of worries lately". She remembered the desperate eagerness with which everyone had seized on this, and had pretended frenziedly that it was an adequate explanation: and then, shortly afterwards, the Davidsons had left, in a whirl of gabbled politenesses and glassy smiles. She remembered how she had longed for them to go, and never to see them again: and at the same time had dreaded, with a growing, sickening terror, the moment when she should be left alone with her husband.

But strangely, when they were at last on their own, Gilbert had not turned on her in fury as she had expected. On the contrary, he treated her for the rest of the evening with even more consideration than usual, jumping up to open doors for her, to carry trays; and all of it done with a sort of pitying affection which Milly could not understand at all, and which filled her with unease. Only just before bedtime did he refer to what had happened, and when he did it was in terms so extraordinary that Milly was awake the rest of the night puzzling about it.

"I don't want you to think, my dear, that your friends are not welcome under my roof," he began, seeming not to notice the way Milly's mouth fell open at this understatement of all time. "But I would just ask you to be a little bit more careful. Those two today—I know you didn't realise it, my dear, and I'm not blaming you—but those two have been on my tracks for a long time."

"*On your tracks?* What on earth do you mean, Gilbert?" The words were out before Milly had had time to weigh them, and a flicker of irritation crossed Gilbert's face.

"Now, don't pretend to me, my dear," he warned her gravely. "That is something I don't like, particularly from my wife. You know—you *must* know—that many people would like to get at my memoirs. Many, many people!" The last words were spoken with a strange mixture of regret and a sort of unholy triumph: and Milly could only stare.

"Your—your memoirs?" she got out at last.

"Yes, yes—" he gestured impatiently at the piles of newspapers that still lay in yellowing heaps on the table, untouched since the day he had forbidden Milly to move them. "It's all in there—all the material for my life's work. As soon as the material is complete, I shall start on the writing. Till then, I want *no one*—I repeat, *no one*, not even you, my dear—to look at a single word of what is in those papers. Do you realise," (and here the strange brilliance was coming back into his light eyes, and his arms gestured in a wide arc), "do you realise that in every one of those papers there are articles about *me*? Did you realise that? No? Well, now you see why they mustn't get hold of any of them. They mustn't see one single line. They could use it against me, you see . . ."

Milly refrained from asking "Who could?" She was beginning to see, as in a glass darkly, what sort of a thing it was that she was up against, but she would not, as yet, give a name to it. What nonsense!——was all she allowed herself to think. He's talking nonsense! How *could* there be articles about *him* in all those thousands of papers! And with this thought, the worm began to wriggle in the bottom of her mind, the Bluebeard worm, and she knew she would not rest until she knew what *was* in those old papers, so carefully saved, and parcelled up, and arranged . . .

It was on the Monday, over a week later, that she got her chance. Gilbert was going out, as he still did at times, "to see a man"; and as soon as the shadow of his progress up the area steps had ceased to swing in sweeps of darkness and grey light against the dining-room window, she seized on the nearest and most accessible of the packages, and began tugging delicately at the string. It must all be done to perfection. She had already noted the exact position of this package among the rest, and now she must so undo the knot that she would be able to do it up again *exactly* the same . . .

The Times, of June 15th, 1935. Milly pored over the faded pages with a kind of tense, shapeless expectancy, with no faintest idea of what it was she was expecting. Her eyes scanned news of wars, and of wars to come; of fashions; of political speeches, and of cricket; but nothing, anywhere, about Gilbert Soames, in any shape or form. Here and there a passage was marked by a light pencilled line down the side, but never was it anything that (as far as Milly could see) could possibly have been connected with her husband, at any stage in his career. The marked passages weren't even interesting in themselves——just a few lines of a parliamentary speech here, or an announcement about the sales of pet food there . . . Milly shook her head baffled, and moved on to June 16th. Only the same sort of thing again . . . Likewise June 17th . . . and 18th . . .

It was when she was halfway through July 12th that she became aware that the print was harder to read than it had been at first. The grey light had become greyer while she wasn't noticing and only now did she look up to see why.

Gilbert's face, flattened and expressionless against the glass, was watching her through the area window.

CHAPTER XVI

Strangely, the explosion of rage that Milly was waiting for never came. Gilbert simply set to work to parcel the papers up again, applying himself to the task with the same meticulous care that he had shown before, putting on his gold-rimmed glasses now and then to examine a passage more closely, or to check on the number of a page. He did not seem to be listening to Milly's muddled lies—how the string had broken . . . the bundle had fallen off the table . . . she had only been trying to get them back in the right order . . . As the implausible excuses tumbled from her lips, he neither silenced her nor made any comment on what she was saying, but simply went on with his task, peering and muttering, as if he was alone. And when it was finished, and the bundle re-tied to his satisfaction and replaced among the others, he settled himself in his big chair as usual, with his green lamp at his elbow, and the pages of *The Financial Times* hiding his face.

Sitting opposite him in the green shadows, not daring to read or to pick up any sewing, Milly kept waiting for the expected explosion, but still it did not come. It seemed that, for some inscrutable reason, she had got away with it: and it was only gradually, as the days went by, that she realised that this was not the case at all.

The first thing she noticed was that her morning trip down to the shops in the High Road was no longer the free-and-easy affair it had been hitherto. Up till now, Gilbert had given her a generous weekly allowance for housekeeping, and had left her to spend it when and as she liked. But now all this was changed. Now, he wanted to know exactly which shops she was going to . . . what she was going to buy . . . when she would be back . . . and at the end of a fortnight she discovered, with a strange cold feeling in her stomach, that he had been keeping a record of it all . . . the exact time she had left the house each day, and the exact time she had returned . . .

But by then there were already other changes that had forced themselves upon her awareness. Each day he had been closing the shutters and fastening the doors a little earlier, at first imperceptibly, and then at an increasing rate, as if he was trying to win some mysterious race against the golden October days, and reach the dark ahead of them. Soon, it was barely two o'clock when the flat was plunged in lamplight, and evening was upon them.

Evenings had always been the worst part of the day, and this gratuitous extension of them was terrible. Milly did not know how she was going to endure the hours till bedtime, with Gilbert silent behind his newspaper, and herself sitting in tense and bitter idleness in the chair opposite. Sometimes she would let her eyes wander along the worn leather backs of the books on the shelves at her side, and lay plans for slithering this or that volume out without a sound in the hope of reading for a little without

Gilbert noticing. But rarely did she manage it. At the faintest sound of movement—or sometimes even before that, when the whole thing was still only a plan churning in her mind—he would lower his paper, or rouse himself from his doze, and look across at her.

"Are you bored, my dear?" he would ask politely. "Then let us talk," and laying down his paper he would sit waiting for her to say something. She tried: sometimes she tried quite hard, racking her brains for something that might amuse him, but it grew harder and harder. Their life was narrowing daily: they were cut off more and more from anything that might have provided conversation. Milly could almost hear the creaking as the walls closed in on them.

"Let's have a cup of tea," she sometimes said, as an excuse for darting into the kitchen, but lately he had taken to coming out after her, ostensibly to help her carry the tray, but in fact, Milly knew, it was to check up on her. Because several times lately, when she had made the tea by herself, he had questioned her when she came back to the dining-room. What had she been doing? Why had she been so long? How could it take—here he would consult his old-fashioned gold watch—twelve and a half minutes to make a cup of tea? She was filling the kettle too full on purpose, he accused, so as to spend extra minutes away from him.

This was so exactly the truth—and yet it sounded so mad when put into words—that Milly denied it hotly, with a sense of genuine indignation, and at last he seemed mollified. But it was only a few days after this that she found, under his pillow, with the record of her shopping expeditions, another, newer record: a list of all the times that she had spent alone in the kitchen each day, worked out to the nearest half minute. Some of the items were mysteriously underlined in red, and marked with a small cross in Gilbert's neat, cramped hand.

It was on the morning when she made this discovery that Milly made up her mind that she had had enough. This was it. Packing only her night things and a spare cardigan, Milly set off for the shops at her usual time that morning, promising to be back by twelve at the latest. She walked, briskly as always, until she was out of sight, and then she began to run: to race, as fast as bus and tube would carry her, to Felicity's.

Felicity was one of her old acquaintances from happier days: an old acquaintance of Julian's, too, of course, but that couldn't be helped. As she hurried through the watery November sunshine towards Felicity's flat, Milly toyed longingly with the idea of making a clean breast of everything: of pouring into Felicity's sympathetic but over-enthusiastic ears all the pent-up follies and miseries of the past months.

But it wouldn't do. Felicity would no doubt be all kindness and concern, and quite uncensorious (well, after her own three divorces, she could hardly be otherwise) but the trouble with kind, uncensorious people is that they are incapable of keeping anything to themselves. Their kindness makes them want to share the delights of gossip with all and sundry, while their uncensoriousness makes them blissfully unaware that the spicy news they are spreading is particularly discreditable to the victim. Within days—hours, very likely—of Felicity's learning that Milly had left her new husband, a dozen versions of the story would be winging their way across the Atlantic, each one more scurrilous than the last. How Julian and Cora would enjoy taking their gleeful pick from the rich and varied menu thus set before them free of charge!

Felicity was naturally surprised to see Julian's ex-wife after so many months of non-communication, but she seemed quite pleased, and agreed amiably enough to Milly's plea to be allowed to stay for a few days: and if, out of her long and varied experience of matrimony, she took with a pinch of salt Milly's story about Gilbert being away for a few days "on business", and about being nervous of sleeping alone in the flat—well, there had been times when Felicity herself had been driven to dishing out this sort of rigmarole on her own account, and the last thing she would do would be to call another woman's bluff. She did not know yet what this Gilbert character had been up to, but she knew very well from her own personal experience that when women told lies it was always the man's fault, he drove them to it, the sod, and so the least they could do was to back each other up. Besides, that way you got the whole story, drama-side up. So she urged her visitor most cordially to stick around for a while. It would be quite a convenience, actually, to have someone here, as she, Felicity, had to be out such a lot, and her current boy-friend (an absolute *sweetie*, you *must* meet him) had recently given her a Siamese cat, and it so happened that Felicity absolutely *adored* everything about Siamese cats except looking after them, and so, if Milly didn't mind . . . ?

The matter having been thus arranged to the satisfaction of both, the two women settled down to a pleasant afternoon of gossipping, answering the telephone to Felicity's friends, and watching television. It was about eight o'clock, and they were idly discussing the question of whether to go out to dinner, and, if so, which of Felicity's admirers should be invited along to pay the bill, when there was a knock on the door: and when Felicity went to open it, Gilbert walked in.

Milly did not even feel surprised. It was as if she had known this was going to happen. She could not even bring herself to wonder how her husband had traced her— whether he had followed her, or had simply gone to the phone box at the far end of Lady Street, and kept phoning all the numbers in her address book until he hit on someone who knew she was here. It wouldn't have taken long. Felicity had been chattering to friends on the telephone all the afternoon, by now half London probably knew of Julian's ex-wife's escapade.

But in any case, there seemed to be no need of a natural explanation. Standing there in the doorway, so straight and still, his hair gleaming like the wings of a white bird, Gilbert radiated a strange power, and it was easy to imagine that he had been guided by some sense not quite of this world; even that he had been magically transported by the powers of darkness through the November night.

What had happened next? All Milly could remember afterwards was that from the moment she saw her husband standing there, so quiet and tall, his eyes glittering like cats' eyes, she had known she would be going back with him. Not for one moment had there seemed to be any choice. She supposed she must have said goodbye to Felicity; must have apologised, and made up some face-saving story to explain Gilbert's sudden appearance when he was supposed to be away "on business". Anyway, the next thing she could clearly remember was sitting in the corner of a taxi, in the dark, with Gilbert sitting very straight and still beside her, and not speaking a single word. She remembered the bright lights of the West End reeling away behind them, to be replaced by the dim sodium lights across the river, fewer and further between as the taxi wove its relentless way towards their home.

She did not know what her punishment would be: but she knew enough, by now, to guess that whatever it was, it would not fall immediately. Rather it would come upon her piece-meal, over the next days and weeks, almost while she wasn't noticing. She would not know when it began, nor when, or by what route, it would reach its unimaginable end.

Even after they were home, Gilbert still did not speak: nor did Milly defend herself, or make excuses. It had gone beyond that. Only after Gilbert had gone all round the flat, bolting and securing the doors and windows, did he finally bring himself to make an observation. Wandering casually towards the bookshelves, and searching along the rows of old leather-bound books, he came upon the volume he wanted. He turned the pages thoughtfully, then paused for a minute. As he read, he began to laugh, that strange, silent laugh of his, setting his gaunt body jolting soundlessly, as if there was a time-bomb ticking away somewhere deep inside him:

"You know what the ancient Scythians did with their runaway slaves?" he said to Milly from across the room, and without raising his eyes from the book. "They used to blind them!" He laughed again, gently, as his eye travelled down the page. "They made just as good slaves, you see, like that, as they only had very simple tasks to perform. It didn't matter at all."

The chiming of Mrs Day's ornamental gilt clock roused Milly from her daydream. Three o'clock already, and nothing done!—not to mention the precious reading time frittered away to no purpose! Jumping up from the telephone corner where she had been sitting, immobilised by memories, ever since that disturbing telephone call for "Mrs Barnes", Milly determined to think no more about any of it. Collecting her dusters and brushes, she set off for Mrs Day's bedroom—usually the storm-centre of operations—to tackle the by now familiar medley of cigarette ends, underwear, coffee cups and evening dresses, with a cross Persian cat asleep in the middle of it.

But the memories were not so easily dispelled. All the while she was squeezing flimsy, glittering garments into the packed wardrobe, trying to find hangers for them all, Milly felt the past lingering all about her, like a taste in the mouth. It would not leave her alone, with its if's, and if only's, and supposing's.

Supposing she had refused to go back with Gilbert that evening? Supposing she had said, boldly: "No, Gilbert, I'm sorry, but I'm not coming. Felicity has invited me to stay, and I'm staying!" What would have happened then? What would have been the course of her life thereafter?

Even as she posed the question, she knew that it was futile. What happened had happened. It had had to happen. The sense of inevitability was as strongly with her now as it had been then, when, unresisting as a puppet on a string, she had followed Gilbert down all those stairs and into the waiting taxi. There was nothing else she could have done. That was how it had seemed then: that was how it still seemed now, when she looked back. It had been fated: she seemed to have had no option: she had been a pawn in the grip of forces outside her control.

This, of course, is the way people usually do feel when they have come to grief through taking on grave and extensive responsibilities for fun. When the full weight of their casually undertaken commitment finally comes to rest on their shoulders, and there is no longer any way out, then it is that they experience this sense of helplessness, this feeling of being a pawn in the hands of fate, a plaything of the gods: and they rarely remember, by then, that it was they, first, who treated the gods as playthings.

It is amazing how much your hands can accomplish without, apparently, any assistance from the mind at all. By the end of the afternoon, Milly had completed all her usual tasks in Mrs Day's flat, and had set off for home, with only the briefest spells of conscious attention to what she was doing:—one when the cat brought half a lobster into the bathroom for her inspection, and she had to decide what to do with it: and the next when the swing doors of the block of flats thrust her forth out of the lush central heating into the gusty winter night, with a wet wind lolloping in from the sea, stinging her into momentary consciousness as it caught at her face, and at her ears, and at her gloveless hands.

CHAPTER XVII

After that evening, Gilbert's deterioration was swift and terrible. It seemed to Milly that there was something almost purposeful about the way he forged onward towards the abyss, as though nothing and no one should stop him. He seemed, at times, to be seeking the Dark Night of the soul with an intensity and passion that other men have devoted to the search for gold.

She knew by now, of course, that he was ill; and when her belated resort to the local doctor produced nothing helpful, she tried to calm her growing panic by telling herself that it was an illness, like any other illness.

But it wasn't like any other illness; that was the trouble. And then there was always the feeling—inescapable for the trapped onlooker—that the patient has somehow *chosen* to be ill in just that way rather than in any other: that if he had been a nice kind person to start with, he would have gone mad in some nice kind way . . .

Maybe there is some grain of truth in this: Milly had no means of knowing, as she had been acquainted with her husband for less than a year, and had anyway devoted precious little of her time so far to trying to understand him. Now, when it was too late, she did try to make some sort of contact with his disintegrating mind, if only for her own safety: but by now such efforts were futile.

It was the day after her abortive attempt at escape that Gilbert nailed up the area door; and that same evening he fixed bolts on the dining-room door, inside and outside. Now, when Milly wanted to go shopping, she had to go up the dark basement stairs to the ground floor, and wrestle with the bolts and chains and double locks on the ancient, peeling front door. Often, as she struggled, Mrs Roach, who inhabited that floor, would hear the groaning and the grinding of the rusty metal, and would shuffle in her slippers out of her fusty bed-sitting-room, and stand watching, almost like Gilbert himself. Milly knew that Mrs Roach disapproved of her—she would hardly even exchange a "good morning" on most days—and this made her nervous and clumsy: it was sometimes five minutes before she finally got the creaking old door open on to the blessed light of day.

But soon even these brief excursions came to an end. Gilbert had taken recently to coming up the basement stairs with her, and taking his stand in the doorway to watch her as she set off down the street. When she came back she would often find him still standing there, watch in hand, and if she had been longer than half an hour or so he would sometimes be actually trembling, with a terrible, silent rage.

Half an hour. Then twenty minutes was all he would stand for, and then ten; and presently there came the time when he forbade her to go shopping at all. He had arranged for Mrs Roach to do it, he informed her, coldly, since she, his wife, was not to be trusted. Thereafter their diet was restricted mainly to things that could be bought at the poky little corner shop—sliced bread and tins of things mostly—since Mrs Roach was reluctant to drag her bloated body further than this, even for generous pay. Soon the milk was tinned too, for Gilbert would no longer allow the milkman to call, insisting that Milly left messages for him hidden among the empty bottles.

And now the time came when Gilbert would no longer open the window shutters at all, for fear "They" would look in. The era of the long night had arrived: and now that it was here, Milly realised that she had been waiting for it for a very long time. She seemed to have known, all along, that this was how it would all end.

End? It was only December even now: and the strange thing was that no sooner had Gilbert achieved the timeless, unbroken night towards which he had been so quietly and purposefully moving all these weeks, than he became passionately, obsessionally preoccupied with the passing of time. A hundred times a day he would ask Milly what the time was, drawing out his watch to check on her answer, comparing his watch with the clock in the kitchen, checking and counter-checking.

Sometimes he would scream at Milly that she was deceiving him, telling him the wrong time on purpose. She would be bringing the lunch in, say, at one o'clock, and he would suddenly heave himself round in his great chair to scold and storm, confronting her with his heavy gold watch with its hands pointing to three, or four or even five . . . No matter how closely she tried to watch, Milly never seemed to catch him tinkering with it; and so presently, in the weird, darkening world that was closing in on her, she began to feel that the watch itself might have become malignantly alive, in league with its master to put her in the wrong.

And now his time sense began to swing like a great pendulum in the dark, gathering momentum. Sometimes he would call for his supper thinking that night had fallen when in fact the bright, frosty day beyond the shutters was only just beginning. At other times—and these were the most terrible of all—he would think that night was day, and would come creeping into his wife's room at dead of night to find out why she was asleep. She would wake, then, from strange uneasy dreams, to find him shuffling around her room, softly opening drawers, peering into boxes, fumbling about among her clothes and other possessions with his old fingers.

The first time this happened, she had called out to him, in spontaneous terror:

"Gilbert! What is it? What are you doing?"—but she had never done so again. So strange had been the look in his shining eyes as he strode swiftly to the bed and leaned over her: and so strange had been the things he'd said:

"Why, my dear, I just wondered if you were ill?" he began, softly. "It seems so strange of you to be lying here, at past midday! It's nearly time for lunch! Aren't you going to cook me any lunch?"

This first time, Milly had argued, and shown him her watch in some indignation: and at last, in reckless determination to prove herself right, she had wrenched open the window shutter and shown him the moonlight filtering down, grey and silent, from the deserted street above.

At first, she thought it was a tom-cat setting up his caterwauling, very suddenly, from the silent area steps. Then she realised that it was Gilbert screaming. He wrenched the shutter from her hand, and slammed it shut, shooting the bolt home, and slotting in the great metal catch.

"So *this* is how they get in!" he jabbered, his voice cracked and shrill with fury. "*This* is how I am being betrayed! In my own house . . . ! By my own wife . . . !"

Less than five minutes later, Milly was only too willing to agree humbly that it was lunch time. That she had overslept. That she was sorry. Anything . . . Anything at all. And thus it came about that, in the small hours of that December night, she had cooked him one of his beloved curries, rice and all, and had served it with a trembling smile, carefully referring to it, in a small, shaking voice, as "lunch".

After this, she had pretended to be asleep, always, when she heard the nightly roamings beginning. Sometimes she would watch, through barely opened lids, as he peered and poked among her belongings, his white hair gleaming and bobbing in the faint light through the open door. At others, she kept her eyes tight closed, listening, willing the soft rustlings to cease, that she might know he had gone away.

And sometimes he had, and then that would be the end of the night's terror, but more often than not he would end by rousing her, and insisting that it was lunch-time. After that first night, Milly never argued again. She got up and cooked his curry, or whatever he might fancy, immediately.

There was something strangely inert, she sometimes felt, about the way she allowed herself to be thus carried along with his insane delusions, and sometimes she was puzzled by it. Fear of him did not seem to be quite the whole explanation, for even her fear, now, was beginning to have a strange passive quality about it, as if she was no longer a real, autonomous being with a real life to be lost or saved. Wherever it was that Gilbert was going, she knew now that he was beginning to drag her with him: already she could feel the tug and pull of it. Before long, as the black storms rose higher in his disintegrating mind, she, too, was going to lose her footing and be sucked along, irrelevant as a spinning twig, towards the darkness where his spirit boiled and churned . . .

It was towards the end of December when Gilbert began to imagine that Milly was trying to poison him, and at first Milly did not take in the significance of the new symptoms. She noticed a slight tightening-up of his surveillance of her activities in the kitchen, she was never alone there at all now, for even a minute. But this was a difference in degree, not in kind, and anyway she was beginning to be used to it now. As she bustled from cooker to sink, she took it for granted now that out of the corner of her eye she would be aware of the tall, waiting figure in the doorway, just as she would be aware of the roller towel hanging white and motionless in its usual place. In some ways, it was less disturbing than it used to be, because he did not pad around helping any more. Instead, he just watched—or sometimes, as it seemed to her, listened. This puzzled her at first: and then one day, she stopped and listened too. She became aware, as he had been aware all along, of the faint, endless tap-tapping of footsteps on the pavement far above. Tap-tap-*tap*, they went: or tappity-*tap*-tap-tap . . . and suddenly she knew, in sick terror, that she must never stop and listen like this again. For she had heard the sounds, just for one telepathic second, through Gilbert's ears, and—just fancy!—they were in code, tapping out messages! So that was why he never took his eyes off her—he was watching for the moment when she would begin to understand, and to tap messages back! How terrifyingly easy it would be!—three cups placed in quick succession on the draining-board—*tap*-tap-tap . . . or the wooden spoon knocking too rhythmically against the side of the pan—trr—trr—trr—as she stirred! After this, she carefully blurred and muddled the sounds she couldn't help making, and hummed noisily as she worked. Perhaps it was not surprising if, after all this, she should have taken little note of the fact that Gilbert was gradually becoming more and more fussy over his food. Such a trifle it seemed, in comparison with all the other problems. It was an odd kind of fussiness, though, and seemed to have little to do with the quality of Milly's cooking—she had, in fact, long since learned how to please her husband (in this department at least) by producing highly spiced, highly flavoured dishes, hot with pimentoes, and peppers, and green chiles. He didn't seem to mind much about the basic ingredients, and thus had noticed no deterioration in the menu since Milly had been limited to the tins and packets of stuff that were all Mrs Roach could be bothered to buy. No, he still liked his food, and ate it with appetite, but he had developed an annoying habit—that's all it seemed to Milly at first—of changing plates with his wife just as the meal was about to begin. Just as she had it all served out, and was already picking up her own knife and fork, he would lean across and slide her plate away from under her very hand, and deftly substitute his own. Usually he would murmur, deprecatingly, some sort of explanation—"You must have the bigger one, dear, I'm not very hungry today", or "Do you mind—I'd rather have the one without so much rice." Sometimes one or both of them might already have started when the long, gnarled fingers slid across the table and closed upon her plate. She never protested, even though she often found it impossible to eat the food thus exchanged. The thought of his fork having touched it, straight from those old lips, turned her stomach. And so there she would sit, pushing the food around her plate, and trying to look as if she was eating. And when she glanced up now and then, and noticed him watching her, his features narrowed with cunning, she did not understand the significance of what she saw.

She had been noticing a peculiar unpleasant smell in the dining-room for some days now, and one evening, early in the New Year, she seized her chance to investigate. Gilbert was for once out of the room for a few minutes, as Mrs

Roach had just come down with the week's shopping, and he was busy in the scullery examining the purchases and putting them away. This was a task he would no longer trust to his wife, and Milly calculated that it would be some minutes before he returned. She knew his slow movements, and the punctilious thoroughness with which he would examine every package: she could hear the low mumbling of his voice even from this distance, as he checked and re-checked each item against the list. Swiftly, she pushed the heavy dining-room door almost shut, and made for the corner of the room from which she was sure the smell emanated. The corner behind Gilbert's great leather chair . . . Somewhere among those ancient leather- bound books . . . Behind them, perhaps, right at the back of the shelves . . .

What she had expected to find, she did not know. When she pulled out the first matchbox, full of old boiled rice, she simply felt that there had been some sort of a mistake. It just didn't mean anything. But when she found the next one, with dried remains of scrambled egg in it . . . and then the one full of mince that had gone green . . . and the one oozing with decaying stew . . . then, indeed, she knew that she had crossed the border into madland, and that there might be no return . . . and now here was the king of madland himself, come back into his own . . . leaning over her, blotting out the last of the light. Darkness blazed from him as from a black sun, and she prostrated herself before it in gibbering, slavish terror. The time of the blackness was come, the black dawn was breaking and there would be no more day. The shrieks and howls from the bottomless pit were already loud in her ears, they came from Gilbert's lips . . . and now she began to feel her sanity itself twisting from her grasp. He was upon her . . . his bony fingers danced like lace . . . he was screaming like a madman—because, of course, he *was* a madman, and at this thought, strangely, her mind snapped back, like good quality elastic, and she was sane again.

He had not killed her, nor even injured her in any way. She could feel no pain anywhere. He must, at some point, have hauled her to her feet from behind the chair, because here she was, standing, with his hands gripping her shoulders, while he howled and shrieked with fear, right into her face.

Fear. This was the first time she had ever observed that fear was what racked and tore him, a degree of fear beyond the comprehension of the sane. And even now, the fact hardly registered. So great was her own terror that she could not even understand his words, let alone the nature of the passion that lay behind them.

Presently, it all seemed to have been going on for hours, her standing there, and his voice streaming into her face. She found she was taking in the gist of it: how she had been putting poison in his food for a long time now; but he had foiled her—ha ha, *how* he had foiled her!—by changing round the plates each time! Did she think he hadn't noticed the way she always refused to eat her helping after they had been changed?

Milly listened almost with interest. And sometimes, Gilbert himself seemed quite to forget that his listener was also the arch-villain of his fantasy, and spoke as if she was a sympathetic outsider, to whom he was confiding his wrongs. He explained how he had been collecting these samples from his wife's uneaten platefuls to send off for analysis, and how the analysis would prove that she had been stealing his sleeping-pills and crushing them up into his food. He had noticed, he confided, that his hidden store of sleeping pills, which he had had by him for years, was diminishing, and he knew his wife had been stealing them, but he could not find where she hid them. He had searched her drawers and cupboards over and over again . . . She was very cunning . . . that was why they had chosen her for the job, because she was so cunning . . .

Barely an hour later, Gilbert was in his usual chair, with the newspaper held in front of his face, as if nothing had happened. Everything was as usual again, except for one small detail: he would not have the light on any more. In the darkness, Milly could hear the twitchings of the paper, and the familiar rustlings, as he turned the pages, and folded them this way and that as if to make them more convenient to read.

He never mentioned the poisoning again. Indeed, there were not many more days, now, for him to mention anything. Already it was the fifth of January.

He seemed to have forgotten his suspicions. He ate the meals Milly gave him, and dozed, and seemed disturbed by nothing, except the light. He hated to have any lights on now. Even his own green lamp he would only switch on now and then, for meals, or to check on the time, and when it was borne in upon him that without a light Milly simply could not cook his meals, he fumbled among his belongings and found her a torch. And thereafter, groping and fumbling, to all appearances as mad as he, Milly produced her meals by torchlight, humbly thankful for this insane concession which spared her total darkness. She knew, and somehow did not mind, that her behaviour had gone beyond humouring him, and that she had become a madman's puppet, battered by terror into a subservience that was close to idiocy.

That way, a ghastly, twilight peace was brought into being, and by giving in to all his mad whims, by following at heel, like an obedient dog, down the twisting path that led to the black caverns of the insane, she managed to maintain this peace, precariously, for four whole days.

And then, on the fifth day, it all began again. For the first time in several successive nights, Gilbert once again roused his wife in the small hours, and demanded lunch. As he flashed the torch into her dazed eyes, and shook her by the shoulder, he seemed strangely eager and alert, like a child bursting with some wonderful surprise that he has been forbidden to tell. Milly had only once before seen his eyes as bright as this, and their strange, silvery brilliance sent a chill through her, like the touch of the finger of death.

Worn out with terror and despair, Milly staggered from her bed at his bidding, threw on some clothes, and stumbled across to the kitchen. And as she stood at the cooker, numb with hopelessness, stirring curry powder and turmeric into the mess of tinned mince and dehydrated vegetables, it came to her, quite suddenly, and with a strange, quiet certainty, that she would never be doing this again.

The feeling faded as quickly as it came, but it left her with a curious sense of power, of being in control of what was going to happen, whatever it might be. And so when she saw that Gilbert was back at his old tricks again— changing the plates round when he thought her back was turned—she almost laughed. She felt that it would be fun—yes, *fun!*—to jerk him out of his idiotic suspicions. By placidly eating the helping he had allotted to her, she would make him see, once and for all, that he was mistaken, and it *couldn't* have been poisoned.

It was horrible. It made her feel sick and awful at this hour in the morning, but she was determined to go through with it. But she had barely had a couple of mouthfuls, when Gilbert's gnarled hand, green in the lamplight, flashed like a snake across the white tablecloth.

"You've changed them back!" he hissed between his teeth. "You've changed the plates back while I wasn't looking!"— and before she had time to protest, the plates were once more changed round, and she now had in front of her the plate from which Gilbert had already begun eating.

So. She had made him see his mistake, all right, but the mistake he saw was one which fitted nicely with *his* picture of the situation, not with hers. Within his system of thought, a wife who could double-cross him by magically re-changing plates under his very eyes, was far more credible than one who merely wasn't trying to poison him at all.

Triumphant, full of sly glee at the thought of having out-witted her, Gilbert fell to, smacking his lips, and plying his fork greedily. Milly did not try to protest, or to point out that she *couldn't* have changed the plates back, even if she had wanted to, since he had been watching all the time. She didn't even try to make any further show of eating what he had so gleefully placed before her. It wouldn't do any good. His delusion was complete now, perfected by months of skilful toil. It was unassailable now by the assaults of reality in any form.

So she just sat, quietly, her hands in her lap, waiting for what she knew was coming.

"Not feeling well, my dear?"

Gilbert's voice, gentle and solicitous as always on these occasions, came to her across the dimly illumined table. "Don't you like this delicious curry, that you made yourself?"

She could not see the sly sarcasm in his eyes, for they were downcast to his plate, from which he was still eating hungrily. But she saw the vulpine look come into his face, and the champing jaws. She watched the familiar narrowing of his features, as suspicion worked inside him like yeast.

Familiar? Well, of course it was, after all these months. But what was not so familiar was the way his face not only narrowed, but then swelled out like a balloon . . . and then narrowed again . . . out, in . . . out, in . . . for all the world as if his skull was breathing, instead of his lungs! For a moment—so accustomed was she by now to helplessly confronting new and terrifying symptoms—she found herself accepting it, raking among her half-forgotten nursing expertise for the significance of a breathing skull. It meant that the brain was breathing too, of course. Breathing-brain, or cerebropulmonosis, was one of the early symptoms of . . . and at this point she noticed, dimly, that her thoughts had become nonsense. She was half-dreaming, on the edge of sleep, right there as she sat. And now—what do you know?—*her* skull was breathing too, in, out, in, out, just like his, swelling as if it would explode. And it was then that she knew, without any doubt at all, that she was drugged.

The curry. Gilbert, in his madness, had imagined that it was poisoned, and it was! He had fancied, in his deluded state, that sleeping pills were crushed into the plateful she had given him, and they were! And in heavy dosage too, for she had only had a couple of mouthfuls before he had changed the plates round all over again. Everything had been done in exact accordance with his mad fantasy—but by whom?

Strangely, with her brain pulsating like a dynamo, and already awash with sleep, she was able to understand it all more clearly than she was ever to do again. It was Gilbert who had done it, naturally. In this moment of drugged dizziness, she could follow his train of thought with perfect ease. What is the most certain way of proving that your wife is trying to poison you? Why, by actually discovering poison in the food she serves to you, of course! And what is the most certain way of actually discovering poison in the food she serves you? Why, by putting it there, of course! The simple, unassailable logic of it struck her as forcibly as it must, a little earlier, have struck him.

Too clever by half, though: that was *his* trouble! It was going to be funny when he found out how he had double-crossed himself, changing the plates round a second time, as soon as he saw her beginning to eat her share! He'd landed up with the poisoned one himself! She giggled weakly, wondering how soon he would find out, and what he would say.

Wait, though. He wouldn't say anything, because by the time he found out he would be dead. That took the edge off the joke, rather. Still, it would be quite funny, all the same. She watched, fascinated, while a bit of rice dribbled down his chin and on to his tie, as it sometimes did when he was over-eager about his food. This time, she wasn't even disgusted. It was almost interesting, to watch it happening for the very last time.

He had laid down his fork. He was staring, first at her plate, and then at his own, as though trying to work out what had happened. Milly watched his puzzlement in a detached sort of way, as if he was already dead, as if it was already no concern of hers. She watched his face grow pinched and grey as some new and monstrous suspicion began to work inside him like a digestive juice, breaking down data from the outside world and re-constituting it into the special kind of nourishment needed by his fantasy. She watched his eyes narrow, and knew herself to be watching, as if it was a physical process, the building of the new suspicion into the old. She could see him joining, dove-tailing, filling in the cracks, until the job was perfect: and then, and only then, did he speak:

"You're lying!" he said to her, very softly, and leaning towards her across the table, intimate as a lover in the dim light. "You've lied to me all the time! You've pretended to put poison in my food to frighten me! You thought it would frighten me into letting that precious doctor come! You knew he was after me. You knew he was in league with them, he's been trying for years to worm his way into my house, only I've been too clever for him! And now you, my own wife, thought you'd trick me into letting him in by telling me I'd been poisoned! Didn't you? Now, don't lie to me, my dear, it is no use at all, I can see into your mind. I've seen into it all the time! Do you think I haven't seen you slinking off to his surgery, when you'd sworn to me you were only going shopping? Do you think I haven't watched, and waited, and timed you, and found out just how long you spent in there plotting against me? I have a record of it, I've kept a record . . . and of the phone calls, too. Did you think I didn't know what you were up to, sneaking off to the phone box, and betraying my whereabouts to him . . . promising to let him in when he came to get me . . . You, my wife, betraying me . . ."

Gilbert's slow rising from his chair was like a snake uncoiling. Never taking his eyes from his wife's face, he worked his way round the table towards her, holding on to the edge of it with one hand, and feeling for his keys in the depths of his trouser pocket with the other.

Was the drug beginning to take effect at last? He must have had ten—twenty—times the dose that she'd had. When he spoke, his voice was still firm, but strangely monotonous:

"You thought you'd tricked me, didn't you? You thought I was fool enough to believe that you really *had* given me poison! What sort of a fool do you take me for? Do you think I couldn't see right into your evil, treacherous mind, right from the very beginning? *I* knew what you were up to—of course I did!" Here the strange and terrible laughter began: it rocked him, silently, from deep within, until he had to clutch at the back of her chair for support. As he stood thus, half leaning over her, his next words seemed to hiss down into her ears like wind.

"That is the last trick you will ever play, my dear. What I am going to do to you now will make it quite, quite certain that you will never be able to play any more tricks, ever again. But first, we must fix the door. We must fix it so that no one will go in or out any more. There will be no need. After this, there will be no need . . ."

Snatching the keys from his hand was surprisingly easy. So was the push she gave him, which sent him staggering backwards, right across the room, and before she could know where or how he had fallen, she was gone. Outside the door . . . locking and double-locking it, and shooting home the great bolts that Gilbert had fixed there only a few weeks ago. From inside, she could hear a floundering, thumping sound, but by the time she dashed past the door again, with coat and handbag, it had ceased. She fancied she could hear another sound now, fainter and much more sinister: a scratching noise, a small scrape of metal, as if he was fiddling, somehow, with the lock . . .

The next thing Milly knew, she was in the street, running, running, through the icy January dark, and although she knew it could not be true—for had she not locked the door, fixed the great bolts, and hurled the keys, the only set of keys, far away into the night?—even though she knew all this, every nerve in her body, every cell of her racing blood, told her that Gilbert was already on her track. Why wasn't he dead? Or in a drugged coma at least? What was the strange strength of his madness, that could fight off the onslaughts of such a dose? Let him die!—let him die *quickly* she prayed, as she raced along. Let him die before he can get the door undone . . . before he can somehow break down the bolts . . . master the lock . . . ! The sound of her own footsteps echoing in the empty streets seemed to have multiplied, until now it seemed that there were footsteps everywhere, racing as she was racing through the winter blackness that was not yet morning. A race, a race to the finish, between her, and Gilbert, and Death. The three of them, strung out along the dark streets, with her (so far) in the lead; then Gilbert, gaining on her relentlessly with his long, stiff stride, the lamp posts spinning away behind him; and lastly Death, pounding along in the rear, the icy air of the January dawn whistling through the sockets of his eyes.

It was only after she had been travelling round on the tube for quite a while that Milly's heart began to slow down, and she gradually took in that she was safe. Gilbert must be dead by now, or so deep in coma that nothing would ever rouse him. And it was not until later still that the implications of this began, gradually, to force themselves upon her slowly clearing consciousness. When they found him—when the police came to investigate—they would find the door locked and bolted on the outside; they would learn the cause of death, and that the dead man's wife had suddenly and mysteriously disappeared. In the face of all this evidence, how could she ever convince them that she hadn't murdered him?

She had, of course. That was the trouble.

By sitting watching while he ate the drugged meal, by locking him in the room so that he could not go for help, by taking no steps herself to inform doctor or police: by all these omissions and commissions, she had killed her husband as surely as if she had done it with her bare hands.

CHAPTER XVIII

Milly reached up and touched her hair. It was damp with the sea-wind, and her face was stinging from the blown spray. From these things, and from her icy hands, she knew that she must have been walking home from Mrs Day's along the sea front: but she remembered nothing of it, so totally had she been reliving the awful weeks that had brought her former life to an end. Looking about her now, she saw that she was nearly home. Already it must be quite late, for the little lighted shops on the corner of Leinster Terrace were just beginning to close, and at the sight of these familiar landmarks, the black memories fell away, like an illness when recovery has set in.

She was here! She was safe in the present! These were the lights of Seacliffe, and this salty wind that whipped at her scarf and through her hair was the wind of now! The past was gone, she had escaped from it for ever: and that night, her dreams, for the first time, were all of Seacliffe. Strangely, they were not very happy dreams, a thread of stress and anxiety ran through them all. She dreamed that she had lent Kevin Mrs Graham's typewriter, and somehow could not return it in time, she was hurrying with it towards a bus stop, and the driver would not wait, though she shouted at him, and waved the typewriter as she ran, trying to explain to him about Mrs Graham's degree in Sociology, and how angry she would be. Next she dreamed that she had lost a parcel of clothes, and Mrs Mumford would not let her leave the house till she had found them. "But I never even groped them!" she seemed to be protesting, with the meaningless intensity of dreams—and woke to the sound of torrential rain beating against her window, and the grey, half-light of the winter morning warning her that it must already be nearly nine.

It was bad enough getting to Mrs Graham's in weather like this, but walking from there to Mrs Lane's was worse still. She had no mackintosh, or umbrella, the way was almost all uphill, and by the time she arrived her scarf clung like a bit of limp washing round her soaked hair. As she slopped through the puddles at the side of the house, and pushed open the side door, she prayed that there would be some heating on somewhere. She had had enough of all those bright open fires that would be glowing in every room once Phyllis had "got things organised".

A housewife who is still trying to get things organised after eighteen years is unlikely to spring many dramatic improvements on you between Monday and Wednesday; and so Milly was unsurprised to find the heating arrange-ments unchanged—small, bronchial oil-heaters muttering and scolding in odd corners of the high, draughty rooms. The kitchen was a nice surprise, though: all the burners of the gas cooker had been turned full on, including the oven, and the dry, airless heat wrapped itself round Milly's chilled body like a warmed blanket the moment she stepped into the room.

Lovely! As she stood right up against the open oven door, the heat puffing gloriously against her soaked skirt, Milly hastily forgave Mrs Lane—Phyllis, that is—for all that imaginary driftwood, and for the undelivered loads of coal.

But where *was* Phyllis—Milly was training herself to think of her employer by her Christian name, as requested, but it was difficult, particularly since Phyllis still persisted in addressing her, Milly, as "Mrs Barnes". It was the sort of inverted snobbery you had to expect, Milly supposed, from people rich enough to own a draughty great house like this, with cobwebs all over its ornate, inaccessible ceilings, and an acre of neglected garden. Such indifference to the opinions of the neighbours argued money on quite a big scale . . . and it was at this point in her musings that Milly heard the unmistakeable sound of a row going on. Voices, suddenly raised, came from somewhere across the hall—from Mr Lane's study, it must be . . . Squelching cautiously across the kitchen in her still-soaked shoes, Milly pushed open the door into the hall and listened, agog with curiosity.

Alas: the proverb about eavesdroppers is usually all too true: rarely indeed do they hear any good of themselves.

"I said the *filter*!" Mr Lane (it could only be him) was yelling. "What the hell's happened to the filter? Can't you tell that bloody woman to leave my things alone?"

Milly stiffened, and raked her conscience. What filter? What did it look like? Was it made of tin? Or paper? Or plastic? Could she have thrown it away as rubbish? Or added it to Michael's electric train set? Or put it away in the knife-drawer with all those apple-coring gadgets and the cake-icing outfit? None of these suggestions were quite the right kind of oil to pour on the troubled waters behind that study door, so she just kept very quiet, glad to be where she was. When a man is carrying on like this, it is good to be the one who is not married to him.

She could hear a soft pitter-patter of words from Phyllis now, evidently meant to be conciliatory, and then Mr Lane's voice bellowed forth again:

"Well, get rid of her, then! Why can't you ever get a decent, capable cleaner who understands her job? *Other* women don't have all this trouble with their servants!"

It might have been Julian himself speaking! *Other* women can do this . . . other women can do that . . . other women seem to manage . . . Milly, lurking out in the hall, shivered with sheer thankfulness that, on this occasion, she was merely the erring domestic, and not the hapless wife. Some one else, this time, had to smooth it all down, calm the raging husband, and get the matter put right without offending the char, or the cook, or whoever. Look, Mary/Doris/Maureen, I wonder if you could possibly . . . if you wouldn't awfully mind . . . you see my husband is rather particular about his . . . and so if you *could* possibly do it this way and not that way . . . Placating, groveling, abasing herself before them, and all the while aware of Julian in the background, despising her, maddened by her devious timidity ("Why don't you *tell* them what you want done? Are you mistress in your own house, or aren't you?").

"Are you mistress in your own house or aren't you . . . ?" Mr Lane was shouting, and Milly's heart twisted with pity for poor Phyllis, knowing exactly what she was going through. She longed to burst into the study crying: "It's all right, it's all right! I shan't be offended if he shouts at me, I shan't give notice! I daresay it *is* my fault about the filter, just tell me what the wretched thing *is*, and then I might remember what I did with it . . . and anyway, it'll probably turn out that he lost it himself, and then that'll be your fault, too !"

". . . how the hell you can expect me to remember what I put in which drawer!" Mr Lane was blustering defensively, and from the way the drawer slammed shut, Milly knew that the filter had turned up in it, exactly where he had put it himself. "It's impossible ever to find anything in this bloody house! The whole place is like a pigsty! What does that damned woman do with herself all those hours you pay her for?".

"Hush, Eric! She'll hear you!" Phyllis was trying to speak in an undertone, but her voice was squeaky with dismay. "I think I heard her come in . . . !"

"You 'think you heard her come in'! Well, that's just great, isn't it? Is *this* what she calls half past two? You let her come swanning along at ten minutes to three, and—"

"*Quarter* to, dear," Phyllis interposed nervily, and Milly could almost have shouted at her. It would only make him angrier; and it wasn't as if a matter of five minutes this way or that affected the principle of the thing.

". . . tell her you're not standing for it! Tell her that if it

happens again, she can bloody well look for another job!"—
and if Milly had only realised that this was the parting shot,
she would have been able to leap out of sight in time. But as
it was, she miscalculated the timing entirely. She had
assumed that still to come was the bit about being ashamed
to bring his friends home, and about his shirts never having
any buttons on . . . and so when he burst from the study
like a charging bull, he was only just able to skid to a halt in
time to avoid colliding with her.

He was not a big man. The red, engorged face and the
small bloodshot eyes were barely on a level with her own,
and the first thought that flashed through her mind was:
He's not like Julian after all! Not a bit like Julian!

"Ah! Er! G-good afternoon, Mrs Barnes," he stammered:
and giving one hunted glance into the study behind him he
turned and fled up the stairs as fast as—or perhaps even
faster than—his dignity as master of the house would allow.

Milly shrugged. The husbands were all like this—terrified to a man. At the beginning of her career in domestic
service, she had sometimes indulged vague, Jane Eyre-ish
daydreams, in which the unhappily married husband of one
of her employers found himself watching her as she
worked . . . felt himself soothed by her quiet efficiency . . .
and increasingly aware of the wordless sympathy in her
modestly downcast eyes. But she knew by now that you
could keep your eyes modestly downcast for ever, and
radiate enough wordless sympathy to power the whole of
the Marriage Guidance Council, and not one of these husbands would notice a thing. How could they, when at the

first tremor of Daily-Helping in any part of the house, they would be off like mountain deer, dodging from ledge to ledge until the danger was over? Milly amused herself for the first part of the afternoon by studying Mr Lane's itinerary as he slunk from room to room, alerted by Milly's dread footfalls approaching, or by the menacing hum of the vacuum cleaner, moving in for the kill.

Milly wondered how Phyllis was going to tackle this business of her lateness. "Tell her she can bloody well look for another job," had been Mr Lane's suggestion, from the safe distance at which he had been at pains to put himself, but Milly knew very well that whatever else Phyllis said, it wouldn't be *that*. The charge of unpunctuality was not unjustified, Milly well knew. It was impossible, sometimes, to get away from Mrs Graham's on time, what with lunch so often being delayed, either because Professor Graham was late, thus keeping them all waiting, or else because he wasn't, thus interrupting his wife's train of thought just as she was about to type her final sentence. Milly couldn't go until she had cleared up lunch, and naturally she couldn't clear up lunch until it had been eaten. And then there were Alison's vitamins, often trodden deep into the carpet, and needing ten minutes' hard scrubbing to remove them. They again couldn't be cleaned off the floor until Alison had finished throwing them there. So, one way and another, Milly rarely got to the Cedars before twenty or quarter to three, and so far there had been no fuss about it at all. Now, of course, there would have to be one.

"Er! Mrs Barnes!" Phyllis gave a bright little laugh and edged further round the kitchen door, clutching the door-knob with hands that Milly knew were sweating. The poor woman looked as if she were going to her own execution.

"*What* a wet day!" she gasped out, with a ghastly, fixed smile on her face, and not looking at Milly. "Oh, dear, yes! *What* a stinker! The rain, I mean. Doesn't it? Oh, Mrs Barnes, how *clever* of you! Doing all those! Oh, you *are* making them look nice!"

It was true, actually: and if only Phyllis hadn't always said this about everything, Milly would have glowed with pride. All this blackened Edwardian silver had been quite a find, really. In her afternoon jobs, Milly was always on the look-out for tasks which would get her off her feet for half an hour or so, and so when she came across this lot on a top shelf of the icy great room called the library, she had pounced on them and borne them off in triumph to the nice warm kitchen. And so now, half an hour later, here she was, sitting happily at the kitchen table, rubbing the beauty back into one blackened teapot or sauce-boat after another, while lovely warmth puffed against her back from the oven, and her aching legs rested surreptitiously on the bars of a chair under the table.

"Oh, it *will* be nice to have them done!" Phyllis jabbered nervously. "Oh, Eric *will* be pleased! He's always saying . . ."

I bet he is, thought Milly: and wondered at the same time if this was the lead-in? If so, how was it going to go? How was the unfortunate Phyllis going to work round from Mr Lane's alleged delight in the polished silver to Milly's short-comings in the matter of punctuality?

"Eric *does* so like to see things looking . . ." Phyllis went on, her words gathering speed as the crunch drew nearer. "Well, a man does, doesn't he, when he's fond of? I mean, so much of it has been in his family since. He was only saying today how nice the house looks since you've been coming, Mrs Barnes."

Having overheard the actual tenor of the conversation to which Phyllis was presumably referring, Milly found it hard to suppress a slight start, but Phyllis seemed to notice nothing, and continued: "And so we were wondering. It's only a suggestion, Mrs Barnes. I mean, it's not as if. We. I. Eric thinks. From *our* point of view, I mean, if you were here as long as possible? So we thought, I thought, if you *could*, by *any* chance, get here by quarter past two instead of half past . . . ?"

Then, when the wretched woman is a quarter of an hour late, it'll still only be half past, and Eric won't know a thing about it: Milly could have finished the unspoken part of the sentence for her. It was a shame—it really was—that all this conglomeration of lies was to achieve nothing.

"I'm terribly sorry," began Milly—and she meant it—"But it's my other job, you see. I can't leave there until after two, and so . . ."

"Yes, yes! Of course, of course! I quite understand! Don't worry about it for one moment . . . !"

Poor Phyllis! This panic-stricken servility—Milly saw it clearly now—was largely forced on her by the fact of being rich. Moralists have been saying for thousands of years that riches are a burden: and now, in the twentieth century, it has suddenly become true, in a perfectly straightforward and practical sense. In the old days, Milly mused, anyone who could afford to own all this real silver would also have been able to afford someone to stop it getting tarnished like this. Anyone rich enough to live in a large house like this, with its vast fireplaces and high, ornate ceilings, would also have been rich enough to employ a team of living-in servants. Sturdy young girls in aprons and print dresses would have lit the fires, polished the grates, and brushed the cobwebs off the ceilings. The coal-man would have come of his own accord, and there would have been someone working full time in the garden. Service on that sort of scale was what money used to buy: now it can only buy things. And so the rich *do* buy things—what else can they do?—and as their possessions pile up, and there are still no extra hands to polish them, or send them to the cleaners, or get them repaired, or even to put them away so, inevitably, does a special kind of plushy squalor begin to invade the homes of the great—a squalor that grows, like mould, on cheques and dividends, and multiplies, at an accelerating rate, with every increment of income. No wonder wealthy husbands become so irascible—the more money they bring home, the more messy and disorganised their homes become and the more distracted their wives ("I can't understand her, she's got *everything*!"—never realising that just as *something* inevitably takes up *some* of your time, so *everything* is liable to take up all of it). No wonder that the less efficient of the wives (like Phyllis) were tending more and more to turn their backs on the whole thing, and to pretend to be poor. This way, they hoped, gracious living would no longer be demanded of them, nor an elegant appearance; and while this did not eliminate the problem entirely, it certainly lightened it. A problem tackled in a torn jersey is a problem halved.

Milly finished the last of the ornate Victorian cakestands, pushing her cloth in and out of the now-shining scrolls and curlicues, and realised, with a shock, that it was already nearly five. No time for the bathrooms now: even the hall and stairs would have to be skimped. Oh, well; that's what came of possessing two bathrooms *and* a lot of valuable silver: you couldn't expect to have all of them clean at once. She'd give the bathrooms a real good do, Milly promised herself, next time she came.

Next time? When she got home that night, she found Jacko sitting on the stairs, waiting for her.

"Thank God!" he greeted her dramatically. "We thought you were never coming!"

A man, it seemed, had called to see her that afternoon. No, he hadn't said what it was about—just that he wanted to make some enquiries. Sort of po-faced he'd been, like he might be from the Town Hall: Jacko hadn't liked the look of him at all.

CHAPTER XIX

The police! In that instant of certainty, it was not fear that engulfed Milly's consciousness, but fury—speechless, impotent, fury.

After all this time! Just when I've really put it all behind me! Just when I've discovered that I don't even feel guilty! Just when it's all properly over, and my new life has really got going! It's not fair! It's not fair!

". . . but it's all right," Jacko was saying—and his voice, which had seemed infinitely far away, suddenly snapped near again, and hope twanged back. "It's all right, Barney! I told him you didn't live here! I told him we'd never heard of you!" He looked so pleased with himself: Milly felt the shock subsiding. Surely, if it had been the police, they wouldn't just have accepted the word of a long-haired student, and gone meekly away? Come to that, how had Jacko guessed . . . ?

"Jacko, that was sweet of you, but how could you know that I didn't want to see him?" she asked, warily. She tried to remember which of her life-stories it was that she had told to Jacko and Kevin: not one that included being on the run from the police, that was certain.

"Well—'enquiries', of course," explained Jacko knowledgeably. "It's just another word for 'trouble', everyone knows that. I mean, they aren't going to be enquiring whether you want five thousand pounds, gift-wrapped, for your birthday, are they? Besides, it wasn't just you, Barney: it was the Mums I was worrying about. She can't bear tenants who attract officials to the house, it's like if they brought in lice, or leprosy. And you can't blame her, really . . ." here he lowered his voice, and his eyes took on a nostalgic, faraway look, as of battles long ago: "Like the time Miss Childe got a man in to look at why her food cupboard wouldn't shut properly, and it all ended in a van-load of inspectors swarming in to measure whether there was sixteen cubic feet of space in the downstairs loo . . . the Mums never got over it. So you see, Barney, we must keep him away from the house at all costs—or else pretend that he's your long-lost brother, and even that not after 11 pm. But not to worry—" here Jacko got to his feet, and squared his rumpled shoulders proudly—"I'll look after you, Barney. If that creep comes back, I'll see that he gets what's coming to him!—I say—" the knight-errantry faltered a bit as they set off up the stairs towards Milly's room, "You don't mind do you? I thought I'd better stay in your room for the evening in case anything happens, so I've moved some of my things in."

He had, too. The hi-fi set—the tape-recorder—a pair of shiny boots—half a dozen books on economics lying open on the chairs and on the bed. Milly looked around doubtfully, wondering if she wanted protection on quite this scale.

"No, I suppose I don't mind," she said. "It'll save gas, anyway." This was magnanimous, because it was most decidedly not *her* gas that was being saved: a fug like this could not possibly have been built up by less than three of her precious shillings from the saucer on the mantelpiece. "Is Kevin coming in too?" she added, mentally dividing her bread, milk, and tin of Scotch broth into three, and adding a third of a banana each.

"No, well. That's the thing, actually." Seeing him now clearly, under the glare of the bare electric light bulb, Milly noticed for the first time that he looked pale and tense: the jaunty manner sat uneasily on him, as though Jacko was finding the part of Jacko suddenly rather a strain.

"What's happened?" she asked, and suddenly it all came out. Nothing to do with the Town Hall man at all—he had evidently been a mere incident in Jacko's harrowing afternoon, no more than a convenient excuse for button-holing Milly the moment she came in. No, his real preoccupation was quite other than this, and centred (so Milly at last gathered from his circumlocutory narrative) on the presence—yes, she was still there—of a certain Janette in Kevin's and Jacko's joint bedroom. She had, it seemed, been closeted there with Kevin for "hours and hours", while Jacko had had to camp out like a refugee in Milly's room, with nothing to do but write his essay on Statistical Method (which anyway didn't have to be in till next week, and so it was a cock-eyed waste of time working on it now), and to brood on what was going on behind the forbidden door. It was lucky, he conceded in a choked voice, that there happened to be all those spare shillings in the saucer or he would have frozen to death, on top of everything else.

Milly had heard of this Janette before. She was the shadowy, amorphous girl-friend who always seemed to have come yesterday, or to be coming tomorrow, but was never here today. When Jacko or Kevin mentioned her, which was not often, they spoke of her with a sort of off-hand resignation as if she was a neighbour's cat for which they felt a vague responsibility: and now here was Kevin triumphantly locked in the bedroom with her, and Jacko, white and near to tears, locked outside it.

"There hasn't been a sound since teatime," he gulped. "They must be . . . They're . . ."

Kid's stuff, Milly remembered, and now here was the jaded veteran of a thousand sexual encounters not even daring to pronounce the correct words.

She consoled him as best she could. Yes, she had to agree, they probably *were*, but so what? This Janette, she wasn't specially *Jacko's* girl-friend, was she? No, no, of *course* she wasn't! Nor Kevin's either! That was the whole *point*, didn't Milly see? It wasn't *serious*, they'd *agreed* it wasn't serious, and now . . . and now . . . !

It wasn't that it was boring, far from it. but Milly was getting hungrier and hungrier, and flattered though she was by being chosen as Jacko's confidante, she found herself watching, with increasing fervour, for some gap in the jeremiad into which it wouldn't be too heartless to insert a suggestion about opening the tin of soup. In the end she got her way by roundabout means: by first getting Jacko to put some sad music on the record-player, then something a bit less sad, and by the time a loud pop song was drumming through the room, and Mrs Mumford had yelled up to them to turn that noise down, the mention of food no longer seemed blasphemous. It was just then, as it happened, that Kevin and Janette reappeared, very cheerful and friendly, with a bottle of cider and a packet of frozen kippers. With these substantial supplements to Milly's tin of soup, there was plenty for everyone, and even Jacko began to cheer up. Soon, Mrs Mumford was yelling up the stairs a second time. She expected *some* consideration, she shrieked, and did they know what the time was? The third time, she didn't yell, but stamped up with a tray of tea and freshly-baked mince-pies, and demanded that a waltz be put on the record-player. If they were determined to shake the house to pieces with their great elephant feet, she scolded, they might at least do it dancing something that *was* a dance. What, they didn't know *how* to waltz?—she'd show them, if it was the last thing she did! And though it *wasn't* the last thing she did, not by a very long way, she *did* show them; and they showed her how to gyrate to *their* rhythms, and by the end of the evening Milly was finding it incredible that anyone could ever want to make Enquiries about anything. Life is so simple, if only you don't make Enquiries about it, and if the Town Hall man had turned up then and there, Milly would have told him.

He didn't, though, nor was there a summons for her in the post next morning, nor a policeman waiting outside Mrs Graham's flat to arrest her as she went in. And though Mrs Graham's phone went several times during the morning, it was never for Milly. Through the wall, she could hear Mrs Graham's voice, bored and irritable, exactly as if it was her husband each time, but of course it couldn't have been.

Only when she arrived at Mrs Day's that afternoon did something happen which forced Milly to think again about her unknown visitor of last night. As usual, there was a note waiting for her, in Mrs Day's wild writing, but this time it wasn't about the *strrt grr*, nor about rinsing the *hwrf grool* in three lots of cold water: it was a telephone message. A Mr *Loops*, it seemed, had *phouled* asking for Mrs *Baines*, he wanted to get in touch with her *ooplardy*, and would *phoul* again this *umpternoon*.

He wouldn't, though. Milly made sure of *that* by taking the receiver off. Then she set about her work with unusual speed and concentration. No reading today; no lounging about on sofas, or speculating on why there should be a scarlet dog-harness on top of the deep-freeze, and no dog. Mrs Day's new flower-patterned tights, slit neatly open all down one leg, left her incurious. She just wanted to get finished, to get out of the place. Even though the telephone was effectively silenced, she still felt uncomfortable every time she caught sight of it. She pictured Mr *Loops* (or was it *Soap*, or *Reeves*?) fiddling about right now, at the other end of the wire, dialling and re-dialling, calling the operator . . . It seemed to bring him horribly near.

She finished her work much earlier than usual, while it was still just light, and as she hurried home through the damp, gusty twilight, her nerves were all on edge, as if she knew, already, the news that she was going to hear.

Yes, the man had been here again; and this time he had not been so easily put off. He had attempted to start an argument about Milly's non-existence, and Jacko had only managed to get rid of him by pretending that he, Jacko, was in a fearful hurry, already late for a lecture. At this, the man had given up—but not before looking at Jacko in a very funny way, and saying he would be calling back later on.

"Well—thanks, Jacko," said Milly dazedly. She was still in her outdoor things, she had not yet closed the front door, and now there was no need. Turning around, she walked out into the night.

At first, she could not decide where she was walking, or why; but gradually, as her dazed wits cleared, she realised that she was after all doing quite a sensible thing. She only had to stay out until Mrs Mumford's locking-up time, and her persecutor would be foiled, at least for tonight. After the magic hour of eleven, Mrs Mumford would admit nobody, on any pretext, and Milly would be able to sleep in peace. Briefly, she thanked heaven for the pockets of narrow-mindedness that still linger on, especially in small towns like this. With a permissive London landlady, she would have been doomed.

Doomed? What a drama she was making of it all! Why was she allowing a second visit from this same man so to throw her?—it was no more, and no less, sinister than the first one. He was no more likely to be a policeman or a detective today than he was yesterday—less, if anything, because surely police working on a murder case move faster than this? Having alerted their victim by a first visit, surely they wouldn't just leave her to her own devices for another twenty-four hours? Not that it wasn't prudent to make herself scarce for the evening, all the same. "Like he might be from the Town Hall," Jacko had said: and if she was going to have to make up a whole new batch of lies about her insurance stamps, or her tax-assessment, or something, then she didn't want it to happen at home, with Mrs Mumford hovering attentively in the background, checking the new lies against the old.

Milly felt that she had walked a very long way, but it couldn't actually have been more than a mile or two, because she was only now coming into the straight, wide road that led to the station. It couldn't be very late, either—not more than half past six or seven—because the brightly lit little booking-hall was alive with commuters just off the London train. They were pouring out from the lighted entrance, pulling up their collars, re-tying their scarves as the wind caught them: and Milly was suddenly and disconcertingly reminded of her own arrival here, nearly four weeks ago. For a moment, as she watched the hurrying, anonymous people fanning out into the dark, she had the strangest feeling of going backwards in time. Just as she had arrived here on a night of damp, gusty cold, the station lights flickering weakly in the wind, so, now, she seemed to be returning, on just such a night, by the way she had come . . . back into the train . . . back to Victoria Station, joining once again the creeping queues, head down, scarf once again pulled across her mouth to avoid recognition . . .

back, back, into the Underground, circling round and round, backwards, backwards, spiralling back and back until she was thrust out into the icy streets of the January dawn, her heels once again clattering in the emptiness as she ran. Ran, and ran, but the other way, this time, towards and not away from that basement in Lady Street, where Gilbert was still waiting, watch in hand, checking on how long she had been away.

Milly rubbed her eyes. She shook herself, and stamped her cold feet. It was all right: that old crone silhouetted against the lighted tobacconists was not Mrs Roach, she couldn't be, this was Seacliffe, not Lady Street. As she blinked, and stared around, trying to get her bearings once again, she had a swift impression of a crest of white hair, glimpsed above the heads of the hurrying crowd; but in a moment it was gone, and the nightmare was gone too. She was here! She was now! The awful power of the past was receding, slipping back into the dark as suddenly as it had come, and she could scarcely even feel, now, the places where its icy fingers had momentarily touched her soul.

Idly, to fill in some of the time till eleven o'clock, she wandered into the station cafeteria, buying a newspaper as she went. As before, she found herself a table by the radiator; but this time, she had a cup of coffee and a roll and butter of her own, properly paid for. Her own newspaper to read, too. No need, this time, to peer and twist this way and that to catch a glimpse of other people's. Her feelings, too, were changed, and although she scanned carefully every column, every paragraph, for something about the

Lady Street Murder, there was a curious lack of urgency about it. It was as if she knew, already, that this was not the direction from which the blow would come.

CHAPTER XX

"Ah, *there* you are, Mrs Er! I wonder if *you* can help me? People keep ringing up and asking for a Mrs Barnes! All yesterday, and now they've started again today. I can't get on with *anything*! *You* don't know anything about a Mrs Barnes, do you, Mrs Er? It's not someone *you* know?"

Mrs Graham was sitting with her hand resting irritably on the telephone, looking harassed and aggrieved. She always reacted to having her time unexpectedly taken up as another woman might to having her handbag stolen, and she was looking at Milly, who had just arrived, with a mixture of appeal and accusation.

"No," said Milly. It was not so much a lie as an automatic reaction, like blinking the eyes in response to sudden movement. The turmoil of shock and alarm which had flooded over her at Mrs Graham's words had rendered her quite incapable, for the moment, of deciding whether to lie or not to lie. The weighing-up of the question whether it was more dangerous to deny her identity than to admit it, was simply beyond her. So, "No," she said, and watched the room spin round her, with Mrs Graham's face revolving in the foreground, like a white ping-pong ball on the end of a string. Gradually, the whirling furniture slowed down, came to a standstill. Mrs Graham's face came to rest too, came into focus, and Milly began to hear the words formed by her moving lips.

"It couldn't be more inconvenient!" she was grumbling. "I'm just starting to summarise the Class C2 responses, and I seem to be twenty interviews short! Twenty! It will invalidate the whole survey! And all that fool of a Miss Bracken can say is that she thinks they were all sent in! *Thinks!*—I ask you! And then she has the cheek to suggest that I should simply extrapolate from the interviews I *have* got! *Extrapolate! Me!* I may not be the most punctilious researcher in the world, Mrs Er, but that's one thing I'll never do. I'll never extrapolate!"

One felt there should have been a roar of applause at this heroic declaration: but all Milly could find to say was "No". "No, I should think not, indeed!" she amended hastily, as Mrs Graham's raised eyebrows warned her that her response had been altogether too tepid. To find herself accused of condoning the evils of extrapolation as well as of murdering her husband was *too* much, and for a moment she just stood there, while her problems swayed like shadowy swing-boats in front of her, huge and ungraspable, and steadily gathering momentum.

They were closing in on her. They were moving in for the kill. No use, any longer, pretending that someone wanted to offer her a job, sell her an encyclopaedia, or ask her opinion about a new washing-up liquid. Indeed, it wasn't just "someone" any longer, it was a whole host of them, assembling to hunt her down. "People keep ringing up," Mrs Graham had said: even allowing for exaggeration, the words could hardly refer to fewer than three. They knew where she worked now, as well as where she lived. And that

Mr Loops yesterday . . . he was in the plot with the rest of them, of course he was, which meant they had tracked her down to Mrs Day's as well . . .

"In the plot"—"tracked her down"—"They"—"Them"— Where had she heard these words before? In the urgency of her panic, Milly did not pursue the thought. The important thing, now, was to plan her getaway—either a simple physical one in the form of packing up and getting on a train, or a more subtle one based on lies, and more lies, told with expertise and panache.

Who better qualified than her for such a task? Toughened as she was by a prolonged survival-course in deception, she would be able to out-lie the lot of them; against her impassioned falsehoods they would break themselves as against a rock, and she would be free . . .

But how much did they already know? The first principle of successful lying is to assemble in front of you all the data already irrevocably in the hands of your opponent, and see how it can be rearranged to your advantage. You can't subtract anything, of course, but you can add bits, and if you are clever you can twist a bit here, alter a sequence there, until the whole tenor of the thing seems to be changed, and they are left staring in blank dismay at the case they thought they had against you, and wondering what has hit them.

But first, you have to find out exactly what their case is: what data they have so far succeeded in assembling against you . . .

"*Data* isn't the problem!" Mrs Graham was proclaiming (how had she got on to this from the extrapolations?). "Any fool can collect the *data*. It's the interpretation that counts, especially with the D-E's. As I keep trying to make Miss Bracken understand, the 'Don't know's' aren't just . . ."

"No, indeed!" said Milly heartily—and Mrs Graham stared at her, startled, but vaguely pleased by support from this unexpected quarter. "I do so agree with you, it's what I've always thought myself," continued Milly recklessly. "But this woman who rang up, this Mrs Barnes, did she say what she wanted?"

Milly had deliberately muddled the issue, got it all wrong, so that Mrs Graham should overlook her odd persistence in the pleasure of putting her right. There are moments when an ounce of confusion is worth pounds of apology and explanation.

"Who?" Mrs Graham looked vague for a moment. "Oh, you mean all those wrong numbers! No, Mrs Er, it wasn't the Barnes woman who was *ringing*, it was . . ." here she paused, studying Milly's IQ as one might study the physique of the man who has come to move the grand piano.

"Oh, well," she concluded, with a sigh that conveyed more clearly than words the boredom she felt at the prospect of trying to make such as Milly understand. "Never mind. It's not important. Though I do wish people would listen to reason, I really do. That man this morning, he just wouldn't take 'no' for an answer, he kept saying he *knew* she was here. Apparently the woman has run away, or something, and he all but accused me of harbouring her! *Me!* As if I've got nothing better to do!"—here she rattled a fresh page into the typewriter, signifying unassailable busy-ness.

"And now, Mrs Er, if you *wouldn't* mind . . . ? I'm an hour behind already, it's been just one thing after another the whole morning . . ."

Milly gave up, and retired, chastened, to get on with her work. Through the ceaseless clackety-clack of the typewriter behind the closed door, she kept listening for the telephone, but it only rang once. From the bored, slightly aggrieved tones of Mrs Graham's voice, it might have been absolutely anything: Professor Graham saying that he was going to be late (or early) for lunch, someone wanting to borrow a book, or perhaps a friend or relative in sudden, desperate trouble, and expecting Mrs Graham to interrupt her typing to listen to it. Mrs Graham's vast and unselective capacity for boredom could have embraced the lot. Milly listened through the door until her ears sang and her very jawbones were tense, but she could pick up no clues. And after a while, soothed by the droning of the Hoover and by all her familiar tasks, Milly gradually gave up thinking about the problem. Anyway, there was nothing she could usefully do. As with any cat-and-mouse game, the mouse stands to gain most by remaining in his usual hole, alert and inconspicuous, relying on his smallness, and on his intimate knowledge of the terrain. It is the cat who must stick his neck out, make the rules, and generally get things going.

CHAPTER XXI

Milly stood for a number of minutes after she had arrived at Mrs Day's, staring down at the telephone and wondering if she would feel safer if she took the receiver off or if she didn't. The pale winter sun, higher and higher every day now, was flooding in through the wide window, showing up every finger-mark, every dingy streak, on the elegant white instrument. Milly noticed, wonderingly, that her fingers were fidgeting to get at it with a damp cloth, just as if nothing had happened. They seemed as if they were separate animals altogether, quite unconnected with herself, and with her seething brain, lashing itself into a fever of indecision as to whether to leave the thing alone to do its worst, or to silence it, as could so easily be done. It was like deciding whether to give tranquillisers to a savage guard-dog. To do so, you have to go uncomfortably close, and yet not to do so may result in being torn to pieces later on. There is no way of guessing in advance which will work best: no evidence one way or the other. No one knows, least of all the guard-dog.

Milly picked up the receiver and laid it gently on the polished table, and at once it began muttering at her in feeble protest. Straightaway, like an over-anxious mother with her crying baby, she snatched it up and restored it to its proper place; then wished she had left it off after all. The whimpering would have stopped in the end. Off with it, then—the spoilt thing!—let it whine itself to sleep, with her safely out of hearing! She would shut the door on it, she would run to the other end of the flat and switch the Hoover on till it was all over! Then, at last, her nerves would begin to relax, and she would be able to get on with her work safe in the knowledge that the telephone not only *wouldn't* ring, it couldn't!

Safe? What sort of head-in-the-sand logic was this? By disconnecting the telephone she was cutting herself off from the *awareness* of danger, not from danger itself. The danger was still there. Biting its nails, perhaps, in some nearby telephone box—maybe only a stone's throw away— and getting more and more impatient with the monotonous line-engaged tone. Tactics would be changed . . . and the first she would know of anything amiss would be the sound of the lift moaning to a halt out there across the landing.

By then, it would be too late. Whereas if she left the tele- phone in working order, she would at least get some sort of advance warning—enough, surely, to enable her to go racing down those six flights of softly carpeted stairs (no lifts, thank you!—she felt trapped enough already!) and out into the wild, wide, windswept world, where surely she would have the same fifty-fifty chance of freedom as a deer, or a fox, or any other hunted thing?

Already she could feel flight mustering in her limbs, speeding up her heartbeat. Her hand, as she re-connected the telephone yet again, was trembling with a build-up of muscular energy as yet un-needed. From her brain the alert had gone forth, and throughout her body general mobilisation had begun: Milly found it hard, with this turmoil of activity going on within, to slow herself down to the pace of dusting . . . of handling ornaments . . . of washing up wine-glasses, putting them away on the high shelf of the cupboard. A slender glass stem snapped, brittle as ice, and tinkled sadly to the floor . . . Milly felt herself moving among Mrs Day's fragile possessions like a battering ram. Already the sensitivity had gone from her fingertips, the delicacy from her movements: all her finer sensibilities were already in cold-storage, packed away to leave room for the essentials—strength, speed and cunning.

When the telephone finally did ring, it was almost a relief. Milly knew, now, exactly what she was going to say to them: she was inspired, the lies almost told themselves. No, she would tell them, she wasn't Mrs Barnes, Mrs Barnes was no longer working here. Oh, yes, there *had* been a Mrs Barnes, certainly there had, she had worked here until—when was it? Two?—three?—weeks ago. Would that be the Mrs Barnes they were looking for? And no, she was very sorry, she couldn't tell them where Mrs Barnes was working now she had moved—gone after a job in Birmingham, someone had said. There'd been some sort of trouble about her references, or something, and she's had to leave in a hurry . . .

That would fox them! A big place, Birmingham. They could hunt down Barnes-es there for weeks on end, and as fast as they eliminated one lot, another batch would appear . . . Barnes after Barnes, rolling in without pause over the smoky Midland horizon.

And meantime, the Seacliffe police would have stopped bothering. Once the search had moved out of their district, they would surely lose interest . . . they must have plenty else on their minds, with hooligans smashing up deckchairs, and everything. And as for the big men in London—Scotland Yard, or whoever it was—surely their enthusiasm, too, would flag once the trail had grown as cold as this? London . . . Seacliffe . . . Birmingham . . . and already the dockleaves and the nettles beginning to sprout on Gilbert's grave, somewhere or other in the crowded, neglected cemetery you could just see from the top of the bus as you travelled towards Morden.

They didn't solve all their murder cases: how could they? No doubt they did their best, but you can no more trace every murder to its bitter source than you can trace the course of a stream beyond the place where it merges into marshland, spreading out into a formless no-man's-land of bog, and reeds, and treacherous patches where, if you are not careful, you can sink nearly to the waist.

Surely Gilbert's murder stood as good a chance of going unsolved as any? There was nothing newsworthy about it, nothing obviously bizarre to challenge the ingenuity of police or detectives, or to stir the popular imagination. The victim was not a beautiful young girl, the suspect was not a member of high society. If Milly could only put them all off the scent for even a few days, she would be safe. Their other files would begin to pile up . . . their in-trays to overflow . . . After all, the police are only human, and in any human transaction, if you can once get muddle and procrastination working on your side, you're home.

"Barnes? Mrs Barnes? No, I'm afraid not . . ." Now that it came to the point, Milly found herself gabbling nervously. The lies, spoken out loud, sounded less convincing than they had in the imagination, and she was hurrying to get to the end of her rehearsed speech before her nerve cracked. "No, I'm afraid there's no one of that name here at the moment. But there was a Mrs Barnes working here not long ago. I wonder if that's the one you mean? She left—let me see—two or three weeks ago, I think it must be. Someone told me she was moving—to Birmingham, I think they said . . ."

"*Barney!* Have you gone nuts, or something? What the hell do you think you're playing at?"

"*Jacko!*" The relief was so great that for a moment it was indistinguishable from the terror that had preceded it, and Milly just stared at the pink wallpaper in front of her, and waited for her blood to start flowing again, and for her brain to start comprehending the miraculous new turn of affairs. "Jacko! Why didn't you—? Your voice sounded all—! Oh, Jacko, I'm so *thankful*! I thought you were—!"

"Yes. You sounded like that's what you thought," Jacko commented drily, his voice sounding very small and far away. "Look, Barney, what the hell's going on? Have you got the sack, or something? We rang you about sixty thousand times this morning, and the hag kept saying you didn't exist . . ."

"Jacko! At Mrs Graham's, you mean? So it was *you*, then, all the time! Oh, but how marvellous . . . !" The relief, the sudden lifting of fear, was almost more than Milly could sustain. The pale sunlight seemed to dance in the room, the very air shimmered with freedom, such freedom as she had never thought to breathe again.

Was it three breaths of it she drew, or four? Then Jacko's voice again:

". . . and so we tried to put him off, just like we did the Town Hall wallah yesterday, but it was hopeless. He just wouldn't believe us when we said we'd never heard of you; and you see, Barney, by that time the Mums was poking her nose out of the kitchen, wanting to know what it was all about, so we just couldn't keep it up any longer. Well, I mean. But I wouldn't worry too much, Barney, really I wouldn't. He seems terribly harmless, this one, like he couldn't hurt a fly if you paid him. He must be about a hundred for a start, you should just have seen his mop of snow-white hair. Said his name was Soames."

CHAPTER XXII

An hour had passed, and Milly still had not stirred. The room was in shadow now, the brief winter sunlight had faded from the rosy walls and gleaming mirrors. It was already quite hard to read the figures on the dial of the telephone, at which Milly was still staring, vacantly.

She did not know how long she had gone on talking to Jacko, nor how long she had been sitting here since the line had gone dead.

There was no reason to move. It seemed to her, now, that she had known all along that this was how it was going to end. All the time she had been on the run, dodging the police, watching the headlines, concealing her identity . . . all this time she had known, somewhere deep inside her, that it was not merely the Law from which she was fleeing, but something much more terrible. Her fear of being arrested for murdering Gilbert had been genuine enough, but it had all the time masked a quite different fear, one too terrible to confront: the fear that she had *not* murdered him. The fear that somehow, somewhere, he had survived, biding his time, perfecting his plans for her punishment. He had waited while the moon waxed and waned once, and now he was on the move.

No, Jacko had assured her: he hadn't told the old boy her address at work; he wasn't *quite* a fool, thank you. Though it was always a bit of a help (he pointed out aggrievedly) if people would tell you what the hell they were up to before they let you in for this sort of thing. And no, he didn't know where the poor old carcase had gone now, he hadn't said. And yes, of course he, Jacko, would phone her if anything cropped up. She could count on him and on Kevin too, even though nobody ever told them anything.

So Gilbert was already on the prowl through the darkening streets: peering into the cafés, the bus shelters, his white hair raked into a cockatoo-crest by the wet wind from the sea.

How long would it be before he found her? That he would do so in the end, she never doubted. Already the feel of him was all about her, she seemed to feel the strange power of his madness guiding him as he roamed the ill-lit streets, staring left and right, through lighted windows and through solid walls, with his shining, visionary eyes.

Ridiculous! was she taking leave of her senses? Madness was a disability, not a rare and valuable gift! It rendered a person *less* able to achieve his purposes, not more! Where a sane person would seek his objective in a strange town by asking the right questions, following up the relevant clues, a madman would be driven hither and thither by a bizarre logic of his own, getting nowhere, banging up against the relevant facts only at random, like a fly in a window. Milly felt her strength returning. The sheer, gibbering terror had passed, and she began to take stock of her situation.

Here, at Mrs Day's, she was comparatively safe, at least for the moment. No one, mad or sane, would be able to trace her to this address in the space of a single afternoon, via such a trail of mis-information as they were certainly going to encounter as they went. Like a mediaeval baron surveying his moats and drawbridges, Milly reviewed the obstacles that such a person would have to surmount. First, Mrs Mumford, tight-lipped, minding her own business if it killed her. Then, Jacko and Kevin, lying tirelessly on her behalf to all corners. And, lastly (if they ever got so far) there was Mrs Graham who, in her sublime unconcern with things which only involved other people, didn't even know that Milly had a name, let alone an address, or a continued existence beyond her, Mrs Graham's, front door.

She would stay here, then, here in Mrs Day's flat, for as long as it was possible to stay. Why, perhaps Mrs Day would take her on as a proper housekeeper, living-in! It was just what the flat needed, actually, someone permanently around to clear up after the all-night parties, to iron the crumpled finery, put the orchids in water . . . and it was just then that she heard the sound. The soft whine of the lift gliding to a halt . . . the doors sliding open, smooth as cream.

Well, and what of it? There were other flats on this floor, weren't there? It could be anybody . . . absolutely anybody.

It was funny, certainly, that there was no sound of footsteps after the opening of the lift doors, but not so funny that it need set the veins pulsing in your temples like this. Were not the carpets in this building thick and soft, the acoustics carefully planned to deaden footfalls? Absurd, then, to imagine that someone must be lying in wait out there, or advancing soundlessly in ancient white gymshoes . . .

She seemed to know, though, what the next sound was going to be, and when she heard it, the shock was the shock of recognition rather than of fresh terror.

It had all happened before, that was the thing: happened exactly as it was happening now, only at a different door, opening on a different flat . . . the slow fumbling at the latch . . . the faint scratching of a key inserted by unsteady fingers, and then the door swung silently open . . .

"Oh!" said the girl, and for a few seconds she and Milly stared at one another in mutual stupefaction, each separately trying to reconcile a turmoil of imaginary expectations to a completely unforeseen reality.

The newcomer was a heavy, thick-set young woman, with a big, freckled face devoid of make-up, and she was wearing a grey jersey and navy blue skirt which (Milly found herself inanely reflecting) the exotic Mrs Day wouldn't have been seen dead in.

Where on earth did so unglamorous a figure fit into Mrs Day's glittering life? Friend? Relative? Or—yes, that was the most likely—she must be a betrayed wife come to have it out with her husband's mistress! That's how she'd come to be in possession of the door key, of course: she had found it in the pocket of his suit when she was sending it to the cleaner's, and then (driven by curiosity and by the chronic insecurity of the plain and dowdy wife of an attractive man) she had searched the rest of his pockets . . . had come across the love-letters, the pressed orchid . . . No wonder, after all that, that the poor girl had been a bit non-plussed at the sight of Milly! Probably she had never seen the legendary Mrs Day, and was right now trying to fit Milly to the part, twisting her hands agonisedly as she did so, with her doughy jaw dropped open.

"I'm afraid . . . !" began Milly, and "I thought . . . !" interrupted the girl; and then they both gave up simultaneously and stared at one another again.

"I've come for my coaching," the girl volunteered at last—and at the sound of the hesitant small voice, Milly suddenly noticed how very young the visitor was, and how paralysed with shyness—noticed, too, the bulging briefcase she was clutching.

"Mrs Day—that's our headmistress—she said just to let myself in, as she'd be late. I—I'm sorry . . . she didn't tell me there'd be anybody here . . . It's my A-level physics, you see, I was away all last term . . ."

A headmistress! How one lives and learns! For the second time in five minutes, Milly found all her presuppositions being turned upside down, and her mind was still spinning from this second effort of readjustment, when the buzzer sounded on the front door.

For some reason, she wasn't frightened at all this time. Somehow, she assumed that it must be Mrs Day herself, and was all agog with curiosity at the prospect of actually *seeing* this many-sided character. "Yes?" she said confidently into the mouthpiece, and heard the caretaker's voice in reply:

"Mrs Barnes? Good, you *are* still there, I thought you might have gone. Your husband's here, Mrs Barnes, he's come to call for you. I'm sending him up now."

CHAPTER XXIII

Running, running, running, all over again, through dingy, ill-lit streets, only this time there was so little sense of escape. She remembered how her lungs had laboured, just as they were labouring now, seared by the freezing night air. Only then there had been a taste of dawn in the January darkness: now, the black night was only just beginning. There had been hope then—though she had scarcely been aware of it—hope of escape, of a new life somewhere on the far side of despair, of new worlds yet untried beyond the horizon of her experience. She had thought then, as she raced through the dark, deserted streets that zig-zagged away and away from the basement in Lady Street—further and further, ever safer, ever more anonymous—she had thought, then, that she was actually escaping: that if she could only run fast enough, and far enough, then she could be out of it all, her very identity left behind like an empty packing case with all the rest of the debris.

Not now, though. From the moment when she had flung herself out of Mrs Day's flat, and out of the life for ever of Mrs Day's astonished pupil, she had known, in her heart, that there was nowhere to run; that this was the end of the road.

Oh, she had run, just the same: had run like a mad-woman, down all those flights of richly carpeted stairs, round and round . . . down and down . . . There was a curious moment when Gilbert must have been barely two yards away, as the lift slipped up and past her, gliding upwards in the opposite direction to her headlong flight.

She had not even glanced towards it. On to the bottom she had sped, without pause or backward look. Nor had the startled voice of the caretaker delayed her. The heavy glass door swung back against his exclamation of surprise and protest, slicing it off, and she was out and away, hurling herself from the lights and warmth of the flats as from a high rock, plunging headlong into the dark beyond.

Yes, she had run, all right. She was still running, her breath coming in short, painful gasps and her heart lurching. Already she had reached the outskirts of the town. The houses were smaller, and shabbier, the street lights dimmer and further and further apart, until presently there were no more lights and the darkness was unbroken, except for an occasional orange gleam from a window as a curtain was twitched aside and a face peered out, idly censorious, to see who it could be, running so fast and so noisily through a respectable suburb at such an hour.

Still she ran on, and after a while she felt the road change to something rougher under her feet. She found herself stumbling against cobbles—or was it dry tufts of winter grass?—And now she could just see that the path ahead of her was forking in two directions, one winding up towards the downs, the other curving down to the right . . . it must be towards the beach. Already there was a salty tang in the air, and that sense of emptiness and uncluttered distance that is unmistakeable: the sea could not be far away.

It did not matter which of the two paths she chose, for she knew by now that she was running nowhere. The options were at an end. Whichever way she chose now, to left or right, it would still be the way back. Back . . . back . . . by the same way she had come . . . It had come to pass just as she had foreseen it—was it only yesterday?—as she stood at Seacliffe station watching the London trains come in. The past had got her. It had caught up with her at last. She could feel the weight of it, dragging her backwards and downwards, even while her legs still went through the motions of running. It was like riding to your death on a stationary bicycling machine.

Strange how her legs would not give up, even now! Still they ran: ran, and ran until her heart seemed to be beating some strange tattoo behind her ribs . . . tapping out messages . . . telling her something . . . She could hear voices, just as Gilbert had once heard voices:

"Milly!" they mocked: "Milly Barnes! *What* a name to choose!" and as she ran faster, trying to outdistance them, she seemed to hear their laughter, rollicking in the dark air that raced away behind her.

They had given themselves away, though! She knew now what they were after. They were after her new self, her new identity.

How could they be so unfair? She had worked so hard on this new self, with such skill and with such determination. Out of the jumbled-up remains of a broken, terror-stricken criminal, she had succeeded in piecing together a perfectly respectable Milly Barnes, a re-conditioned, good-as-new model, capable of earning its own living, even of making friends for itself.

"Milly Barnes! Milly Barnes! *You're* not Milly Barnes, there's no such person!"

She had not outdistanced them after all! They were back . . . they were all around her! They were seizing on her . . . laying hands on her new self . . . confiscating it, as if she had been smuggling it through the customs! "It's mine!" she kept crying, "I've got a right . . . !" but all she could hear was their maddening laughter . . . and now here were their hands, tweaking at her, pulling her back, weighing her down, until her legs could carry her no longer, and she sank to the ground.

She knew, really, what it was she had done, and why They had been sent to fetch her. She wasn't supposed to be here at all. She was a reincarnated soul without a passport . . . somehow, she had slipped illegally between the frontiers of life and death, dodging the regulations, jumping the queue, getting herself re-born before her time.

And now they were pulling her back, dragging her down to the place where she belonged. "You're not getting away with *that*, my girl!" she heard them say, amazingly clear and loud against the noisy thudding of her heart. "Re-birth isn't *that* simple—whatever made you think it was? And so now it's right back to the beginning for you, Milly Barnes, with it all to do again—and *properly*, this time . . . !"

Milly opened her eyes. She found herself staring ahead into a sky so black and so full of stars that at first she thought she had died, and was floating free of the earth's atmosphere, heading out into space.

But then, after a few seconds, she became aware of a pressure against the back of her skull and against her shoulder-blades. She was lying on the hard ground, flat on her back, staring up into the incredible night sky, completely cloudless, and scoured by the cold into this unimaginable brilliance.

What time was it? How far had she come? Painfully—she must have bruised her shoulder in falling—she raised her head, and far away over the black sea she saw the crescent moon sinking, and knew that it could not be very late—not later then nine, anyway.

How long did that give Gilbert to track her down? Say she had fled from Mrs Day's at about six—what would he have done first, when he found her gone? He would have glided down in the lift again, he would have sought out the caretaker. "She went *that* way," he would have been told. "Towards the Avenue . . . No, I'm sorry, sir, there was nothing I could do, she was going like a mad thing. I tried . . . I called out to her . . ."

And then what would Gilbert do? She saw him pacing stiffly across the dark town, the strange, predatory look sharpening his features, until he seemed to be sniffing the night air, to left and right, like a beast of prey. And people would help him, of course they would—a white-haired old man in such a state of anxiety and concern. "Yes, she went in *that* direction," they would say, pointing, and "Yes, we wondered if she was all right, but we didn't like . . . Oh, not at all, only too glad to be of help . . ." and on he would come, on, on, sniffing this way, sniffing that way, until at last all the muddled directions, all the well-meant advice, all his own strange, supra-normal perceptions, would begin to focus in a certain definite direction . . . would converge, at last, on this spot where she was lying.

She must move! She must hide! She must *do* something! Milly staggered to her feet, and on limbs stiff and almost numb with exhaustion, she tried to begin running again. But in which direction? She had a mad feeling now that Gilbert was everywhere. Ahead, crouched in the dry winter grass. Behind, padding soft as a shadow through the outskirts of the town. Up in the Downs he would be lurking, too, his white hair like tufts of sheep's wool, just visible through the dry, crackling gorse and winter furze: and down there at the sea's edge also she would find him, looming up behind the break-water like one more rotting timber, his terrible silvery eyes shining in the light of the moon.

Nowhere to turn . . . No way to run, and yet run she must, for fear had possession of her limbs and would not let her be.

She came at last to the beach, at the point where the parade petered out into a slippery concrete ramp. She scrambled over the damp stone, and landed, with a scrunch of pebbles, on the shingle beneath.

The noise was terrible. For several minutes Milly crouched, absolutely still, under the shadow of the ramp, waiting to see if she had given herself away.

No sound. Nothing: and at last she ventured from her hiding-place, tiptoeing painfully over the stones, until at last she reached the limits of the shingle belt, and felt her feet sinking into soft, powdery sand.

The tide was far out, and as Milly moved towards the distant line of foam at the water's edge, she had a strange sense that she was no longer moving at random; she was walking towards a rendezvous, to keep an appointment fixed long, long ago. And it was no good turning round and walking the other way, for if she did the rendezvous would be there, as well.

The soft sand had become firm under her feet, then wet, and wetter still, until now, as she approached the curving scallops of foam that defined the limits of the almost waveless water, marking it off from the glistening expanse of sand, she felt her feet sinking in once more, squelching at every step. She could feel the water soaking in above the soles of her shoes.

Far off to the right—a hundred yards or more—she could just make out the breakwater, gaunt and jagged against the starlit water. The treacherous light of the moon seemed to be playing games with the black timbers, they stirred and wavered in front of her tired eyes . . . one of the taller, narrower ones almost seemed to be detaching itself from the main body—lurching with a strange, lollopping gait out across the sand.

The Voices. Was it in moments of great and unendurable fear that they came to you? They were not mocking her this time, they were not even calling her "Milly" any more— "Milly Barnes" was just a bad joke that had come to an end.

"Candida!" she heard them call, faint and far away: and then, nearer and clearer, "Candida! Candida!"

The syllables of her old name, her real name, beat upon her out of the past, their rhythm rang like the hooves of a galloping horse alongside the quiet sea.

She put her hands to her ears, she tried to black out the sound of the past thundering towards her; she stared, with dilated pupils, across the faintly-gleaming stretches of sand which spread away into the darkness as far as she could see.

Was she going mad? The black upright timber *had* moved nearer . . . this was no trick of moonlight . . . ! it had detached itself from the breakwater, it was rocking towards her across the glimmering sand. In a few moments it would be near enough for her to glimpse the white hair, flying wild under the moon.

"Candida!" the voice came again, "Candida? What in heaven's name . . . ?"

She did not believe it. Even after she had recognised the voice beyond all possibility of doubt; had recognised the swing of his shoulders, too, as he ran she still did not believe it.

All the same, it was necessary to say *something*.

"Hullo," she said, in a small voice. "Hullo, Julian!"

CHAPTER XXIV

Gilbert was dead. At first, that was all she could take in of Julian's tirade, as he sat beside her on the breakwater in the light of the dying moon, berating her for her folly, just as he always used to do.

Gilbert was dead, had been dead for nearly a month now. This was the third time Julian had repeated the information, and yet still she kept asking the same inane questions, seeking confirmation by repetition. What about the Mr Soames who had called at Mrs Mumford's? Gilbert's brother, naturally. Surely she knew he *had* a brother? The poor devil was nearly out of his mind with the worry and strain of dealing with his late brother's affairs single-handed (he was quite a lot older even than Gilbert had been), and with the complications arising from the fact that he wasn't legally the nearest relative. *She* was—and she had chosen to disappear! To go swanning off on a seaside holiday under a false name, leaving everyone in this mess! Did she, by any chance, realise just exactly how much trouble and expense she had caused? Lawyers—Bank managers—ground landlords—they'd all been going crazy trying to get in touch with her . . . and now, to crown everything, he, Julian, had been compelled to fly over from Boston, at vast inconvenience, to help sort it all out!

Gilbert was dead. The words drummed through her brain, deadening the sound of Julian's scolding. He was dead, and no one, now, would ever know that she had murdered him.

For there had been no inquest—no awkward questions. The harassed, overworked young doctor had scribbled a certificate of Natural Causes (Gilbert was an old man, after all: what more likely than that he should suffer a stroke or a heart-attack?). And as to the door, locked and bolted on the outside, there was no mention of this at all in Julian's story; and so it must be presumed that, somehow, no one had noticed it.

It would be Mrs Roach who had undone the bolts, for it was she (Julian had explained) who had found the body. She must have undone them without comprehension, her slow mind not taking in their significance. No doubt Gilbert's habit of locking and bolting everything was so familiar to her that it no longer made any impact: she must have failed to put two-and-two together and to realise that, on this occasion, it could not have been he, himself, who had fastened the door. And afterwards—naturally enough—the shock of finding him dead in his chair would have put the matter right out of her mind.

Dead in his chair. In his great leather chair, with the green-shaded lamp at his elbow. Strange to think of him sitting there, just as he had always sat, at peace for the very first time.

Far out across the black water the moon was setting. Staring out along the jagged silver track, Candida thought about her responsibility for Gilbert's death, just as she had tried to think about it once before, when she was still Milly.

She had murdered him: that, she had already faced. What she had to face now was the knowledge that she was not going to be punished for it. No one, now, would ever know what she had done. No blame would ever attach to her, no penalty would ever be exacted.

Fixing her eyes on the magical silver track, that led from the infinite right to her very feet, Candida waited, as she had once waited when she was Milly, for the first pangs of the terrible, haunting guilt that would be with her to the end of her days. Guilt that would gnaw secretly at the dark roots of her being, giving her no rest. Guilt on this sort of scale must be waiting somewhere for her, somewhere under the glittering vastness of the sky?

All she could feel was an unutterable thankfulness that Gilbert was dead. Dead like the dinosaurs, and Shakespeare, and the kings of Babylon. Dead as she would one day be, and Julian, and the glistening ribbons of seaweed that today slapped so proudly against the timbers under the winter moon. Are we to ask of each and all of these deaths, Whose fault was it?—However did it happen? Under the shadow of the millennia, such questions dry upon our lips; they become a blasphemy against the benign cycle of birth and death, against the miracle of evolution under the turning circle of the stars. Even the humming of a gnat contains more of truth and wisdom.

She could feel no guilt at Gilbert's death: only a confused sense of participation. But his life—Ah, that was another matter! Whatever small wrong she might have done him by killing him paled into insignificance by the side of the wrong she had done by marrying him.

That was the wickedness. There, if anywhere, lay the lifelong guilt. She had married not merely without love—plenty of women have done *that*—but without the faintest desire for anything he could provide at all. She had not even married him for his money, or for the security he could offer—for even these motives can leave a man with some shred of self-respect, some shred of pride at having provided his woman with at least *something* that she needs.

No, she had left no shred of anything for Gilbert. She had not married him for anything he had, or was. She hadn't married him as a person at all, but as a thing, a handy weapon, a stick with which to beat her former husband.

Well, and did a man like Gilbert deserve anything better? He was a crafty and bitter old man, even before he went mad. All his life he had quarrelled with everybody, distrusted everybody, destroyed every relationship that had ever come his way. What had he ever done, or been, that he could expect anybody to marry him for love?

She had never thought before of how it must have seemed to him. After a bitter, lonely life of enmities and hatred, now here, suddenly, is a woman who mysteriously seems to *like* him! Who actually seeks his company! Nobody has ever sought his company before—and good riddance, damn them!—but here, at last is someone who *does*! A woman, too . . . Not unattractive . . . not much over forty . . . Can it be—can it possibly be—that something new and magical may yet be going to happen to Gilbert Soames, in this last decade of his life? Can it be that here, at last, is the woman who will break down his frozen inhibitions, soften his bitter, vindictive spirit . . . ?

No. Well, naturally not. That sort of thing just doesn't happen. His new wife left his inhibitions exactly where she found them—and was thankful to do so. She shrank from his fumbling touch. Instead of love she gave him fear . . . instead of friendship, defensive withdrawal. Just as everyone had always done . . . She was one of Them after all . . . !

Candida understood about Them now, as she had never done while Gilbert was alive. For now she, too, had known what it was to hear the faint, menacing whisper of their approaching battalions, had felt, once or twice, the first tentative touch of their icy hands. She had known what it was to hear Them down every harmless telephone . . . to see Them in every careless gesture.

It was because she had been on the run, of course, in fear of her life: for it is fear that brings Them flocking. They can smell it afar off, like vultures hungry for blood.

What fear was it, then, that had brought Them flocking around Gilbert, flapping and screeching, confounding his judgement and finally blotting out his sight? Fear of something he had once done? Some enemy he had once made, long, long ago? Perhaps, if she had been a quite different sort of a wife, he might have confided to her his dark story, or such of it as he still remembered, during the silent, deathly evenings. Now, no one would ever know.

247

It wasn't her fault! It wasn't *she* who had driven him mad: he was already far gone on the course of which she saw the terrible climax, long before she met him. Once she realised what a state he was in, she had done what she could. She had done her best, in the face of the awful odds.

Naturally, she couldn't have been expected to do for him the things which a woman who actually loved him would have done: to have put her warm arms round his stiff, wary body: to have answered his cold, formal kisses with warm, spontaneous ones: to have said, sometimes, "Don't be such an old silly!" or "You *know* that that's nonsense!" when his bizarre delusions first began peeping through.

Did he, in the beginning, imagine that Candida was going to love him like that? Did he daydream, like a foolish adolescent, of a real flesh-and-blood relationship, utterly beyond the capacity of his warped and frozen soul?

What right had he to dream such an impossible dream? Or to go to pieces when Candida couldn't make it come true? No one could! Probably no one could even have given him ordinary friendship, or even companionship, so hollowed out was he by the long years of bitterness and suspicion.

All right, so they couldn't. Then they shouldn't have married him. To marry someone in the clear knowledge that nothing can be given, nothing received—that was the wickedness: and no wickedness on his side would ever cancel it out, or justify it. On that August day, in the Brixton registry office, she had committed a crime against Gilbert far worse than the crime of murdering him—and yet one for which the Law provides no penalty at all. Strange.

Suddenly, Candida felt herself Milly again: buoyant, carefree, impervious to remorse because she had only just been born. Candida felt in her own bones Milly's toughness, her zest for survival, her hard-won capacity for cutting off from her former self and living each moment as if nothing had ever happened before.

The Voices had been wrong. They had been talking platitudes, as Voices so commonly do. "You can't run away from yourself" had been the theme of their discourse: but the truth is that you can. She had. She had become Milly, and as Milly she had acquired an entire new repertoire of strengths and skills—not least of which, she now realised, was the recapturing of some of the special qualities of childhood: above all the child's untramelled eagerness to explore the next minute, the next hour, as though it was a voyage round the world. All these new skills and aptitudes, so painfully acquired by Milly, were now at Candida's command, to use exactly as she wished. If she chose, now, to by-pass guilt and remorse, and to concentrate on getting on with the rest of her life, she could easily do so. Milly had provided her with the techniques.

And in fact, when it came to the point, it hardly seemed a matter of techniques at all: it seemed the most natural thing in the world simply to put it all behind her, as Milly would have done.

Cautiously at first, and then with increasing boldness, Candida made herself face the things she had done. Without self-deception or self-justification she contemplated the full extent of her folly and wickedness in marrying Gilbert, and thereafter escorting him blindly to his death.

Still she felt nothing that could be identified as guilt. All she could feel was a vague and not unpleasing sense of her own superiority to the blinkered, self-centred bitch she had once been.

Was this a special sort of detachment peculiar to the twice-born, a privileged kind of opting-out? Or was it simply that it is almost impossible for anyone under fifty nowadays to experience guilt in the true, crippling sense in which our grandparents experienced it? Nowadays we are told constantly that we are all riddled with guilt-feelings, and that it is this over-developed sense of guilt that is at the root of all our ills, but surely, by now, this is more of a folk-memory than a fact? It was true once, no doubt, but can it possibly be true still? We have been told so often and for so long that no one is ever really to blame for anything: that it is all due to what Mother did, or Father, or Society. And what Mother did is itself the result of what *her* mother did, and of the pressures of Society in *those* days . . . cause behind cause, rolling in out of the infinite, as far as the eye can see or the mind can reach, leaving nowhere any place where guilt can come to rest, can settle and take root . . .

"And of course that Roach woman wasn't much help!" Julian was saying—and Candida jolted herself out of her reverie to listen—"Apparently the old harridan had been going around telling everyone you weren't married to Soames at all, that you were 'No better than you should be'—I think that was her phrase. And of course everyone believed her—why not, in this day and age?"

Why not indeed. In the darkness, Candida was smiling. How ironic that the old woman, in her would-be malice, should have done her victim such an utterly unlooked-for service! Because, of course, this misconception delayed considerably the moment when anybody began seriously to search for Candida. All the while they were assuming that it was merely Gilbert's mistress who had (so conveniently for all concerned) seen fit to make herself scarce, no one evinced the least interest in her whereabouts. It was the missing brother they were after at that stage, for he was the presumed next-of-kin. It was he who must sign the papers, pay for the funeral, sort out the incredible chaos of Gilbert's accumulated possessions. And it was only after this brother had been found, and had been ineffectually muddling with Gilbert's papers for several days, that it came to light that Candida really *was* Mrs Soames, really *had* been married to Gilbert. Then, of course, the search for her started in earnest.

". . . I hate to say it, my dear Candida, but I've never in my whole life encountered such an incompetent way of disappearing! First you give yourself some daft phoney name, and then what do you do but straightaway sign a cheque with it! So, of course, the first thing Brother Soames finds on the doormat is this letter from the Bank, asking who the hell is Milly Barnes?

"Mind you, *he* seems to have been pretty slow in the uptake, too. Apparently he just shoved the letter in among the rest of the papers, and forgot all about it. It took *me* to point out that it might be an idea to find out who this Milly Barnes was—Not that I hadn't already guessed, of course— who else would be acting so plumb daft? And anyway, I'd already heard from Felicity What's-her-name that some-body'd seen you two or three weeks earlier hanging around Victoria Station, looking as if you'd committed a murder, or something. So, putting two-and-two together . . ."

Of course. It had been a daft thing to do. By hanging around a main line station all through the rush hour you are exposing yourself to just about as high a statistical chance of being recognised as it would be possible to achieve if you were specially trying. And as for Mrs Mumford's cheque— that had been idiotic, too, but how else could she have got a roof over her head that night?

After that, it had all been easy for Julian. Victoria . . . Seacliffe . . . Leinster Terrace. Candida could visualise the impatient scorn with which Julian would have brushed aside Jacko's implausible lies . . . the effortless charm by which he would have manoeuvred the tight-lipped Mrs Mumford into telling him everything she knew, including the fact that her newest lodger worked for a Mrs Graham—had, in fact, offered this lady's name as a reference, only Mrs Mumford had never taken it up, on account of her low opinion of refer-ences in general (how courteously, in the interests of his ulterior motive, would Julian have listened to these opinions, betraying neither boredom nor impatience, charming to the last). And then the phone calls to Mrs Graham, and finally a visit to her in person, and the extracting from her of the information that her Daily Help worked also for a Mrs Day.

From *Mrs Graham*? *Information*? But Mrs Graham had never bothered to learn so much as her name!

Not her name, no. But her other jobs, yes. Because this was something that affected *her*, Mrs Graham. The fear of piracy by her dearest friends had never been far from Mrs Graham's mind since that first morning, when Mrs Day had rung up with that treacherous offer of five pence an hour more.

So, on from Mrs Graham's to Mrs Day's . . . and Candida knew the rest.

Or most of it. Why, though, had he referred to himself as her *husband*, in talking to the caretaker?

She felt Julian give a tiny start.

What a quibble, he protested! Christ, after nearly twenty years of marriage, it was a slip anyone might make!

The moon had set now; and though the filmy rim of the water could no longer be seen, a soft gobbling sound in the shallow water at their feet warned that the tide had begun to turn. In the starlight, Candida could just make out the sulky hunch of Julian's shoulders, and knew that he was discomfited, and in a moment would think up something to blame her for.

"You never answered my letter," he said, aggrievedly; and for a moment Candida stared at him, in total bewilderment.

"What letter . . . ?" she was beginning—and then, suddenly, she knew.

Answer it! That letter which she had torn into a thousand pieces . . . the letter which had goaded her through the nights and days, had driven her onward like one possessed, into folly, wickedness, and crime . . . *Answer* it!

"Oh, I was going to," she replied lightly, her eyes on the hurrying swirls of the awakening water, just visible in the starlight. "I was going to, but you see I was waiting for the mustard and cress to come up first. I wanted to see if it spelt R.A.T."

He laughed; and she felt a tremor of surprise go through him. Suddenly she realised that in the old days she had never cheeked him like this in answer to his bullying. This was something new. Something that Milly had bequeathed.

". . . I suppose it was then that I got my first inkling of how impossibly touchy and possessive Cora could be," Julian was saying. "You see, the crazy thing was she'd more or less *written* the damn letter for me—we were both a bit drunk at the time, and I remember how we laughed when she suggested the bit about the aunt! But no sooner had I posted it than she turned on me like a mad thing! Storming at me that I didn't love her, that secretly I still loved *you*, or I could never have sent you a letter so pointlessly, so deliberately cruel! She accused me of trying to sting you into some kind of reaction, by any flamboyant, childish means I could devise, and declared that this proved I still cared! And by God, Candida, I've been thinking about it a lot lately, and I realise she was right! I *did* still care! I still do! Candida, when my divorce comes through, will you marry me?"

The cheek of it! The unutterable, brazen impertinence! Now that Cora had thrown him over, now that he was no longer quite the brilliant success he had once been—*now*, Candida was good enough for him again!

For this was how it must be with him: she could see it clearly now. That Boston research job must have been a step *down*, not a step up . . . perhaps he had overestimated the permissiveness of the permissive society, particularly where it impinges on the medical profession: perhaps he had found, to his dismay, that the betrayal of an innocent wife *does* still cause raised eyebrows in some quarters, even nowadays.

Whatever it was, his conceit must have taken a beating, and so now here he was, with ego bruised and bleeding, limping back to Candida. And without so much as a word of apology or remorse!

How often had she dreamed of this very scene, during the long nights in the empty Kensington flat, and during the lonely, drifting days! Julian magically back again . . . pleading with her to forgive him . . . begging her to marry him all over again . . . to give him one more chance!

There had been all sorts of endings. Sometimes, after a wonderful scene of remorse and forgiveness, she had fallen into his arms. Sometimes, proud and aloof, she had spurned him, watching, with icy scorn, as his haughty features crumpled . . .

Out in the dark, a small wind had risen with the turn of the tide. Candida could hear the tiny waves lapping restlessly at the foot of the breakwater, limbering up for their journey up the dark sand. Against the starry blackness, she could see

Julian's dark bulk, but not his face. After twenty years, she did not need to see his face: from the set of his shoulders, from the tilt of his half-seen jaw, she knew exactly the expression of self-satisfied expectancy he was wearing; the smug look of a man who has no doubt of victory.

Julian, my boy, you've got another thing coming. This isn't the Candida that you remember, all meek and compliant. *This* Candida has Milly in her, a woman of whom you know nothing!

"Will you marry me?" he repeated, still with that cocksure confidence in his voice and bearing.

The conceit of the man! The insufferable, unbelievable smugness! The monstrous, insupportable arrogance!

"Yes," she said.

Her friends, naturally, were less than whole-hearted in their congratulations. "Some people never learn!" they confided to one another wryly, with a shake of the head.

But Candida *had* learnt, of course. The only thing was that, as is so commonly the case, the lesson she had learned from her experiences was quite other than the one which seemed so obvious to the onlookers.

Also by Celia Fremlin

Uncle Paul

Waterstones Thriller of the Month

'Fremlin packs a punch.' Ian Rankin

'A slow-burning chill of a read by a master of suspense.' Janice Hallett

The holidays have begun. In a seaside caravan resort, Isabel and her sister, Meg, build sandcastles with the children, navigate deck-chair politics, explore the pier's delights, gorge on ice cream in the sun. But their half-sister, Mildred, has returned to a nearby coastal cottage where her husband – the mysterious Uncle Paul – was arrested for the attempted murder of his first wife.

Now, on his release from prison, is Uncle Paul returning for revenge, seeking who betrayed him, uncovering the family's skeletons? Or are all three women letting their nerves get the better of them? Though who really is Meg's new lover? And whose are those footsteps . . . ?

'The grandmother of psycho-domestic noir.' *Sunday Times*

faber

Also by Celia Fremlin

The Long Shadow

'Splendid . . . Got me hooked.' Ruth Rendell

'A dark delight: Barbara Pym with arsenic.' Clare Chambers

Jolted from sleep by the telephone, Imogen stumbles through the dark house to answer it. At first, she can't quite understand the man on the other end of the line. Surely he can't honestly be accusing her of killing her husband, Ivor, who died in a car crash barely two months ago.

Soon, Imogen finds her home filling up with unexpected Christmas guests, who may be looking for more than festive cheer. Has someone been rifling through Ivor's papers? Who left the whisky bottle beside his favourite chair? And why won't that man stop calling, insisting he can prove Imogen's guilt?

'Fremlin's sly, subtly feminist take on the ghost story is a gem.' *Sunday Times*

faber

Also by Celia Fremlin

The Hours Before Dawn

Winner of the 1960 Edgar Award for Best Mystery Novel

'A lost masterpiece.' Peter Swanson
'Fremlin was a genius.' Nicola Upson

Louise is desperate for a good night's rest. Forget the girls running errant in the garden and bothering the neighbours. Forget her husband who seems oblivious to it all. If the baby would just stop screaming, everything would be fine.

Or would it? What if Louise's growing fears about the family's mysterious new lodger are real? What could she do, and would anyone even believe her? Is she dreaming – or is this a nightmare? Maybe, if she could just get some sleep, she'd be able to think straight . . .

'Few people can chill the blood like Celia Fremlin.' *Daily Telegraph*

faber